I0730187

Lust & Lace

Contents

The Elevator Game

Her footsteps echoed in the empty corridor, the staccato of her heels sharp and unforgiving. Ella felt the building settle around her, as weary as she was after another week of unrelenting deadlines. She pulled her hair free of its severe twist, hoping to ward off the headache beginning to pulse behind her eyes. Her office was quiet now, only the shuffling of the night crew left to remind her that time was running late. She'd promised herself that she would make it home before dark, that she would break the cycle of being the last one out the door, the one the others eyed with a mixture of suspicion and awe.

She moved with determination, her body's slow unwind apparent in the looseness of her posture. Her green eyes stood out, burning with a self-imposed intensity even as they scanned the deserted workspaces. When she reached the end of the hall, she glanced back toward the empty cubicles, once buzzing with low chatter and the thrum of ambition, now a landscape of sleeping computers and low-lighted desk lamps. Even the cleaning staff had retreated to their own corners, leaving Ella alone with the rhythmic clatter of the overhead lights. It was typical, she thought, how the place seemed to fold in on itself once she was ready to leave.

The week had been relentless, and the space around her mirrored the cavernous stretch of her own energy. She let out a breath, long and controlled, pushing past the simmer of exhaustion. She was determined to get home early for once, refusing to let herself give in to the comforts of staying late. There was no point - everything that needed to be done was done, as usual. She couldn't escape the weight of their looks though. They were impossible to ignore, those fleeting glances from colleagues who imagined her devoid of warmth and humour, who saw her coolness as proof of some unflappable inner flaw. She was a professional anomaly - too serious, too focused, too confident for their tastes.

And yet, despite all that, Ella took a sort of grim satisfaction in knowing she outpaced them. She held onto that, tucked it beneath her jacket like a shield. Her shoes clicked against the floor as she reached the elevator, each step counting down the minutes she was supposed to spend in transit. She could still make the early train, she told herself that she could still reclaim the evening for herself. The thought was just shy of optimistic, and she winced as though caught in some betrayal of her own restraint.

The fluorescent lights wavered above her, flickering in a distracted pulse. Ella paused, feeling the energy shift. Her skin prickled with the anticipation of sudden change. Just the electrical system struggling under the pressure of its long hours, she thought. She stood straighter, smoothing her jacket, and pressed the elevator button. The doors didn't open.

The strain of the last week seemed to collapse inward, an entire orbit redirecting itself against her plans. The lights dimmed again, and this time they struggled to regain their former brightness. She felt the pressure of her own presence in the room, in the office, so unyielding that it pushed everything else out of focus.

Ella took another breath, steadier this time, convincing herself that it was nothing but an inconvenience. Nothing she couldn't overcome. Even as the minutes piled up around her like unwanted paper on a desk, she stood rigid against the uncertainty. Her entire career, her life, was predicated on the idea that she alone could control the things that others let slip away. The space around her felt as though it conspired to break that resolve.

Finally, with a heavy sigh of surrender she decided to take the stairs. As though in answer, a stuttering power surge sent the lights through another cycle of blinking indecision. She blinked back, firm and stubborn in her intent, daring the universe to challenge her. But it did.

The fluorescent lights stuttered and stalled, and the next time they dimmed, they did so with an air of finality. Ella felt the floor tremble beneath her, as though it too had reached the limit of its endurance. The entire building flickered out of existence around her, leaving her in complete and unexpected darkness. The sudden absence of sound and movement left her with a startled, bitter taste in her mouth. Her body stilled, but her thoughts unraveled in an urgent torrent.

The profound darkness pressed in, as insistent and intrusive as a stranger's hand. She hated this - being vulnerable, exposed, at the mercy of external forces. She inhaled sharply, the breath solidifying into something heavier than frustration, more complex than anger. She waited, counting her own breaths, hoping the darkness would reveal some flaw, some give in the situation she found herself in. Instead, it only tightened its hold.

There was noise now, distant and shifting. Footsteps, voices, the hum of panicked reactions. She was not the only one left. The thought both comforted and unsettled her, turning over her previous certainty in an ironic twist. She strained to hear, her body tense and alert. Her mind cycled through possibilities, discarding each as fast as it arrived. She had almost convinced herself to begin moving, to assert her control over this unexpected detour, when a voice rose from the shadowed hallway.

"Ella!" A mix of curiosity and amusement coloured her name, punctuating the gloom. It carried through the space with a sense of entitlement she knew all too well. The sound of it made her square her shoulders, even as she felt the tug of exasperation at her own inability to plan around such chaos.

The building had exhaled, releasing its pent-up energy in the frenzy of early quitting times and hastily made plans. Only the residue of such urgency remained, dust settling on the ghostly hum of the air conditioning. Jace soaked in the rare calm, relishing the freedom of an empty floor. He felt taller without the crush of other bodies around him. He felt in control. He slouched against the elevator's closed doors, letting the silence fill his ears like the crash of distant waves. This was his favourite time, the lull between his last meeting and the start of the weekend, the anticipation of unwinding.

His body stretched with the ease of a man who never worried about the things he couldn't change, of a man who had always found ways to mould the world to his liking. He ran a hand through his hair, the gelled perfection giving way to something looser, more careless. There was no one left to impress but himself. He strolled down the corridor with the self-assuredness of someone who knew the world would wait. His pace was unhurried, his path indirect. The day stretched long and supple before him, and he intended to take full advantage.

He could never understand why Ella didn't do the same. Didn't see the charm in knocking off early, taking time to let the stress evaporate. He guessed she liked the hard lines of effort and precision too much. Jace smirked at the thought, the challenge of it. He'd just have to find out how late she planned to stay this time, how close she'd cut it before admitting defeat and heading home. He almost laughed at the predictability of her unyielding dedication.

He took a turn and climbed a flight of stairs. The dust motes in the air were lazy with the lack of competition. No sound but the distant whoosh of the ventilation and the hum of lights above his head. He rarely noticed these things, too caught up in the interactions that filled his days. Now, in the lull, he saw the details that fled in the wake of full-throttle schedules and meetings that tumbled over one another like children playing in a backyard. He let them soak into him like sunlight. Let the knowledge of Ella's floor calling him drift into the forefront of his mind.

She was as constant as a star, burning bright and singular, he thought. Jace knew what he'd find before he reached her office, knew that she'd still be behind her desk, her hair like a dark flame, a neat stack of work ahead of her, papers pinned beneath her fierce determination. Sure enough, when he reached the landing, he could see the light spilling from her office door, casting a long rectangle of brilliance onto the otherwise dim hallway.

He paused, savouring the moment. He felt that usual mix of curiosity and admiration, along with a spark of disbelief that someone could be so damned devoted. His movements, slow and deliberate, turned the corner and moved closer, one eye on her door. It was like finding a rare specimen in its natural habitat, untouched by outside influence. Jace liked to think of himself as that outside influence, a potential disruption to the seamless flow of her plans.

He'd never had anyone ignore him as effectively as Ella did. Her indifference was a force of nature, as persistent and undeniable as he was. A spark of something stubborn flared within him. A desire to break that indifference, see it splinter into a reaction. He was almost certain he would enjoy her reaction, whatever it might be. Her cool regard had started as an affront, but now it fascinated him. The edges of a challenge had dulled into a finer game, one that was strategic and demanding of his wit.

She was something else, something he couldn't name but knew he wanted to know. He smiled as he came up with a new angle, a way to intersect with her life as neatly as possible. He was sure she'd cut her losses soon, and when she did, he'd be right there. He liked to think of it as a tactic. She'd likely think of it as an annoyance.

The more she ignored him, the more he found himself trying to push against her boundaries. He couldn't say why it mattered, only that it did. He was thirty-two, at the top of his game, used to others trailing in his wake, and he wasn't about to let one woman's indifference undo him. It had become personal in a way that both infuriated and amused him. He couldn't wait to see if she'd look up when he stopped by her office, to see if she'd even flinch.

The thought made him laugh out loud, the sound cracking like a whip in the quiet space. He'd play it casual, nonchalant, and make her roll her eyes in that dismissive way he knew she thought of as polite. He was counting on it. The unpredictability of her predictability was an irresistible paradox. He only hoped it would be more than that this time, that she'd give him something different to work with.

He was almost to her office when he heard her footsteps. Ella, ahead of him by just a fraction. He stopped and leaned against the wall, biting back his amusement. He was about to round the corner when a flicker of the lights caught his attention. They blinked and shuddered, and he felt the universe pull the rug from beneath him. Jace froze, suspended between anticipation and a sudden shift he couldn't yet name.

Her name hung in the darkened hallway, too loud and too familiar. It bounced off the walls, impatient, and came back to settle against her skin. It made her fingers twitch. She spun, pivoting sharply in the low light, just in time to catch the silhouette of someone tall and assured in their pursuit.

"Not this time." She muttered under her breath, the words more wish than command. Ella squared her shoulders against the vague shape of Jace and moved toward the stairs, determined not to engage. She had too much else to worry about. Her steps were firm, confident, like the meeting notes she compiled in ruthless order. If she just made it around the corner, she thought, she'd be out of sight. His voice couldn't reach her there.

But she knew how this went. She could almost hear him laughing, his ability to shake off her dismissals something she both resented and secretly admired. Even when he wasn't in front of her, Jace's presence was an intrusion, an unavoidable detour. Ella rolled her eyes, not breaking her pace. The dark didn't stop him, she was sure. Nothing did. Her jaw clenched as she imagined him angling for a way to catch her, her already tenuous plans disrupted by his relentless and almost ridiculous persistence.

She hit the stairs with urgency, letting the mechanical rhythm of her descent crowd out her thoughts. Her hands gripped the rail, a lifeline to some shred of self-imposed sanity. But when she reached the next floor, her confidence faltered. The lights were an unreliable flutter overhead, winking out in tandem with her resolve. They left a cold emptiness behind each time they failed, a preview of the night's trajectory. Ella paused for only a second, less than a breath, then continued to the elevator.

The looming shape of Jace haunted her mind more than the flickering darkness, and she shook her head. She wanted to believe she was beyond his reach. She convinced herself that her focus would keep him at bay, a shield he couldn't penetrate. She convinced herself that her independence could not be compromised. He didn't seem to notice the elevator's irregular lighting or the strange stutters of sound that sent goosebumps racing up her arms. Or maybe he didn't care. Maybe Jace was immune to disruption of any kind, immune to the cold stare of Ella's resistance. It both baffled and annoyed her.

She was almost to the elevator when she turned her head and found that the space behind her was empty. There was nothing but silence, and it unsettled her. Had he given up this time, she wondered. It would be unlike him. Unlikely. A rare victory, if she managed to avoid his intrusion. She allowed herself a moment to breathe, a pause in her rushing momentum.

She heard the low chuckle before she saw him, and her moment vanished into the void. He was just down the hall, his shadow stretching long and determined. Her pulse quickened, caught between irritation and something else, something with more charge. Ella picked up her pace, willing herself to remain in control. Her body felt tense and ready, poised to spring forward. With a barely audible sigh, she pushed the elevator button. The slight trembling of her hand told her more than she wanted to know. She waited, seconds feeling longer than entire workdays. Jace gained ground, and she felt the weight of his attention like a spotlight, unwanted and intense.

"Hello Ella," he called, his voice casual and unconcerned by the strained darkness, "am I going to catch you before you bolt this time?" She tried not to smile, but the corner of her mouth betrayed her with the slightest twitch. A flicker, then gone. She turned to meet his eyes, green against the shadows, only acknowledging him once she was sure the elevator was on its way. His grin was lazy and wide, the expression of someone who'd had all the time in the world to work out his plans. Someone who never doubted he'd get what he wanted. He had her cornered, but she was too practiced at evasion to let it show.

"I thought everyone had left by now." She said, her voice as cool as she could manage. A challenge more than a statement. Jace shrugged, his silhouette an unyielding smudge in the hallway's flickering light.

"You know me. I like to stick around, see who else is here." His grin widened, confident and slightly mocking. He knew it would get to her. He liked that it did. The elevator pinged and the doors opened, spilling dim light over both of them. Ella stepped inside with the swift precision of someone used to slamming doors before anyone else had a chance to cross the threshold.

"Still running from me, I see." Jace said as the doors began to close. "Always." She said, almost softly as though acknowledging an unwritten rule. As though conceding just enough to give him hope. His foot caught the door, and with one smooth motion he slipped into the elevator beside her. The doors clicked shut, enclosing them in an unnaturally tight space. Ella felt the walls shrink inward, her ability to command her own escape just as effectively trapped.

She wasn't prepared for the jolt, wasn't prepared for the grinding sound of cables, the sudden and absolute stop. The elevator shuddered, its halt as brutal as a full stop on a racetrack, as unexpected as the space between herself and Jace shrinking to zero. Her hand flew to the wall, then back to her mouth, as though she could swallow her surprise. And then the lights died.

Everything was dark. Everything was motionless. Ella's heart pounded in time with the metallic echo of her thoughts. She tried to will her eyes to adjust, tried to see Jace's reaction in the perfect black of the elevator car. But she couldn't see a thing. The uncertainty pressed against her, insistent, reminding her that she had less control over this situation than any before. The pause stretched, and she realised she was holding her breath, as though waiting for the world to right itself. As though it might.

Jace's presence loomed, no longer a shadow she could dismiss or slip away from. A thrum of something almost electric ran between them, thicker and more potent than even the utter absence of light. It tangled around her, wrapped itself around her certainty like an untended vine. Ella fought the feeling of its restriction. Fought her own increasing sense of helplessness.

The darkness was a living thing, expanding and contracting with the sound of her breath. She counted to ten and back again. Her thoughts careened in widening circles. The elevator should have moved by now. The lights should have returned. She wished she hadn't noticed how close Jace was, how his presence left so little room for anything else.

Ella shifted her weight, the movement amplified in the silence. The space between her and the elevator walls felt like it closed in on her with every shallow breath. The usual certainty of her actions dissolved in the ink-black air, leaving her with nothing solid to hold. She let her hand brush against the wall, grounding herself with the cool surface. She then immediately withdrew it, annoyed at the uncharacteristic display of need.

Everything was so quiet. So close. She inhaled, slow and deep, measuring her response to the claustrophobic feel of the space. She could almost sense Jace's amusement, a palpable thing she wished she could bat away like a fly.

With a flick of her wrist, she pulled her phone from her pocket, her fingers clumsy in the dark. The sudden glow of the screen was a shocking brightness. Her eyes, adjusting, picked out the contours of Jace beside her. It wasn't as reassuring as she'd hoped. No bars, no signal. She locked the screen again, unwilling to give him the satisfaction of seeing her futile attempts to find a way out.

Her own impatience crowded out any sense of self-control. She bit the inside of her cheek, her mind a relentless spin of options. She had never liked the thought of being trapped. The irony was not lost on her, though she would never admit it. Instead she exhaled sharply, almost a sigh, and tucked the phone back into her pocket. The stillness stretched taut between them. She could feel his eyes on her, even in the darkness. Ella wondered how much longer she could keep up her silence before the situation forced her hand. Forced her to acknowledge him.

"Not quite the way you planned to spend your evening, I take it?" Jace's voice cut through the dark, cocky and amused. The words buzzed against her skin, equal parts irritation and provocation. Ella fought the impulse to respond, to give in to the easy banter he always seemed to initiate. Her silence wasn't as reassuring as she hoped it would be. When she didn't answer, he shifted, and she could feel the movement echo through the confined space. It seemed to go on forever, vibrating with the tension she tried to ignore.

"It's going to be a long night if you keep up that silent treatment." Jace chuckled, low and casual, and the sound drove straight through her efforts to remain unruffled. Her resolve cracked slightly, like the first fracture in a newly paved street. Ella responded with a nod, her usual grace stunted by the unfamiliar weight of frustration. She wished the sound could cover up the awkward stutter of her own pulse, loud and unrelenting in the dead air. She focused on the elevator buttons, though she knew there was nothing she could do that she hadn't already done. A knot of tension pulled tighter in her stomach, an unfamiliar companion to the control she so often wielded with ease.

"I can see you've got your escape plan all figured out," Jace said, his voice edging into a lightness that felt deliberately constructed, "me, I'm going to sit back and relax until someone comes to rescue us. Or until the power comes back. My money's on the latter. " She wished he would take the situation seriously. It felt unfair, how he twisted everything into a game, how she almost liked that about him. The uncertainty clawed at her resolve, at her desire to keep her cool under any and all circumstances. She heard him move again, closer this time, his steps careful and deliberate. It startled her how much she could feel it. How much she was aware of him even when she couldn't see him, when everything was drenched in dark.

"Look, it's not so bad, is it? Some people pay good money for this kind of one-on-one time." There was an ease in his tone that disarmed her, even if she refused to let him know. Ella swallowed, tried to find the right amount of calm to balance her words on. Tried to cover the exposed wire of her sudden uncertainty.
"As far as I'm concerned," she said, her voice a low tremble, "you're not worth the hourly rate you charge. You couldn't have paid *me* for this time with you." A moment of silence, and then she heard him laugh, truly laugh, and the sound vibrated through her, her

body soaking up the energy despite her resistance. Despite her own growing sense of helplessness, she felt the trace of a smile threaten to spread across her lips.

Jace kept the air alive with his self-assured presence, and Ella found herself wondering how much of her life she'd spent actively avoiding moments like these, moments where she couldn't be entirely sure of the outcome. The tension between them was tangible and new, her certainty as rattled as the motionless elevator car.

It was too dark to see anything but the silhouettes of their intentions. Too quiet to be anything but starkly aware of how close they were. How much smaller the space was now that the world had forced them together. Ella remained still, searching for a foothold, some grip on the situation. Jace remained close, a dark figure against an even darker background, his presence warming the air with a promise of waiting things out. The realisation dawned with a clarity that struck deep, as unwelcome and bold as Jace himself - this time, she couldn't avoid him. This time, they were truly stuck.

The heavy air swallowed up the sound of the button, leaving only a faint echo. Jace exhaled, long and loud, filling the space between them with his own amusement. It wasn't as rewarding as he'd hoped. He listened to Ella breathe and wondered how long they could stand being trapped in this state. How long he could stand not getting a rise out of her.

He let the silence grow, certain it would unravel her eventually. It was thick enough to slice, almost solid in its density. His usual tactics met with no success. She was as unreadable as ever, a challenge he could feel but not see in the pitch-black space. Jace hit the emergency button again, a token gesture he knew was pointless. His own impatience almost made him laugh out loud. This wasn't the game he'd envisioned. But it was a game, and that's what mattered. He could outlast her. He was sure of it.

"I'm starting to think this is a setup," he said, leaning back and letting his shoulders slump into the elevator's corner, "is this your way of telling me you wanted some quality time?" The dim outline of her form shifted slightly, the movement full of cool disdain.
"You figured it out," she said, "how clever of you." There was the smallest catch in her voice, a minor note of frustration that sparked his determination to push further. Jace liked the sound of it.
"It's going to be hard for you to run from me in here," he said, his voice low and teasing, "nowhere to go. No excuses." He knew he was pressing his luck, but he liked the feel of that too. He liked testing the boundaries she kept so firmly in place. The thrill of the situation electrified the confined space, even if he was the only one acknowledging it.

Jace waited for another reply, the gap between his question and her answer stretching like an awkward pause on a first date. He let the anticipation build, sure he would wear her down. Sure she would crack first. But the seconds ticked by in the darkness, slow and lazy, and he felt the initial hints of impatience begin to tap against the edges of his resolve.

"Maybe we should try talking about something other than you for once." She finally said. Her voice was cool, but he detected a thin edge beneath it, a thread of discomfort he wasn't used to hearing. Ella, breaking the silence in her own unexpected way, surprised him more than he'd ever admit. Jace let her words settle, mulled over them, tried to find their hidden barbs. When he spoke again, he did so with a lightness that contrasted the tense air.

"Why don't you pick the topic, then?" He asked, unwilling to let her deflect so easily. Another shift, a subtle sound that made the space seem even smaller. He wished he could see her expression, wished he could see how much this annoyed her. He almost liked not seeing, the added layer of guessing, of possibility.

"Okay," she said, "how about what we're doing to fix this? Just sitting here won't help." He could hear her tap the elevator's button panel, a tiny percussion that echoed her state of mind.

"Don't you ever relax," Jace said, shaking his head even though he knew she couldn't see it, "this is like a social experiment. And I have to say it's not going the way I'd planned." He heard her almost laugh, the sound as fragile as a whisper. It encouraged him. Made him press harder, the way he always did. Ella let a breath escape, more exasperated than before. She seemed to weigh her options, trapped between answering and not answering, her silence growing less steady by the moment.

"What was the plan?" She asked, her voice quieter now, but undeniably curious.

"The plan was to see how long it would take for you to stop ignoring me," he said, and he couldn't stop himself from grinning, "I think we've got a record going here." Ella shifted again, this time toward him, the motion marked by the barest brush of her arm against his. It surprised him how much he could feel it. How much she was coming through in the dark. Jace heard her breathe in deeply, the sound as tactile as if she'd reached out to touch him. It thrilled him in a way he couldn't quite define, couldn't categorise. He decided to up the stakes, took a breath of his own, and jumped.

"What are you working on this late, anyway? Trying to prove a point? Trying to win some award I don't know about?" His voice held more than teasing this time. It held real interest. Ella paused, longer than he expected. Long enough for him to believe she'd ignore him again, keep her secret to herself. But she surprised him. "If you have to know, I've been lining up a few side projects. Things that will make what I do look impressive to people other than you," her tone was less cool, less sharp, "the longer the hours now, the shorter they are later. You should try it." He felt the corners of his grin stretch into a new shape. Not a smirk. Not a smile he'd worn in the office. He hadn't seen this side of Ella before, and he wasn't about to let it slip away. The conversation felt easy, even as she tried to drag it back to more impersonal territory. He pushed harder, letting the easy, teasing air stay close, feeling out the limits.

"Is that your way of saying you've got bigger plans?" He asked, knowing she'd have a response ready. He could see the edge of her form as his eyes adjusted to the dim light leaking in around the edges of the elevator. Her pause made him catch his breath, and he wasn't sure why it mattered so much. Wasn't sure why it made him feel a spark of real surprise.

"That's my way of saying I'm not done yet." She said, and neither was he.

Their proximity had its own gravity, pulling them toward each other with an inevitability that made Ella grit her teeth. Her desire to maintain distance from Jace went against the unspoken rules of physics, of attraction, of wanting. The closer he came, the harder it was to stay untouched. The space between them was too small, impossibly so. She felt his presence as acutely as she felt the pressure of her own restraint.

"You know, you should be reporting these projects to me." Jace moved with a confidence that belied the dimness, stepping toward the control panel, toward her. Ella knew his intent was not to fix the elevator. His intent was to find the chink in her armour.

"You're not my boss." She kept her back to the wall, thinking she could remain grounded there, an immovable object against the force of his attention. She hated that it didn't work. Hated that he still had so much pull.

"My position is more superior to yours." Jace came nearer, his outline taking on definition in the low light, and she fought against the urge to shrink away from the inevitable brush of their bodies. As he passed, the fabric of his shirt skimmed against her arm, a fleeting touch that set off sparks between them.

"I don't report to you." She drew in a sharp breath, more in surprise than annoyance. More in something she didn't want to name. Jace lingered at the panel, his eyes on her instead of the lifeless buttons. She knew he'd felt it too, the electric charge. He seemed satisfied by her reaction, but not as much as she expected. Something in his expression changed, shifted from cocky to curious, the shadow of genuine surprise in his gaze. She crossed her arms over her chest, an unconscious gesture that felt too much like a concession.

"Still think this is fun?" She asked, her voice tight. Jace turned to face her, a slow, measured movement that brought him closer than before.

"More fun than a stack of reports." There was a new tone in his words, something she didn't know how to handle. Something less practiced, more sincere. Ella pressed herself further back, but the wall wouldn't give. Her thoughts crowded against her resolve. Against the reality of his body heat mixing with her own, the air charged and alive.

"You have a strange idea of fun." She said. She wanted it to sound dismissive, wanted it to carry the usual edge of resistance. It didn't. Not quite. Jace moved again, and she braced herself for the next brush, the next shock. It didn't come. Instead, he took a step back, giving her space she hadn't expected. It left her off balance. He shrugged, but there was something new in the motion, something thoughtful.

"You have a strange idea of me." The lightness in his voice remained, but it was wrapped in something deeper. He saw more than she wanted him to. He saw that this was affecting her. That she wasn't as impervious as she pretended to be. Ella let out a breath, as if releasing all the tension would force it out of her. As if it could relieve the tightness in her chest. The spark from before still crackled in the air between them. She wasn't sure what to do with it, only that it was there, alive and waiting.

"So what's your plan? Annoy me until the lights come back on?" She asked, struggling to maintain her usual composure, struggling to sound casual.

"I've got a better one," he said, "talk to me until the lights come back on." She bit her lip, trying to smother the smile that threatened to reveal itself. The way he said it made her want to give in, made her want to play along.

"Don't count on it." She shook her head, trying to keep control, trying to maintain her independence. But he seemed to have all the time in the world. He waited, watched her, let her silence work against her. She felt herself slip toward him, not physically but in a way she couldn't resist, in a way that made her face grow warm. It made the rest of her grow warm, too.

"You're not like anyone else," Jace said, and his words caught her off guard more than she would have thought possible, "I mean that. I've never met anyone like you." His eyes were on her, dark and intense in the low light. Her throat tightened, the force of his sincerity unsettling. It was the last thing she expected, the last thing she was prepared for. She tried to come up with a response that would match his unexpected honesty.

"You should get out more." She said, but the humour didn't cover the awkwardness in her voice. He laughed, a real laugh, and the sound made her smile in spite of herself. It chipped away at the walls she'd worked so hard to build. It did more than that - it filled the tight space with a kind of heat she wasn't used to.

Their conversation had taken on a new intensity. Ella found herself caught in the shift, in the unexpected way they seemed to understand each other. How she found herself moving closer, unable to keep the space between them. Unable to hold onto her pretence. She felt his attention on her like a current, and she could no longer tell if it was uncomfortable or electrifying. She could no longer tell if she wanted to push it away or pull it closer. Ella felt the gravity, and for the first time, she stopped fighting against it.

Jace lingered in the new space they'd built between them. He wasn't about to leave it empty, and he wasn't about to let Ella do so either. He drew closer, sure that she wouldn't resist. Sure that the momentum would keep carrying them forward. She could still back away, but he could tell she wouldn't. He could tell she didn't want to. The confidence of that realisation made him bold. The warmth of her body, so close now, made him eager. He inched forward, letting the silence between them hold all the unspoken possibilities. He could almost hear her thoughts, the pull between them like a current through a wire. Jace wanted to feel it at full strength.

Ella's breathing matched his, her body mirroring his movements in a way that thrilled him. Her reluctance from before seemed to dissolve into the air around them, leaving nothing but the charged feeling of anticipation. She wasn't pulling back, not this time. He felt the shift, and it drove him to push further, to test the limits of what she'd allow. He could smell the faint scent of her perfume, the scent he sometimes caught in passing when they shared the same conference room. Here, it was concentrated and inescapable. It wrapped around him like a promise, like the intimacy of the elevator. Jace closed the gap, his breath warm against her ear, his presence undeniable.

"Is this how you treat all your colleagues?" He asked, letting his voice hold a note of daring and challenge. He saw her cheeks flush in the dim light. Saw the way she drew in a breath, caught between excitement and hesitation. Ella remained silent, but it wasn't the silence of resistance. It was the silence of too much to say, the kind of silence that welcomed the words he offered. Jace felt the edge of triumph, but it was coloured with something more - something that tasted like admiration, like genuine desire.

Ella felt the heat of him, felt the rush of the moment as she stayed still. Her earlier resolve had faltered, and she found herself not caring as much as she thought she would. The intensity of his presence matched her own intensity, and it was more thrilling than she expected. More liberating. Her awareness of their proximity burned in her thoughts. She could still push him away, still draw the line she'd been so determined to hold. But the longer she waited, the less she wanted to. Jace moved in even closer, daring and assured. She could almost hear him smile, the twist of his lips as he leaned back just enough to let her see it, let her know it was there. He watched her, saw the struggle in her expression turn into something more fluid, something that blended resistance with desire. His confidence swelled, but it was not the usual swagger. It was tempered by the realisation of how much he wanted this, how much he wanted her to want this too.

"Not so bad when you let your guard down. Does it feel as strange to you as it does to me?" His words were a mixture of challenge and sincerity, a rare combination for him. Ella laughed, a sound more surprised than intended. The tension that held them tight seemed to loosen, and for a moment, she was just a woman in a dark elevator with a man who had more patience and persistence than she thought possible. A woman who found herself letting go.

The power flickered back, and the dim light cut through the space between them like a brief glimpse of clarity. Jace caught sight of her expression, caught sight of his own reflection in her eyes. There was no time to dissect the looks they shared, only the intensity of knowing they'd seen each other in ways they hadn't before. Jace reached out, his fingers adjusting her blouse, claiming it was slightly askew. His touch was a brush of heat against her skin. The contact, unexpected and deliberate, sent a thrill through her that bordered on shock. She flinched, but she didn't move away.

Then the lights flickered out again, plunging them back into the comfort and chaos of darkness. But the memory of that moment stayed, as vivid as the sudden brightness had been. Ella didn't need to see his face to know the look he wore. She felt it, the smirk mixed with something new, something like satisfaction. She felt her own expression shift, the tension between them growing until it was almost too much. Their eyes met in the dark, charged with intent that went unspoken. Charged with the understanding that neither of them had to say a word.

Ella was more at ease than she thought possible, her earlier struggle morphing into something more. Into an acceptance she hadn't anticipated. The momentum carried them forward, leaving her breathless in a way that felt entirely new. The elevator's confining walls turned inward, not against her body but against her intentions. Ella felt the resistance crumble like old plaster. Her plans, her defences, her stubborn autonomy - they left her with a rush of something more primal, something deep and urgent.

The weight of her own restraint was heavier than she'd realised, and when it lifted the air felt charged and alive. The spark of their earlier touch, the thrill of Jace's fingers on her skin reignited a hunger she couldn't quite tame. It spread through her, unfurling with the kind of heat she hadn't felt in a long time. Maybe ever. Ella had fought against this for so long, fought against the inevitability of attraction, of want. Her pulse quickened as the reality of her desire caught up with her. Caught up with the dark, electric charge between them. Her mind was alive with it, with the overpowering need to stop pretending she could remain untouched by his presence.

Everything felt new, more intense than she thought possible. The tension collapsed into something undeniable, a pulling force that set her body in tune with his. Each brush, each shared breath, brought the urgency of the situation to a fever pitch. The pressure of holding back dissolved, leaving her free to feel everything at once. She was startled by the depth of it, by how quickly she let herself tumble into the realisation that this was about more than just proximity. More than the thrill of a chance encounter. Jace's words echoed through her, the promise of being different when she let go. It rang true now. Her old life, her old intentions, seemed too thin to hold her. Seemed inadequate to the strength of her own feelings.

She was tired of resisting, tired of acting as though she didn't want this as much as he did. As much as the heat in her body told her she did. The struggle between control and release balanced on a sharp edge, but she knew which way she would fall. Knew that it wasn't as terrifying as she had once believed. With the collapse of her defences came the acceptance that this was real. That she wanted him, wanted the breathless charge that wrapped around them, held them close in the impossibly small space of the elevator.

Letting go was inevitable, but it felt like something more. Something vast and necessary. She leaned into the feeling, the rush of blood and need. She leaned toward Jace, her resolve softening with the knowledge that surrender was its own form of power. The darkness and the urgency took on new forms, wrapping her in the warm promise of everything she hadn't allowed herself to want. Of everything she was now ready to admit she did want.

Her independence, the guard she kept so fiercely intact now seemed less important. Seemed smaller than what she felt, what she let herself feel without the constraint of rules and plans. The raw desire that thudded through her was as emotional as it was physical, a revelation that left her breathless and ready. The space around them was alive, the potential of what was about to happen making every breath and every touch intensify her decision. Ella hung in the moment before everything changed, the precipice of her own control. The air pulsed, their bodies moved toward each other, and she was poised on the edge of fully giving in.

She couldn't stop her mind from running through all the reasons this was a bad idea, all the ways she'd fought to keep him at arm's length. But none of them mattered now. They held as much weight as tissue paper in the rain. Every word he spoke soaked through her, filled her with the thrill of its potential. The urgency of her thoughts matched the rapid pulse of her body. Ella felt like every reason she had ever constructed crumbled under the pressure of the moment. The old truths she held onto disintegrated in the heat of their proximity. Jace's words, his voice full of flirtation, pushed her closer to the edge. She didn't mind.

Each inch between them felt charged with energy, a magnetic pull that left her dizzy with its force. She had been feeling this way for so much longer than she was willing to admit. Even to herself.

She saw it clearly now like a bright flash that wouldn't let her turn away. Her breath was fast and shallow, a tempo that mirrored her heartbeat. Ella was so close to surrendering, so ready to let go of everything she had built around herself. It scared her, but it excited her even more. Jace seemed to know it, to sense the shift in her stance. Her pulse quickened with every glance he stole, every word he offered.

The struggle between wanting him and maintaining control teetered on the verge of resolution. The friction of his attention, the gravity of her own, stretched thin and tight like the elevator cables above them. Like the last shreds of her resolve. Her mind raced, each thought faster than the one before it. She wanted this. Wanted him. The desire and the nearness folded into one. The tension was electric, leaving her gasping in the aftermath of it. It matched the flicker of excitement that ran through her body like a live wire. Ella leaned into the feeling, into Jace. The lightheaded abandon of it swept her away, until all she could feel was the inevitability of their touch.

She couldn't stop herself now. Her breath caught, and she knew the decision was made. It was as thrilling as it was inescapable. Ella gave in to the heat, to the desire, to everything that pressed against her from the inside out. Her old reasons vanished, leaving nothing but the bright shock of the moment. She knew Jace was aware of the change, knew he was waiting, just as breathless. Just as ready. The air was thick with anticipation, every touch and every word charged with the promise of what came next. The tension grew, filled the space until there was no room for anything else. Until it had to break.

A jolt shook them loose, broke the tension that held so tightly around their bodies. They collided, full of surprise and uncertainty, and when the laughter came, it rushed out like steam from a pressure valve. Ella didn't remember the last time she laughed like this. Maybe she never had. The elevator's movement caught them both off guard, their balance as fragile as the breathless anticipation they'd been wrapped in. Jace stumbled, his shoulder brushing against hers, and the shock of it sent them reeling in more ways than one.

Ella's laughter was raw and unrestrained, a sound that filled the small space with an energy she'd never expected. It broke through her with the force of something long buried, something more profound than she'd been prepared to admit. Jace joined her, his own laughter spilling out, as surprised and uncontained as hers. He leaned back, the walls pressing in against them but feeling bigger now, full of the echoes of their unexpected release. The satisfaction of seeing Ella like this, of seeing her free, thrilled him more than he thought possible.

The collision of their bodies had startled them into something deeper, into a connection that rang true and clear in the dimness. Ella felt her own restraint unravel, leaving her wide open, and she loved the way it felt. She hadn't known, couldn't have guessed, how much she needed to let go. Jace watched her with a kind of wonder, her transformation almost too much to take in. It wasn't a transformation at all, he realised. It was a revelation. His laughter held a note of triumph, but it was not the victory he'd imagined. It was sweeter, realer. The laughter softened and settled into something quieter, something more shared. They were both surprised by it, surprised by how right it felt to let go of everything but the moment. Ella leaned back against the wall, catching her breath, feeling lighter than she ever had.

"I don't think I've laughed like that in a long time." She said, her voice still threaded with the tail end of mirth.

"You're missing out," Jace said, his eyes on her, full of an admiration she hadn't expected to see, "I told you it wouldn't be so bad if you just let go." The teasing note was there, but so was something deeper. Ella shook her head, half in disbelief, half in acknowledgment of how much she'd changed in such a short time. "I should've known you'd have this all figured out." She said, but the words carried none of the resistance she'd once kept between them. Jace shrugged, but the gesture was full of warmth.

"I like this side of you," he said, surprising even himself with the simplicity of it, "didn't think I'd ever see it."

"Neither did I." Ella admitted. She met his gaze, the intensity of it less intimidating, more welcome, than it had ever been.

"Neither did I." The repetition was an acceptance, a claim on her own freedom. Their laughter lingered, a soft hum in the air, the resonance of something broken open and left unguarded. Ella's new sense of freedom wrapped around her like a blanket, comfortable and warm, as if the tight edges of her world had been loosened and left her at ease. Jace saw the change in her, felt it in himself. He wasn't sure when he'd crossed the line from wanting to win her over to simply wanting her, but it didn't matter now. The crossing was complete. The line was gone. They were both stunned by how the elevator's simple jolt could lead to such an emotional release. They were both thrilled by it too. It was an outcome neither had anticipated, but one that left them closer than ever.

"I think I needed this." Ella said, her voice still buoyant with the remnants of laughter, with the freedom she was beginning to embrace. Jace grinned, unable to contain the pleasure of seeing her so unguarded.

"Maybe I needed it too." He said, softer now, the depth of his own realisation sinking in. He hadn't expected this to be so intense, so transformative. But it was. The understanding of their shift, of how fundamentally they'd changed pulsed between them. The air felt electric, felt like everything she'd been afraid to let it be. Ella took a deep breath, her internal reflection leaving her more open than she'd ever allowed.

The tension she'd held onto slipped away, and in its place was something real, something undeniable. She didn't feel confined. She didn't feel trapped. She felt free. She felt ready for whatever came next. It was more than she'd hoped for, more than she'd imagined. Beside her, Jace shared in the moment. Shared in everything. The light snapped on, then off, a rapid pulse that left everything exposed in sharp relief. Jace moved toward her with purpose, with intent.

"You're different when you let go." His words were soft but hit her with force. She absorbed them like a shock, felt them in her core, and in that moment nothing else existed. The raw intensity of his voice and the warmth of his body wrapped around her in a way that was both terrifying and exhilarating. Ella's breath caught in her throat, a strangled exhale that felt like the only thing tethering her to reality. She couldn't believe how much it affected her, how deeply she felt the truth of his words. She was different, and she knew it. She knew that letting go had changed everything. Her old self felt like a shadow now, like something she could only see in contrast to what she'd become.

The lights flickered, casting the intimacy of the moment in shadow and light, the transition of her own emotions mirrored in the chaos of illumination. She stood in stark contrast to the woman she'd been before. Jace saw it. She felt it. The charged atmosphere solidified their connection, made it more real, more vivid. It enveloped them, leaving no room for uncertainty or second-guessing. Jace's presence was electric, and it was all she wanted, all she could focus on. Nothing else mattered. The world outside was distant, irrelevant, reduced to a memory of motionless elevator cars and late nights at the office. All that remained was the heat of Jace's words and the way they settled into her, the way they rooted themselves in her breathless certainty.

The intensity filled the space between them, a physical force that held her tighter than she'd ever let anyone hold her before. Ella accepted the change, embraced it with a sudden and unexpected eagerness. Her thoughts raced, flickered with the same rapidity as the lights. They filled her mind with the urgency of her own desire, with the thrill of finally admitting to herself how much she wanted this. How much she wanted him.

"You're right." She whispered, the words both a surrender and a claim. Her voice didn't waver. Her resolve, once so solid, had melted into something else, something pliant and warm. Jace's eyes met hers, the dim light barely enough to make out their depths, but she didn't need to see them clearly to know the expression they held. The unspoken promise hung between them, an offer she was more than ready to accept. Everything felt new, felt electric. Ella was caught in the brilliance of it, in the rapid shift that had left her exposed but unafraid. Her breath came fast, came shallow, matching the rhythm of her heartbeat.

The realisation was stark and undeniable. She didn't want to go back to the way things had been. She didn't want to return to the safe but empty confines of her independence. She wanted more of this, more of Jace, more of everything that rushed through her with the force of an unexpected storm. She embraced the shift with a recklessness she hadn't known she possessed. The surrender left her powerful, left her open to whatever came next. Ella knew she'd crossed a line she didn't want to step back over. The change thrilled her, terrified her, and filled her with an anticipation that tingled against her skin. She was poised, waiting for the next moment, knowing it would be as intense as the one before it.

They filled the space between them, electric and undeniable. Ella caught her breath, caught the look in Jace's eyes. She wasn't prepared for how much it affected her. Wasn't prepared for the thrill of finally closing the gap. Her heart raced, outpacing even her wildest thoughts. She hadn't realised how intense this would feel, how intense his gaze would be. It drew her in with a gravity she couldn't resist, pulled her closer with an urgency that matched the rapidity of her own desire. Jace's eyes were dark, full of intent and invitation. The dim light carved sharp lines of shadow and depth across his features, and she knew she was seeing him clearly for the first time. Knew she was seeing more than she'd ever let herself admit.

The thrill of closing the gap was more than she expected, more than she could have imagined. Every inch disappeared, replaced by a heady, potent closeness that left her breathless. Jace moved toward her, the shift in his gaze matching the shift she felt in herself. Every touch, every glance was charged, and she let herself soak in the feeling. She let herself accept how much she wanted this, how much she wanted him. The gap closed, leaving no room for hesitation or doubt. The air was thick with tension, so thick that it pressed against her skin like an eager hand, like the promise of what they'd been moving toward all along.

The elevator couldn't contain it. The tight press of their bodies, the heat, the urgency - it was more than the small space could hold. Ella leaned toward Jace, felt his breath, felt everything, and knew it was about to explode. The air pulsed around them, a living thing that wrapped them tight and left no room for restraint. It was more than heat, more than anticipation. It was a force that pushed them together, pulled them in with the inevitability of something too powerful to resist.

Jace moved closer, and Ella moved too, the intensity of their proximity making her gasp. She felt his breath warm on her skin, felt the electric charge between them, a bright and crackling line that connected her to him. The urgency thrilled her, overwhelmed her, made her forget everything except the thrill of being pulled into his orbit. Ella felt the tension rise like the temperature in a boiler, climbing until it reached the point of no return. Until it was too much to hold in. She looked at Jace, and his eyes told her what she already knew - he felt it too. He felt the tight press of the moment, the urgency of their closeness, the thrill of their uncontainable desire. Ella didn't hold back. She didn't want to. She let herself go, let herself lean fully into the force that pulled her toward him. Her final surrender was a release, an opening, a rush of heat that left her breathless and full of want.

Their lips met in a kiss that was passionate and all-consuming, a kiss that was the culmination of everything, the confirmation of what had been simmering between them from the start. The tension broke in an explosion of heat and closeness. They wrapped themselves in it, in each other, and nothing else existed. The outside world faded into a blur, the only reality the urgent, undeniable force that held them together. The kiss broke, but the tension between them didn't. Ella's breath came in ragged bursts, and Jace's eyes were dark and filled with promise. They stayed close, bodies pressing together, as the elevator lurched into motion. As the world slipped away.

The closeness was intense, too intense for them to pull back, too potent for them to care about anything but the moment. The lights flickered, but it was nothing compared to the charge between them. The intensity left them breathless, their bodies hot and urgent against each other. The elevator moved, but they didn't care. It was only them. Only this. The reality of what they'd shared left the rest of the world in shadow, left everything but their connection in the blur of motion outside. The moment felt infinite, felt as if it held the pulse of everything they'd been waiting for. Everything they'd denied themselves. Ella's breath hitched as she pulled him closer, as she let go of anything but the sheer thrill of being right here, right now.

Jace's satisfaction was raw and bright. He'd broken through, reached the side of her he knew was there. The side he'd wanted to reach from the start. The realisation of it hit him hard, as hard as their bodies pressed together. The depth of their connection left them both stunned, more than either of them expected. It was real. It was electric. It was all that mattered. The power died and took the light with it. The darkness came as a shock, sudden and disorienting, but Jace was ready for it. Ella wasn't. She felt his fingers find hers, his grip solid and warm, and the unexpected contact sent a shiver through her.

The elevator jerked, the motion throwing them off balance. The blackness that followed was overwhelming, erasing the vibrant moment they'd shared. Ella's heart pounded, each beat a reminder of how quickly things could change. She didn't expect it to hit her so hard, didn't expect to feel the rush of disorientation that pressed in around her. It was as if the world had inverted, flipped from charged intimacy to the stark absence of light and sound. But Jace was there, already closing the distance, already reaching for her. She felt his grip, solid and reassuring, and the warmth of it steadied her more than the light ever had.

"I promise you're safe." Jace murmured, his voice a low hum against the dark. The simple words carried more than reassurance. They carried intent, a promise of connection she felt in every nerve. Ella accepted his touch, accepted the new dynamic with a thrill that pulsed through her, that pulsed through their joined hands. The simple contact felt profound, more intimate than the kiss, more real than the heat of their earlier desire. The elevator was still and quiet around them, but Ella's thoughts raced with the sudden shift, the newness of the moment. She was surprised by how much she welcomed it, how much she let herself lean into the feel of his grip.

The silence was full, alive, and so were they. Jace didn't need to say anything. Ella didn't need him to. He pulled her in, pulled her close, and she melted into the kiss with the kind of intensity that left her gasping for more. Her hesitation was brief, a fleeting thought that vanished as their lips met. The kiss was electric, a rush that surged through her and left no room for doubt or resistance. It was everything she wanted. Everything she didn't know she could have. It overwhelmed her, swept her away on a tide of heat and urgency. Ella pressed closer, let the depth of it consume her, let it confirm everything they'd been moving toward, everything they'd been avoiding until now.

The kiss took her breath away, left her wanting, needing more. It took her resistance and turned it into something wild and free. Ella let herself get lost in the feeling, in the heat, in the truth of what they'd become. Jace held her close, closer than she'd let anyone hold her, and the profound sense of connection wrapped around them, tighter than skin, tighter than their own breath. The kiss was everything, the kiss was all. The kiss was the unspoken promise made real, made right. The elevator was still, but they were not. Ella felt the world slip away, felt Jace pull her closer, felt the tight press of his body and the heat that consumed her. It was more than she thought she could hold, and it was all she wanted. And then the momentum shifted.

The kiss was a spark in a gas tank, and the explosion was inevitable. Ella's breath hitched as Jace's tongue pushed past her lips, hot and insistent with a rhythm that sent shivers down her spine. His hands were everywhere, clutching at her thighs, grabbing her breasts, tugging at the fabric of her skirt like it was the only thing standing between them. She moaned into his mouth, the friction sending a sensation through her that made her shake.

Jace's satisfaction was raw and bright, finally breaking through Ella's barriers. As he reached the side of her he knew was there, he lifted her skirt and his fingers found the top of her lace panties. The intensity of their connection left them both breathless and wanting more. Ella could feel him pressing into her thigh like a brand. She ground against it, desperate for more, her body throbbing with need. He growled low in his throat, a sound that made her pulse, and he backed her into the elevator wall, the cold metal a sharp contrast to the heat of his body. His fingers trailed deeper into her soaked panties, and he ripped them off with a single, brutal tug.

"Jace." Ella gasped as his fingers slid between her folds, teasing her clit with rough, deliberate strokes. She was dripping, and he buried two of them inside her without warning. Her knees buckled, but he caught her, holding her up with one arm while the other thrusted inside her intently.

"Hush," Jace muttered against her neck, his breath hot on her skin as he bit into her flesh, "you're so fucking tight. You have no idea what you're in for. I'm gonna make you scream." She didn't doubt it. She felt him against her, thick and heavy in his tight pants.

"What if someone hears us." Ella's heart pounded as Jace's skilled hands explored her body like a map, each touch leaving a trail of her juices in its wake.

"Maybe they'll just think we're calling for help," unzipping his pants, his cock was thick and heavy in his hand, glistening with precum, "and even if they could tell, no one would know it's us. No one would ever think it could be us." He didn't give her time to process his words or catch her breath. He plunged into her without warning or mercy. Ella let out a scream as he filled her completely in one powerful thrust. She dug her nails into his shoulders as he stretched and claimed every bit of her. She clung to him, ravenous and soaked, and he showed no signs of relenting. His pelvis smacked against hers, the wet sound of skin on skin reverberating in the small elevator, mingling with their passionate moans and grunts.

"Ella." Her name was a curse and a prayer, a raw plea that filled the small space and consumed them both. Ella's back hit the wall, but she didn't care. She was lost to him now, lost to the heat and the need. Every inch of her was his, stretched and full and burning with desire. Her head spun with the intensity of it, her thoughts nothing more than flashing lights and excited shudders. Each stroke sent shockwaves through her body, making her grip tighter around him. She bit down on her bottom lip to keep from crying out as he reached deeper inside her with every powerful thrust. The friction was incredible, making everything inside her clench and shudder as he hit that spot over and over again. And then the walls started to shake.

The elevator hummed, a low, mechanical purr beneath the symphony of their ragged breaths and slick, slapping skin. Jace's hands were everywhere - pinning Ella's wrists above her head, his fingers digging into her delicate flesh as he slammed into her with a force that made the walls tremble. Her back was flush against the cool metal, her curves pressed hard enough to leave imprints, but she didn't care. Her spine arched, her hips bucked, and her legs wrapped around his waist like a vice, drawing him deeper.

"Jace." She gasped, her voice a broken mess, raw and desperate. His name dripped from her lips like honey, sweet and sinful, and he growled in response, his teeth grazing the shell of her ear. The sound vibrated through her, sending sparks down her spine as he angled himself just right, hitting that spot inside her that made her vision blur and her thighs quiver.

"Fuck Ella." He groaned, his voice thick with lust, his breath hot against her neck. His cock was a force of nature, pounding into her with a rhythm that was relentless, unyielding. She could feel every inch of him - the way he stretched her, filled her, owned her. The head of his dick dragged against her walls, teasing her with a precision that was almost cruel. Her body was on fire, every nerve ending screaming for more.

Her nails raked down his back, leaving angry red trails in their wake, his hips jerking forward with a brutal snap that made her cry out. The elevator jerked slightly, the motion only adding to the chaos of sensation as Jace thrust in and out of her. The sound of their bodies slamming together was obscene - wet, filthy, and frantic. Sweat slicked their skin, the air thick with the scent of sex and desperation. Ella's legs tightened around him, her heels falling from her feet as she urged him on, her body begging for release.

"You feel that?" Jace moaned, his voice a dark promise as he pulled back just enough to look her in the eyes.

"Jace—"

"Feel how fucking deep I am? You're mine, Ella. Every fucking inch of you." And then he was moving again, his thrusts harder and faster.

"Fuck Jace." Ella's moans were loud, unrestrained, echoing off the walls as he pounded into her with a ferocity that left her shaking. "Fuck, you feel so good." Jace growled, his voice raw with need. He lifted one of her legs over his shoulder, changing the angle so his cock hit that sweet spot inside her that made her eyes roll back. She couldn't speak, couldn't think. All she could do was feel his cock hammering into her, his fingers digging into her hip, his breath hot on her skin. She was close, so close, and when his thumb found her clit again, rubbing circles that set her on fire, she shattered.

"Come for me." Jace demanded, his voice rough and commanding. Ella screamed, her body convulsing around him as her orgasm tore through her. It hit her like a freight train, her insides clenching around him as waves of pleasure crashed over her. Jace didn't stop. He kept fucking her through it, his pace relentless, until he finally came with a groan. She clenched around his cock, milking him for all he was worth, and Jace swore loudly as he followed her over. He buried himself to the hilt, his cum flooding her in hot, thick spurts as his hips jerked against hers. They stayed like that for a moment, pressed together and breathing hard, their bodies still connected.

Jace pulled out slowly, his cock glistening with her wetness and his cum as he stepped back. Ella's legs gave out beneath her, and she slid down the wall with a soft whimper, her body still trembling with the echoes of her orgasm. Jace reached down, his hand rough but gentle as he helped her to her feet. The elevator moved, but they didn't. The soft jolt broke nothing but their breathless laughter, nothing but the stillness that had wrapped them tight. Jace pulled Ella's skirt down over her, smoothing out the creases in her blouse. Before she could say a word, he tucked her loose hair behind her ear and leaned in close, resting his hand on her shoulder.

"Are you going to be less uptight from now on?" Jace held her in his gaze, his grip as sure and steady as his own breath, as sure and steady as the way he felt.

"Yes." Ella's thoughts spun, a dizzying spiral of desire and disbelief. She couldn't believe how intense it had been, how quickly everything had changed.

"Good girl." Jace's fingers traced her skin, leaving her with the soft warmth of his touch and the even softer warmth of his presence. They collected themselves in the quiet aftermath, in the softness of their shared breath and bodies. Jace bent down to collect her panties from the floor. She held out her hand to retrieve them, but just as quickly he snatched them from the air and placed them gingerly in his back pocket.

The elevator doors slid open, spilling the light from the lobby into their dark cocoon, forcing them into a world that felt too bright, too real. Ella hesitated, not ready to let go of the moment, not ready to let go of Jace. He gave her a grin, wide and full of promise, and she felt the ground tilt beneath her feet. They stood on the threshold, the starkness of the outside world a jarring contrast to the warmth they'd shared. Ella felt the light and reality wash over them, felt the sudden shift from intense intimacy to the buzz of everything else.

"Same time next week?" His teasing demeanour brought a new warmth to her cheeks, a new rush to her pulse. She felt the exhilaration of change, felt the confusion of how quickly everything had turned. They hung in the air, as vivid and full as the rush of heat she felt in response. As full as the change she felt in herself. Ella's reaction was immediate, a mix of thrill and uncertainty, a rapid beat of thoughts that spiralled with the unexpected truth of what she wanted.

And then she watched him walk away, leaving her in the harsh lobby light that had broken them from their fleeting dalliance in the elevator. The unspoken promise of what was to come wrapped around her, held her in the bright reality of the moment. It was a shift she didn't want to end. It was a change she was ready for. As she hailed a cab and headed home, she felt a sense of anticipation for what the future might hold. Change was in the air, and she was ready to embrace it, no matter where it might lead her.

Room Service

The city glowed below, a shimmering constellation of neon and glass as Natalie stepped into the cavernous solitude of the penthouse suite. Behind her, the door clicked shut with a sound that seemed to echo all the way to the horizon. She stood there for a moment, still wrapped in her woolen coat and her own taut ambition, feeling the emptiness press in from all sides. A sleek glass wall unveiled the Manhattan skyline - a spectacle that might have filled her with wonder on any other day. But today was not any other day. She set her suitcase on the pristine white bedspread, the silkiness of it yielding to the pressure. The hotel was meant to be an escape, a lavish break from a life dominated by late nights, legal briefs, and endless negotiations. Yet even here, amidst the carefully curated opulence, she found herself imprisoned by the thoughts she had tried to leave at the office.

The suite itself was modern art, cool and immaculate, each piece of furniture strategically placed like a calculated offer. The plush carpet stretched luxuriously underfoot, and the rich marble accents promised indulgence at every turn. Natalie imagined what her colleagues would say, knowing she had splurged on such an extravagance. She forced herself to admire the view again - the expanse of skyscrapers flickering like votive candles. But it was no use, she couldn't stop her thoughts from ricocheting back to the grind that awaited her Monday morning.

It was a last-minute case that brought her to this point of fatigue, a contract dispute that spiraled into an all-nighter. She needed distance from the chaos, but her mind wouldn't grant it. There was a mockery in the way she lugged the suitcase into the suite - heavy, determined, as though transporting more than just clothes and toiletries. She stared at it now, the leather gleaming in the low light, a reminder of how tightly wound she'd become. A reminder of everything she thought she could leave behind.

Natalie rubbed her temples and exhaled, pulling herself into the centre of the room. Her heels clicked on the polished floor, the only sound aside from the muffled hum of the city below. She was exhausted in a way that sleep couldn't cure, exhausted from the need to be always the one who wins. Her friends said she was driven, her mother called it obsessive, her colleagues thought she was competitive. She preferred to think of herself as dedicated, but the truth was that she didn't know how to switch off.

The coat slipped off her shoulder as she stared out the window, one glass wall away from the world. She hoped that the wine she brought would dull the sharpness in her mind, that the quiet would soothe what felt raw and unraveled. As the low light brushed the contours of the room in soft gold, she imagined an alternate universe in which her mind was as spacious and open as the suite itself. A universe in which she could sip wine and savour each note, rather than down it as an anesthetic.

A breath, deep and deliberate, expanded her chest. She let her hair fall out of its bun, the silky weight a gentle distraction from her crowded mind. She allowed herself to indulge, for a moment, in the idea that she could sink into this luxurious isolation. Yet even as she fought to claim this night as her own, Natalie felt it slipping through her fingers like silk. Her fingers traced the rim of the wine glass, and she caught her reflection in the window, all ghostly elegance and distraction. Her thoughts leapt back to last week's negotiations, the details she might have overlooked. They slipped into the imagined conversation she'd have to mediate when she returned. The words crowded her, always so many words. For once, she wished them away.

"Stop." She said aloud, the sound a faint challenge against the persistent quiet. She moved around the suite like a visitor in her own life, running her fingers over the plush upholstery, the edge of the marble table. Everything bespoke elegance, simplicity, the ultimate form of control. Everything was just as she had requested. And yet her fingers hovered over her phone, the screen blank and inviting. The inbox might hold urgent messages, new deals, fresh fires to put out. It was a pull she resisted, but just barely.

She slipped out of her blazer, folding it neatly and placing it on the bench at the end of her bed. A glass of wine now full, the bottle a promise of more. She slipped off her heels, and with it, a modicum of tension. Her stockinged feet sank into the carpet, warmth creeping up from the soles, but her mind remained restless. She wished, for once, to escape into the night like a different woman - someone unconcerned with anything more than this moment. She wished she could lose herself in the anonymous magic of a New York weekend, in a city where possibility hummed at all hours. The view from the windows told her it was within reach. The hours stretched out in front of her like a golden road to dawn.

The suite felt too large, a museum, a stage. And she, a singular figure unsure of her own script. Perhaps, she thought, this is what luxury really meant - the freedom to walk away from one life and slip into another, even if only until sunrise. Natalie crossed her arms, hugging herself, standing in the perfect stillness. She breathed in, a deep gulp of air that felt like diving into the night itself. The lights winked back at her from across the river, and the city hummed with its inexhaustible energy. Natalie's mind, always the restless hunter, for once went quiet.

The pristine suite enveloped her, each meticulously chosen element like a soothing lullaby against her frayed nerves. As Natalie moved from room to room, she peeled off the layers of her executive armor - satin shirt, pencil skirt, stockings - releasing them with the defiance of a prisoner turned escape artist. She took in the space once more, noting the stark perfection of it all. That's when she saw it, the elegant, cream-colored concierge card, propped like a temptation on the glass table. A concierge specifically dedicated to the suites in the hotel. Without thinking, she dialed.

"Miss Campbell," came the voice, deep and polished as mahogany, "this is concierge Leo speaking." The name, so unexpectedly personal, caught her off guard. She hesitated for a moment, her own name perched on the edge of her tongue like a delicate bird.

"This is Natalie," she finally replied, her voice slipping into the confident cadence of negotiation, "in the penthouse." She paused, uncertain whether to say more. Leo's laughter was a warm, inviting sound.

"Yes, Miss Campbell. I can see which suite you are calling from. How can I be of assistance?" His voice wrapped around her, filled with an ease that disarmed her corporate composure. She pictured him - tall, suave, ready to cater to her every whim - and that amused her.

"I know it's last minute, but I noticed the spa was open until ten. Any chance they have a masseuse available?"
"Unfortunately the spa is fully booked for the evening, ma'am," Leo replied, the words stretched out like a cat waking from a nap, "but I can offer you an alternative if you're in need of some relaxation." She imagined his smirk, just on the edge of professional.
"Oh?"
"We have an excellent selection of amenities that we can bring to your room."
"What if I need something more than just a bottle of wine?" Her tone was airy, flirtatious, the hint of mischief even new to her.
"If you head into your ensuite, you'll find an in-room spa menu. Or did you have something more specific in mind?" His sense of playful abandon caught her by surprise.

Natalie let out a laugh she hadn't realized she was holding in. Walking toward the bathroom, she hesitated in the doorway, staring at the large and luxurious spa bath in front of her. It was the grandest bathtub she had ever laid eyes on, a masterpiece of opulence and indulgence. Crafted from gleaming, polished marble, its expansive basin could easily accommodate two people, inviting them to bask in its depths. The rim was embellished with intricate gold leaf patterns, shimmering softly in the ambient light, and delicate carvings of cherubs and vines wound gracefully around its exterior. Plush, oversized towels, as soft as clouds, were artfully draped over a nearby heated rack.

"Miss Campbell," Leo's voice had taken on a gentle and captivating tone, "do you see the menu on the benchtop?"

"Of course, one minute." She gracefully approached the sink, delicately lifting the menu from its ornate stand. Her eyes swept across the pages, revealing a luxurious array of options for a lavish bath experience. There were creamy milks like coconut and almond, promising to soothe and nourish the skin. Exquisite bath salts, infused with minerals and scents of lavender and eucalyptus, promised relaxation and rejuvenation. A symphony of scents awaited, from the calming aroma of chamomile to the invigorating zest of citrus. Silky oils such as argan and jojoba offered deep hydration and a touch of indulgence. The selection of items was completed by an assortment of scrubbers, including soft loofahs and exfoliating brushes, designed to invigorate and refresh.

"Is there anything you like the sound of?" Leo asked, clearing his throat gently.

"I'm not sure—"

"Perhaps you'd like me to put something together for you? If it's relaxation you're after, I know quite the assortment of products to bring you." Leo's voice, an intoxicating mix of smooth professionalism and something else. Something dangerous.

"Do you always offer such personalised service?"

"Only for guests who need it." He replied, his tone warm and mischievous. Natalie laughed, the sound mingling with the evening air.

"Then I look forward to it, Leo." The click of the call ending was like a punctuation mark on a page that she hadn't quite finished writing.

Earlier, the idea of relaxing seemed absurd, an indulgence she could ill afford. But now there was a spark, a sensation as elusive and rare as the empty hours ahead of her. She didn't quite know what to make of Leo, the man who wove promise and provocation into a single thread. Natalie moved through the suite again, seeing it differently this time. The sparseness felt intentional, every detail tailored for her comfort. The early evening light shifted from cool silver to soft gold, dipping everything in warmth. The longer she lingered, the more she realized the room was a cocoon, designed to envelop and transform her.

Unpacking became an afterthought, and she left her suitcase open on the floor, a jumble of silk and wool. Instead, she dressed in the silk robe the hotel had provided and poured herself another glass of wine, the liquid swirling ruby and luscious in the glass. She sank into a plush chair, one robe strap slipping off her shoulder, and revelled in the quiet. She laughed softly to herself, feeling something crack open inside, something she'd thought had calcified under the weight of endless hours and grueling expectations. Natalie sipped the wine, letting it linger on her tongue, the taste bold and unfamiliar. She closed her eyes, savoring it all, and felt the exhilaration of uncertainty.

She walked over to the full-length mirror, every step cushioned by the plush carpet beneath her bare feet. Her coat hung from the back of the chair, forgotten but still holding the shape of her ambition, a stark contrast to the soft curves now wrapped in silk. Natalie felt the weight of the past few weeks pressing down, a hand on her shoulder she couldn't quite shrug off. Exhaustion seeped into her bones, but there was something else too. Something unsteady and exciting, like the first dip of a rollercoaster ride.

The forceful knock on her door reverberated through the quiet room, jolting her upright and almost causing her glass of rich red wine to cascade over the pristine white fabric of her robe. Her heart raced momentarily, but she took a deep breath, carefully setting her glass down on a coaster on the polished oak table. She smoothed her robe, took another calming breath, and made her way to the door. The man stood in the dimly lit hallway, holding an intricately arranged basket of jars filled with luxurious creams, artisanal soaps with swirling patterns, bottles of aromatic oils, and soft, plush sponges. The air became infused with a mélange of incredible scents, from soothing lavender to invigorating citrus, each promising a moment of escape. The calming colors ranged from pale blues to gentle pinks, which added to the basket's allure. Nestled snugly in one corner of the basket was a bottle of exquisite wine, its deep green glass and rich red liquid glinting under the hallway light. In the centre, a small card protruded, its edges catching the light.

"Miss Campbell." His voice was deep and gentle. She was certain it was Leo, though he appeared younger than she had anticipated. He stood tall, with a light shining in his dark brown eyes. His beard was neatly trimmed, and his hair was styled to one side with gel. His shirt fit snugly around his muscular arms.

"Leo," she said gently, holding out her arms for the basket, "thank you for organising this for me."

"It's my pleasure," handing her the basket, he offered her a coy smile, "please call me if you need anything else." She nodded and closed the door, taking the assortment into the bathroom with her.

As she drew her bath, she opened the note from the basket. *Each container has the perfect amount needed for each item,* she read to herself, *empty each one into your bath, except the lotion. Rub this all over your body after the bath.* She held the paper in her hand, scrutinising the handwriting - so neat, too neat for someone like Leo. But the message at the bottom told her that it could only have come from him. *If you're still in need of relaxation afterwards, let me know.* The words were inviting, and playful, but it was hard to tell tone from a handwritten note. Her years of practising law taught her that.

She unscrewed the lid from a small jar filled with bath salts, smelling the mixture of lavender and charcoal before emptying it into the water. She watched as they swirled and dissolved under the plunging water from the tap. Picking up the oil, she smelled the aromas of eucalyptus and mint before pouring it into the water. A candle labelled *Peony and Prosecco* balanced neatly in the basket, and she placed it gingerly on the benchtop before lighting it. The bath milk was a subtle blend of oat and rose, which she poured slowly into the water, watching it mix with the salt and oil. She turned off the overhead lighting, suddenly plunged into an orange cocoon filled with an incredible mix of scents.

She refilled her wine glass, letting the silk robe slide from her shoulders and pool at her feet. Her toes curled into the soft bath mat before she eased into the hot water. As the gentle embrace of the bath enveloped her, Natalie closed her eyes, determined to savour the moment and banish thoughts of work from her mind. She focused on the soothing warmth that seeped into her muscles and the faint aroma of lavender and eucalyptus and mint and rose. The soft flicker of candlelight danced across the walls, casting a tranquil glow. She took a deep breath, trying to centre herself in the present, feeling the tension slowly melt away. However, every so often, a stray thought of unfinished reports and looming deadlines threatened to intrude. But Natalie resolutely pushed them aside, reminding herself that this was her time to unwind and recharge.

The water lapped at Natalie's skin like a lover's tongue, warm and insistent, and she leaned back against the porcelain edge of the tub. Steam curled around her, clinging to her flushed cheeks, her damp hair plastered to her neck in dark, sinuous tendrils. Her nipples pebbled beneath the surface, hard and aching, as her mind wandered to him. His name was a whisper in her head, a low, throaty growl that sent shivers skittering down her spine. She could almost hear his voice - that deep, velvety timbre that made her thighs clench involuntarily.

Her hand drifted lazily over her stomach, fingertips tracing the curve of her hip, the dip of her navel, before sliding lower. The water rippled around her as her fingers found the slick heat between her legs, and she let out a soft, shuddering breath. She imagined him there, kneeling beside the tub, his broad shoulders casting shadows on the tiled walls. His hands - those strong, calloused hands - would plunge into the water, seeking her out, claiming her.

She could almost feel his fingers parting her, the rough pads of his thumbs brushing against her clit in slow, deliberate circles. Her back arched, her hips lifting slightly as she pressed into her own touch, her breath hitching in her throat. She imagined his mouth on her neck, his teeth grazing her pulse point as he whispered filthy promises in her ear. His other hand would slide up her thigh, gripping her with a possessiveness that made her core clench with need.

"Leo." She moaned softly, her voice trembling with want. Her fingers worked faster now, plunging into herself, curling just right to hit that spot that made her toes curl. She pictured him watching her, his dark eyes heavy with lust, his cock hard and straining against his pants. He'd strip off his shirt, revealing that chiseled chest she'd only glimpsed in passing, and she'd reach for him, pulling him into the water with her. The thought of his weight pressing her down, his thick cock sliding into her, made her whimper. She could almost feel the stretch, the delicious burn as he filled her completely. Her free hand gripped the edge of the tub, her knuckles white as she touched herself, imagining it was him. Her breath came in ragged gasps, her body trembling on the edge of release.

"Fuck." She hissed, her head falling back as pleasure coiled tight in her belly. She could see him above her, his muscles taut with restraint, his jaw clenched as he thrust into her with a rhythm that left her breathless. Her clit throbbed under her touch, and she rubbed it harder, faster, until she was teetering on the brink. And then she came, her body convulsing as waves of ecstasy crashed over her. Her thighs shook, her toes curled, and she bit down on her lip to stifle the cry that threatened to escape. She slumped back against the tub, her chest heaving, her skin slick with sweat and water. But even as the aftershocks faded, she couldn't shake the image of him. Leo. His hands, his mouth, his everything. She wanted him. Needed him. And she wouldn't stop until she had him.

Natalie stood up suddenly, watching the water drip from her naked body in the mirror. She hesitated for only a moment, then stepped onto the bath mat and walked to the phone, dialing, her fingers swift and eager. The thrill of hearing Leo's voice came back to her in a rush, like the first sip of a potent cocktail. She hadn't expected to feel this way - bold, reckless, unmoored.

"Good evening, Miss Campbell," he picked up on the second ring, his voice a warm current, "have you finished so quickly?" She took in a quick breath, her body stiffening suddenly.

"I—, excuse me?"

"Your bath, ma'am," Leo said, the playful assurance making her heart skip, "are you feeling more relaxed?"

"Somewhat," she replied quickly, looking down at the pool of water and soapy suds that had collected at her feet, "but—" The hesitation caught at her throat - the bold feeling of urgency had escaped her once she heard his voice on the phone. The fantasy, *her* fantasy, was now reality, and she couldn't bring herself to accept it.

"I wanted to order some room service," she allowed a beat to pass, the air filling with possibility, "is there anything on the menu that you recommend?"

"What are you in the mood for?" His words hummed across the line, the kind of promise that left no room for doubt. Her breath caught for the briefest moment once more before she laughed awkwardly, the sound escaping her like a dare.

"I can't quite make up my mind." Natalie answered truthfully, though she knew she wasn't talking about food.

"You filled in your preference sheet for your penthouse breakfast experience. How about I surprise you?" His words left her feeling buoyant, electrified, like she could float away on his wit and banter. The connection was undeniable, a charged wire between them that buzzed with life.

"I'll leave you to it then." This time, when she set the phone down, the click was less an ending and more an exclamation point. His voice lingered in her ears, as though the suite itself was holding onto the sound. Natalie sank back into the water, her thoughts racing, her body alight with anticipation. The call had left her feeling daring, her usual reserve entirely misplaced in the heat of their exchange. She'd meant to hold on to her composure, but Leo had swept it away with disarming ease. It was exhilarating, terrifying, a rapid unraveling of the tightly wound person she usually was.

And she wanted more. She wanted to see where this thread would lead, what tapestry it might weave in the wide-open space of the hours to come. The shift in her mood was palpable, from weary and uncertain to something brighter, something eager and new. It was a glimpse into the world she'd nearly let slip away - the world of unpredictability, of connection, of playing the game by a different set of rules. She sat up slowly and reached for her wine, the glass as warm and rich as Leo's words. For the first time in too long, the notion of pleasure, pure and uncomplicated, didn't feel like a fantasy. She found herself smiling at the thought, her earlier reservations dissolving like sugar in champagne.

She took a sip, the wine smooth and heady on her tongue. There was an urgency in her that surprised even herself, a need to see how far she could push the boundaries that always seemed so fixed. This weekend was already unlike any she had planned. It held new energy, one that sparked against her skin and made her pulse race. Natalie set the glass down with a sense of finality, a readiness to embrace whatever the evening would bring. For once, she felt the thrill of not knowing, and it was like a shot of pure adrenaline.

This was her night, her New York story, and she was determined to live it with the volume turned all the way up.

Dessert wasn't what she'd expected. Certainly not on her doorstep, delivered by Leo himself. But there he was, tray in hand, his uniform disheveled in the most artful of ways, as if crafted to disrupt her night even further. Natalie hesitated for a split second, but the invitation was too tempting. She stepped aside, allowing him into the suite and into the unspoken game she wasn't sure how to play. He set the tray down with a deliberate pause, letting their eyes meet like the first sip of a forbidden drink.

The evening had been a tapestry of expectation and tension, but this was unexpected. Natalie had intended to unwind with a glass of wine, maybe let the muted hum of the city lull her into rest. But now, all her plans lay scattered like pieces of a game board, one that Leo seemed to know all the rules to. She let the door close with a quiet click, the sound swallowed by the spaciousness of the suite. Leo's presence shifted the air, filled it with a warmth that made her pulse quicken. His confidence was palpable, but not overbearing. It wrapped around her like the city lights, subtle and all-encompassing. Natalie watched him with an attentiveness that surprised her, her earlier resolve to settle in for the night evaporating like a summer shower. She felt exposed, but not in the way that work and life often left her. This was different, softer, more alluring.

She was acutely aware of her appearance - the wet silk robe, her damp hair, the only thing separating Leo from seeing her completely naked a simple piece of fabric. She wondered when the last time was that she had allowed someone to see her like this, unkempt and without makeup. But this wasn't unkempt, she told herself - she had just awoken first thing in the morning nor had she let herself go. She had a bath, and she was perfectly fine the way she looked emerging from it.

"Leo," she said, his name carrying a hint of disbelief and delight, "what have you brought me?" He placed the tray on the marble table with a grace that seemed deliberate, each movement a silent declaration of intention.

"Sit." Their eyes locked, and Natalie felt the world narrow down to just this room, just this moment. His gaze was warm, a soft but relentless focus that held hers captive. She wasn't used to being the one looked at, not like this. Not with such knowing intimacy. She sauntered over to the chair, slowly taking a seat and staring out the window at the city skyline. He stood behind her, hands on the backrest, staring at her reflection in the window. Leaning over her, he removed the cloche from one of the plates to reveal a sumptuous feast that was almost too beautiful to eat.

"To start," Leo murmured, his voice smooth and inviting, "we have a rich, creamy lobster bisque infused with just a hint of sherry, the perfect way to awaken your senses." He poured a single, shimmering glass of champagne, the bubbles dancing to the surface like a promise of something exquisite. She took a sip, the effervescence tingling on her lips as he unveiled the main course - a perfectly seared filet mignon, resting on a bed of velvety mashed potatoes, drizzled with a decadent truffle sauce that filled the air with an intoxicating aroma.

"The filet," he purred, "is cooked to perfection, tender and succulent with every bite melting in your mouth. Pink in the middle, the way all fine meat should be." Natalie couldn't help but smile, the anticipation building as he moved to the final reveal. She watched him in the reflection, his eyes on her when he spoke. She couldn't help but blush at the potential double meaning, pressing her thighs together under the silk. He watched her, looking at her legs as they clenched. With a flourish he lifted the last cloche to unveil a plate of strawberries, each one glistening under a layer of dark, luscious chocolate.

"And for dessert," Leo continued, "a selection of the finest strawberries, hand-dipped in rich chocolate, sweet and indulgent."
"I don't know how I'm supposed to eat all of this myself." She whispered, the combination of flavors, the warmth of his presence, and the view of the city skyline made the moment utterly unforgettable.
"There's no rush," Leo leaned closer, his breath warm against her ear, "you have all night. Try, taste, savour, and you can always save the strawberries for later." She gazed for a moment at the food before looking at his reflection in the window, realising in her reverie that he had already begun to walk toward the door.
"Leo." She turned to him, and he steadied his hand on the doorknob.

"Leo, wait," she stood, walking briskly to her purse and pulling out a crisp bill, "your tip. For this, and earlier."
"I couldn't—"
"I insist." She pressed the money into his hand, noticing the warmth of his skin against hers. The sensation was electric, just as

she had envisioned when she imagined him touching her earlier.

"Tips are included in the price of the suite, ma'am." Leo leaned back slightly, the confidence in his stance unshakeable, as though he knew exactly what impact he was having. As though the entire suite were an extension of him, and he was granting her entry to it piece by tantalizing piece.

"Still," she pressed her hand into his, feeling the warmth and strength from his grip, "I insist." With a small nod and a coy smile, he walked through the door.

Natalie felt a thrill rise within her, the kind that had been buried beneath professionalism and control for too long. His presence was a catalyst, something she didn't know she was waiting for until he stood there, turning her solitude into a shared adventure. Natalie picked up the glass of champagne from the table, her fingers grazing the cool stem. The dessert sat there, a perfect confection, but it was Leo's presence that consumed her. Her desire to see where this would lead, what unspoken agreements they would make, felt reckless and right.

She slipped into the moment and devoured the meal in charged silence, each bite an explosion of flavor that overtook everything else and flooded her senses with a rich, decadent rush. She ate like she was consuming the very promise of what Leo had left behind, like she could taste his audacity and daring, like the food itself was imbued with his heady unpredictability. She relished every morsel, each taste a testament to his expertise, with the menu he had meticulously and passionately crafted just for her.

Leaning back in the chair, she crossed her legs and took a sip of champagne, gazing at the city's glowing lights for what felt like forever until something caught her attention. A white slip of paper was peeking out from beneath the dessert plate. She stared at it for a while, pondering whether it was the receipt or maybe a duplicate of the menu. But it couldn't be that simple - nothing was simple on a night like this. She placed the champagne down on the table gingerly, slipping the paper from underneath the plate and opening it slowly.

Try to relax, Miss Campbell. The world won't fall apart if you remove yourself from it for one night. Her hands shook slightly as she held the note, so tempting and inviting in the words written there. She glanced at the bottom, her heart skipping a beat as she red. *If you're <u>still</u> in need of relaxation afterwards, let me know. I get off at midnight.* She wasn't sure if if was an invitation, or information. If he was asking her to invite him to the suite, or if he was letting her know that her last chance for his professional services would be cut off.

She glanced at the clock - ten minutes. The night had enveloped her, feeling both fleeting and endless at the same time. She had arrived late, knowing work wouldn't allow much time for her to check in before the evening had already began to envelope the sky with darkness. She wondered how long she had spent staring out the window when she arrived, how long she had spent in the bath after she ordered room service, how long she had spent eating. Before she could process her thoughts, before she could even recount the minutes that had lead her to this moment, her hand was on the phone.

"Miss Campbell," came the voice, light and airy and not at all familiar, "this is concierge Michael speaking." Natalie glanced at the clock, just a minute too late.

"Oh," she gasped, "I'm sorry. I was looking for—" She stopped herself, wondering how ridiculous she would sound seeking out a specific person instead of a concierge service for which the line was intended.

"Ma'am, is there something you need?"

"I was looking for someone to come and remove my dinner plates." She hesitated, looking at the table where Leo's note lay exposed.

"I'll send someone up shortly," the voice was polite, but it neglected to carry the earth and grit that she had become accustomed to hearing on the other end of the line, "is there anything else you need?"

"No, thank you." She hung up the phone with an urgency she hadn't intended, cursing herself for sounding so rude and dismissive to the new man on night shift. Cursing herself for missing her opportunity. How time had flown in the last few hours, she thought, and now she was unsure how to spend the rest of her evening. Her mind raced with the improbable and the inopportunity. She wasn't sure what she had planned, but for a few fleeting hours she hadn't thought of anything else to occupy her night. When the suite had been booked, she had planned to read in bed against the familiar hum of New York City traffic.

The book which sat idly in her suitcase now seemed ordinary and absurd. Spending what she had on the room to read a book now seemed ridiculous, when other possibilities she hadn't even considered had been offered to her on an ornate plate covered in a silver cloche, yet she had neglected to remove it in time before what was on offer had been taken away. The knock at the door startled her, but not enough to make her jump. Her thoughts drifted from the book and her night and her fantasies as she walked to the door, tightening the silk sash around her before opening it.

"That was fast—"

"Miss Campbell." Leo was there, impossibly close yet still untouchable, like the cityscape sprawling just beyond the glass wall. The boundary between fantasy and reality blurred, a shimmering line that she was both thrilled and terrified to cross. Leo seemed to know it, sense it, his awareness adding to the dizzying sense of anticipation.

"Leo," Natalie felt the weight of the room shift, all of it focused on the space between them, "I thought you had finished for the evening." The wine, the dessert, the neatly arranged tray - all background noise shifted to the clarity of this moment. Leo stood across from her, an open challenge and invitation, and she knew instinctively that this was something more than what she'd imagined for the evening. Her world, usually so structured and predictable, tilted on its axis, and she found herself leaning into the unexpected tilt.

"I came to return this." He held out his hand, the tip she had given him lingering idly between his fingers. She walked across the room, leaving the door open, and grabbed her wine glass from the mahogany table where she had left it hours before.

"I want you to have it," she lifted the glass to her lips, her eyes never leaving his, "you've more than earned it."

"Why?"

"Are you always this attentive to guests' needs?" Natalie let the wine linger on her tongue, the taste rich and heady, much like the undercurrent between them. The hours stretched out before her, no longer daunting in their emptiness but lush with possibility. She was uncharacteristically off-balance, and for once, she reveled in it.

"Depends." Leo said, and the room filled with the charged quiet of two people daring to see who would make the next move.
"On what?"
"On how much a guest needs my attention." Leo stood in the doorway, a silhouette against the dim lights of the hallway, as if inviting her into the night he had so effortlessly altered. She hadn't known she could feel this way - anticipatory, alive, ready to see what story would unfold. A ding of the elevator startled them both, and their attention turned to the concierge who had not yet noticed Leo's presence at the threshold. She ushered him inside, closing the door and forcing him to hide in the ensuite just in time for the knock at her door. She was flustered, too flustered at the events of the last few minutes, but opened the door nonetheless to get the intrusion over with.

"Miss Campbell," the man said, his voice familiar from her earlier call, "your plates?" She smiled and gestured to the table, watching him with scrutinising eyes as he began to collect them. Her gaze darted to the note which she had so carelessly left open for prying eyes to read, and she awkwardly coughed for his attention.
"Not the desert," she slowly wandered toward him as he looked up at her, "I'm not quite done with those yet." Delicately, she swept the plate aside and set it down on the mahogany side table next to her wine, alone with the note she had so graciously gathered with it.

"Very good," he gathered the last of it before setting them on the tray, collecting everything and heading for the door, "please let me know if you need anything else. I will be at your service until your midday checkout."

"Of course," she said, opening the door for him, "I'll ring if I need anything." With a nod he left, carrying the tray so delicately with one arm as he made his way down the hallway. She watched him enter the elevator, a sigh of relief escaping her lips as she closed the door. Leo was at her side suddenly, glancing at the mahogany table.

"You read my note," he took a step closer, the movement so slight but enough to close the chasm that she hadn't known was between them, "I wasn't sure you had."

"I called downstairs for you, but you had already finished your shift." Her pulse was a wild thing in her chest, a drumbeat echoing the truth she'd avoided admitting.

"To come and see you." He lingered like a question waiting to be answered, each moment of his presence pulling at her carefully woven self-control. Returning her tip was an excuse, Natalie knew that much now. Leo's eyes caught hers, a wordless communication that spoke of uncharted possibilities.

"Why do you need to relax so badly, Miss Campbell?" Leo was impossibly close now, close enough that the world beyond the suite might have vanished, leaving just them and the luxurious silence that dared them to break it. She'd spent her life curating every moment, managing every interaction, but now, standing in this gilded room with Leo, all bets were off. The only thing that mattered was the spark they both felt, the chemistry so electric it practically hummed. Natalie, who always knew the terms, always controlled the negotiations, was suddenly and willingly off script. "I spend my life in boardrooms and court rooms," the words, delivered with casual sincerity, broke over her like a wave, "I command every room I enter because I have to, in order to be heard." They washed away her pretense of distance, of cool indifference, and she couldn't stop the smile that crept onto her lips.

"So what is it you're seeking from your night alone in a penthouse suite? All this space to yourself, all this opulence for a single night. Do you know what you wanted when you came here?" Leo's presence chipped away at her walls with an insistence that thrilled her, and she let it, feeling them crumble like ash. These weren't just questions, they were a gentle disruption, a test of her willingness to embrace what she hadn't dared ask for.

"I'm not alone," she replied, her voice more breathless than she intended, "not anymore." And so she let the evening transform, giving herself to its intoxicating potential.

"Beautiful view." Leo remarked, his gaze never straying from her face. The air was thick with possibility, a lush tension that made her heartbeat louder in her own ears.

"Do you say that to all your guests who stay in the penthouse suite?" She met his eyes, unable to disguise the challenge, the want, in her gaze.

"I don't often find myself alone with guests in their room at this hour." He said, the words dripping with sincerity and heat. It was a surrender, an unspoken admission that neither of them could resist what had started as a playful exchange and turned into so much more. Their connection was undeniable, magnetic, and she felt herself pulled into it, powerless and willing. This was a realm she hadn't entered in years, where longing lived unchecked and passion ran the show.

"And what makes me so special?" Her voice was low, the veneer of professionalism melted away, and all that remained was raw and real. She felt alive, a vibrant pulse of sensation and want. Leo had introduced himself with nothing more than a phone call, but in the span of an evening, he'd become something more - a possibility she hadn't considered, an indulgence she was ready to unwrap.
"Do you need to *feel* special?" Leo replied, and the charged air between them snapped with anticipation. This was her night, their night, a world she'd long thought out of reach. She felt bold, reckless, ready to find out what happened when she let herself be exactly who she wanted to be. They stood in that moment, a breathtaking pause, before she took the leap.

"I need to let go." Natalie felt the warmth of him before anything else, the kind of heat that melted away pretense and left only desire. The night had unfurled like an unexpected gift, and she was unwrapping it layer by tempting layer. His presence had shed its professional skin, leaving behind something raw and magnetic. They weren't playing by any set rules now, and that realization sent a wild spark through her veins. He moved through the suite like it was an extension of him, his ease making the room feel smaller, more intimate. Natalie watched him, anticipation knotting deliciously in her chest. The suite's vastness, which had once dwarfed her, now pulled them into the centre, making it impossible to ignore what simmered between them.

"Here." Leo said, his voice as smooth and dark as the wine he poured. He placed the glass in her hand, the closeness of his body a deliberate brush against hers.

"You're off the clock," she replied, her tone edged with admiration and challenge, "you don't need to wait on me anymore."

"Just making sure you have what you need." Leo said, his eyes locking onto hers, making the simple words feel like a promise. He stood near, so near that the room's earlier opulence became mere backdrop to the immediacy of them. Leo was close enough now that she could catch his scent, an intoxicating mix of citrus and cedar that made her pulse race. She noticed every detail, every nuance, as though she were cataloging this moment for some future retelling. Natalie had imagined the hotel as a refuge from chaos, but Leo's presence turned it into something entirely different - a cocoon for indulgence, for exploring desires that had languished under the weight of work and worry.

"This is a little beyond your job description." She said, her words teasing, daring.

"Maybe," he replied with a playful gleam in his eyes, "but some lines are meant to be crossed." The charged atmosphere around them was alive, pulsating with every unsaid thing. Natalie's heart was a frantic rhythm, her earlier reservations fading into the background as Leo continued to unravel her with every glance, every subtle shift of his body toward hers. He made her feel wanted, seen, and it sent a thrill through her she hadn't known she could experience. As he arranged another drink, his arm brushed against her, a casual contact that ignited like a spark in dry tinder. Her awareness of him, of the skin-to-skin nearness they hadn't yet dared but couldn't stop imagining, made her dizzy with the freedom of wanting.

"How far are you willing to cross?" Natalie asked, the question bold, full of promise.

"As far as you'll let me," Leo's reply was instant, a readiness in it that sent her heart into a wild dance, "I'm going to take a shower, and when I'm done I expect to find you on the bed." Leo's nearness was no longer a distraction, it was the main event. The physicality of him, the sheer presence, set every nerve in her body on fire. His attentiveness, his openness, his commanding presence caught her off guard. It was a vulnerability she hadn't expected, and it made her own desire feel less like a guilty pleasure and more like a right she'd earned. She felt her barriers crumbling with each moment he spent in the room, the walls she'd so carefully constructed reduced to nothing more than background noise.

She nodded once, and watched him as he removed his uniform so nonchalantly on the way to the bathroom. The shower turned on, and without hesitation he had already begun to rinse himself of a day's hard work. Natalie felt as if she'd been granted permission - not just by him, but by herself. Permission to step out of the roles she was used to playing and into one she hadn't realised she longed for. The suite seemed to breathe around her, alive with the kind of potential she'd rarely allowed herself to consider. She didn't know where the night would lead, but for the first time, not knowing was its own kind of seduction. It was a revelation, a reclaiming of something she'd lost in the clutter of expectations and career. It was an awakening, and Natalie welcomed it with every fiber of her being.

She quietly climbed onto the bed, inching her neck ever so slowly to sneak a peek at him in the shower. The steam clouding the mirror made it difficult to see him clearly, but his well-defined physique and strong arms were unmistakable, even through the mist. Then, abruptly, he finished, and she flipped onto her back, her heart pounding with nerves at the thought of him catching her watching. He exited the bathroom, fresh and wet and wrapped in a towel which barely hid the top of his groin. The suite cocooned them in its lavish quiet, the outside world fading to a soft murmur. Leo's voice broke the silence, revealing a glimpse behind the confident mask he wore with such ease. He spoke of the city, of the constant blur of faces and how easy it was to feel alone among them. His words carried the weight of honesty, raw and unguarded, and Natalie felt a twinge of recognition. It wasn't often that she let herself feel this way - unprotected, yet more connected because of it.

"You see so many people," Leo continued, his voice a gentle hum in the quiet, "but everyone's moving so fast, it's like they're afraid to stop and be seen." His vulnerability was a revelation, a tender offering that took her by surprise. She wasn't used to being the one who listened, who comforted. But there was something in Leo's openness that called to her, a sense of shared solitude that made her chest ache with familiarity. She watched him, his features softened by the warm glow of the suite's lighting, and felt a deep resonance with his words. Natalie nodded, a small movement that carried a world of agreement.

"It's different, working in an office. But the feeling, it's the same." Her own voice surprised her, the softness of it, the lack of defenses. His eyes held hers, deep and attentive, making her feel exposed in a way that was strangely comforting. She'd hidden behind her work for so long, let it be the armor that kept her from feeling too deeply.

But now, being here with Leo, she felt that armor loosen piece by piece.

"You probably have more in common with these people than you realise," Leo said, leaning onto the bed but never breaking their gaze, "I've seen it a lot. People who seem to have everything figured out, but really—" He let the words hang, unfinished but full of meaning.

"Really, they don't." Natalie finished the thought for him, the simple admission feeling like a weight lifted. Leo's presence had a way of simplifying things, of boiling them down to their essence. She wasn't just a lawyer here, wasn't just a woman checking into a hotel to escape her life. She was Natalie, seen and understood.

"Do you know what you need this night to be?" Leo leaned forward, his fingers brushing her thighs as he edged onto the bed. It sent a ripple through her, a warm acknowledgment of their shared vulnerability. Natalie couldn't remember the last time she'd felt this way, this seen.

"I don't know." She admitted, the truth hanging between them, bare and beautiful.

"Then I'll decide for you," his honesty, his willingness to drop the façade made her reevaluate the walls she'd put up, "let someone else be in charge for a change." The room seemed to draw them closer, each unguarded moment another step toward an unknown but inviting destination. Natalie's usual instincts to close off, to control, fell away. In their place was a new kind of connection, one that made her feel both fragile and fiercely alive. She'd always thought of them as necessary, as shields to keep her from getting too close to what she might lose. But now, they felt more like prison bars, confining her to a life of obligations and predictable victories.

The room was thick with the scent of her arousal, a heady mix of sweat and the faintest trace of her perfume that lingered on her discarded work clothes. Leo's hands moved with deliberate slowness, his fingers brushing against the smooth silk of her sash as he untied it. The robe fell away like a whisper, pooling at her sides, leaving her naked body exposed to the cool air. Her skin prickled, goosebumps rising as his eyes raked over her, taking in every curve, every dip, every inch of her trembling flesh. He knelt, retrieving his tie from the floor, and with a practiced ease he bound her wrists together, the fabric tightening around her delicate skin. He lifted her arms above her head, securing them to the headboard with a firm knot. Her breath hitched, her chest rising and falling with each shallow inhale.

"You're safe," he murmured, his voice low and gravelly, a promise and a threat all at once, "if you need to stop, just say so." She nodded, her lips parting as she watched him move to the cupboard, retrieving the sash from the second robe meant for a second guest. He returned to the bed, his movements deliberate. He spread her legs wide, tying each ankle to the bedposts with the same care he'd shown her wrists. The silk bit into her skin, a delicious mix of pain and restraint that sent a shiver down her spine. Leo stood back, admiring his handiwork, his cock straining against the fabric of the wrapped towel. He collected his belt from his pants on the floor, the leather sliding free with a soft hiss. He held it up, letting her see it, letting her feel the weight of what was to come.

"Is this too much?" He asked, his voice a low growl. She shook her head, her eyes dark with desire.

"No." She whispered, her voice trembling. The first strike was light, the leather kissing the soft flesh of her inner thigh. She gasped, her body arching against the restraints. He did it again, this time on the other thigh, the sting blooming into a sweet ache. He moved higher, the belt grazing the swell of her breast, the tip of her nipple hardening under the teasing touch. He repeated the motion, each strike a little harder, a little more intense, until her skin was flushed and tingling. He quickly removed a pillowcase from a pillow, wrapping it around her eyes and tying it tightly behind her head.

Dropping the belt, his hands replaced the leather as he leaned in, his mouth closing over one taut nipple. His tongue flicked against the sensitive bud, his teeth grazing it lightly before he sucked it into his mouth. She moaned, her hips bucking against the restraints, desperate for more. His fingers found her clit, already slick with arousal. He teased her, circling it with slow, deliberate strokes. She whimpered, her body trembling as he pushed two fingers inside her, curling them just right. His fingers were a revelation, a slow, torturous promise that made her thighs quiver like an earthquake.

He didn't just find her clit - he claimed it like a conqueror staking his flag in uncharted territory. She was already dripping, a slick, glistening mess that begged for more, but he wasn't about to give her what she wanted. Not yet. He slowed down. Every stroke was a tease, a taunt, and she could feel the heat pooling low in her belly, her thighs clenching around nothing, desperate for something to fill the void but unable to move her legs. She whimpered, a pathetic little sound that only seemed to spur him on, and he chuckled darkly, his breath hot against her ear.

"You're so fucking wet." He murmured, his voice rough with lust. She couldn't respond, couldn't think, not when he was driving her to the edge with just his fingers. And then, just when she thought she might lose her mind, he pushed two fingers inside her, slow and deliberate, the stretch making her gasp. He curled them just right in a way that made her see stars, and she moaned, her hips bucking against his hand. He pulled his fingers out almost all the way, leaving just the tips inside her, and she whimpered again, her pussy clenching around the emptiness. He smirked, his eyes dark with hunger, and then he pushed them back in, deeper this time, the heel of his palm grinding against her clit as he worked her open. She could feel every ridge of his fingers, every knuckle, and it was too much and not enough all at once.

"Fuck," she gasped, her nails digging into her palms, "please—"
"Please *what*," he said, his voice dripping with mock innocence, "you want more? You want me to fuck you hard? Or do you just want to come all over my fingers?" She didn't answer, couldn't answer, but he didn't need her to. He knew exactly what she wanted, and he was going to make her beg for it. He added a third finger, stretching her even more, and she cried out, her back arching off the bed. He fucked her with his fingers, slow and deep, each thrust hitting that spot inside her that made her toes curl. And all the while, his thumb was working her clit, rubbing it in tight little circles that had her trembling on the edge.

Then he stopped again, and she whimpered in the silence. Her panting was all that filled the void, her head moving and searching for something she couldn't see, visionless by the makeshift blindfold. Leo's eyes burned into her like a lion savoring its prey, his gaze a molten mix of dominance and desire. She lay there, trembling, her body slick with sweat, her wrists bound above her head with the tie that bit into her skin just enough to remind her she was his. Her legs, finally freed from their restraints, were still weak and trembling.

With a growl that rumbled deep in his chest, he flipped her onto her stomach, the sudden movement making her gasp. Her face pressed into the mattress, muffling the whimper that escaped her lips. He straddled her thighs, his weight pinning her down. She could feel the heat of him, the raw, primal energy that radiated from his body, and it made her clench around nothing, desperate for him to fill her. His fingers trailed down her spine, slow and deliberate, leaving a trail of fire in their wake. When they reached the curve of her ass, he paused, his touch teasing and taunting. She shuddered, her hips bucking instinctively, but he held her down, his grip firm and unyielding.

"Please," she moaned, her voice muffled by the mattress, "please Leo."

"Please what," he growled, his voice low and dangerous, "use your words."

"Fuck me," she begged, her voice breaking, "please, just fuck me." But Leo only chuckled, a dark, sinful sound that sent shivers down her spine.

"Not yet," he purred, his fingers brushing against her slick pussy, "you're not ready." And then he plunged two fingers into her, deep and hard, making her cry out. His pace was relentless, his thumb circling her clit with just enough pressure to drive her wild. She writhed beneath him, her body arching, her pussy clenching around his fingers as she teetered on the edge of orgasm.

"Leo, please," she sobbed, her voice raw with need, "let me come." But he didn't stop. He didn't let her. Instead, he slowed his pace, his fingers moving in lazy circles inside her, teasing her, tormenting her. She could feel the tension building in her body, the ache in her growing more intense with every passing second. She was so close, so close, but Leo wasn't going to let her have it. Not yet.

"You're so fucking wet," he murmured, his voice thick with lust, "you want it that bad, don't you?"

"Yes," she gasped, her body trembling with need, "I need it." But Leo just smirked, his fingers still moving inside her, driving her closer and closer to the edge without letting her fall.

"Not yet," he leaned down, his lips brushing against her ear as he whispered, "you're going to beg for it first." And she did. She begged and pleaded, her voice breaking with every word, her body writhing beneath his as he continued with his fingers, teasing her clit with his thumb until she was a trembling, sobbing mess. Her chest heaved with every breath, her nipples hard and aching as she dripped with need.

"Leo." She moaned, her voice a broken whisper.

"Now," he growled, "now I'll fuck you." And with that, he plunged into her, his cock stretching her wide as he buried himself to the hilt. She cried out, her body arching as he began to fuck her, his pace hard and relentless. He pounded into her, his cock slamming into her pussy with a force that made her weak.

He fucked her harder, faster, hitting that sweet spot inside her with every thrust. She could feel the tension building in her body again, the ache in her growing more intense with every passing second. She was so close, so close. And then he reached underneath her, his fingers finding her clit once more, and she came undone. Her body convulsed around him, her pussy clenching tight as she screamed his name. But he didn't stop, didn't let up, and she was still coming when he leaned down and bit at her back, swallowing her moans as he continued to fuck her through it.

Her body convulsed, her pussy clenching around his cock as she cried out, her voice breaking on his name. He didn't stop, drawing out her pleasure until she was a trembling mess, her body spent but still craving more. Leo growled, his own orgasm crashing over him as he pulled out, spilling himself all over her back, his cock pulsing with every wave of pleasure. She was a trembling, boneless mess, still pulsing with the aftershocks of her orgasm. The sensation of it all - her vision removed and movement restrained allowed her to feel every inch and every second of him inside her. When it was over, they lay there, their bodies tangled together, their breaths coming in ragged gasps. Leo pressed a kiss to her neck, his touch surprisingly gentle after the rough fucking he'd just given her.

Though she was free from the binds, she remained tethered to the moment, unsure and unwilling to break the spell. Her eyes were closed, perhaps in feigned sleep, perhaps in exhaustion. She nestled against him, her breath warm against his chest as he folded her into him, wrapping her in his own limbs like a cocoon. She drifted there, floating in a haze of afterglow and satisfaction, each breath a lullaby. He whispered her name, a soft murmur against her hair, and she finally let herself believe she was safe enough to sleep, to surrender fully to the darkness. Her sighs slowed, the quiet of her breath matching the quiet of the room they filled with the symphony of their desire.

Morning unfurled with the soft glow of sunrise, its light creeping across the suite in a golden tide. Natalie stretched languidly, the relaxation in her body an unfamiliar but welcome luxury. Her mind was clear, free from the clutter of obligation and expectation. She reached for her phone, an instinctive move, but the soft click of the door stopped her short. Realising that she was alone, Natalie lay back against the pillows, letting the sun warm her skin as she looked around with growing amusement. The sheer luxury of the moment, her mind unburdened, was a rare and precious thing. Natalie couldn't remember the last time she'd felt so unencumbered, so light.

It was still early, too early to accept that the day had begun. The aroma of fresh coffee mingled with the bright scent of morning, filling the room with a sensory richness that mirrored her internal state. Natalie felt awake in a way she hadn't in weeks, months even. Each inhale was a balm, each exhale a release of all the pressure she'd carried. The food was warm, and the coffee was steaming - Leo must have delivered it to her and allowed her to enjoy her leisurely morning nap, she thought.

She walked to the table, standing unclothed in the suite, letting the sun bathe her skin and envelop her in the warmth of an early spring morning. She noticed the note sticking out from beneath the plate, its presence a whisper of the night's audacity. Leo had slipped it there with the same understated confidence that marked everything he did. She loved that about him, this man she barely knew but who seemed to know exactly how to shake her up in the best ways. Natalie's laughter bubbled up, bright and genuine, as she reached for the paper with more eagerness than she cared to show. It was a reminder, she knew, a promise wrapped in teasing script, and the anticipation of its message left her giddy.

She slipped on her silk robe, the fabric whispering against her skin, and gracefully made her way to the elegantly set table. The air was filled with the savory aroma of steaming bacon, perfectly crisp and glistening with just the right amount of seasoning. Beside it lay a generous serving of scrambled eggs, their soft, fluffy texture promising a delightful bite. Golden slices of toast were arranged artfully, lightly buttered. A vibrant array of fresh fruit added a splash of color to the table, with juicy strawberries, succulent slices of melon, and tangy orange segments. A carafe of rich, aromatic coffee sat nearby, its bold fragrance mingling with the other scents, while a sparkling mimosa, with bubbles dancing joyously in the glass, awaited to add a touch of indulgence to the morning.

The note was simple but electric in its implications. *If you ever want to play again, you know where to find me.* The boldness of it took her breath away, much like the man who'd left it. Natalie set it back on the tray, a faint chuckle escaping her lips as she marveled at the delicious turn her weekend had taken. The morning felt like a new world, spun from the threads of their shared night. She felt the pull of curiosity, the thrill of not knowing what would come next, and she embraced it.

Picking up the note again, she let her fingers linger over the words before carefully setting it down once more. It was a symbol, she realized, of everything the last twelve hours had meant. A shift, a change, a vivid splash of color in a life that had begun to feel monochrome. The promise of more, the tease of uncertainty - it all wove together into a pattern that was new and exciting and filled with the kind of possibility she hadn't let herself entertain. Natalie smiled, a bright, unburdened thing, and felt the dawn of new possibilities settle into her skin.

Natalie reclined comfortably into the chair, crossing her legs as her fingers curled around the stem of the delicate glass holding her mimosa. She took a slow sip, savoring the blend of citrus and champagne. Her eyes were fixed on the horizon, where the first light of dawn began to paint the sky in hues of pink and orange. The sun emerged gradually, inching its way up between the silhouettes of two towering buildings, casting a warm glow over the city below.

Amidst this serene moment, Natalie's thoughts drifted to the note resting in her lap. Its words had stirred something within her, a mix of nostalgia and anticipation. She glanced down at it once more, tracing the familiar handwriting with her eyes. A soft laugh escaped her lips, and she felt a sense of closure wash over her.

With a contented smile playing on her lips, Natalie scrunched the note in her free hand, feeling the paper crinkle beneath her fingers. The act felt liberating, a symbolic gesture of moving forward. She leaned over and tossed the crumpled note into the nearby bin, watching it disappear amongst the remnants of yesterday. As she turned back towards the rising sun, the world seemed filled with endless possibilities, and Natalie felt ready to embrace every one of them.

Ink & Skin

Rain dripped from Sam's nose, and he shifted from foot to foot in front of the studio, staring at the hand-painted sign as if trying to decipher a foreign language. The lights inside cast a dim purple glow onto the sidewalk, making the rain puddles look like oil slicks. He checked his watch again as he rubbed the chill from his arms and reached for the doorknob. A tattooed arm yanked the door open before he touched it, and a voice as deep and warm as a bubble bath spoke.

"Don't just stand out there getting wet. You coming in?" A woman with sleeves of tattoos stood framed in the doorway, her dark hair wild and cascading. Her mouth curved into an amused smile as she leaned one shoulder against the doorjamb. Sam jumped back, startled, his feet tangling in hesitation. A flood of warmth spilled out from inside, wrapping him in a sudden embrace of sage and ink.

"You lost?" She asked, though the question came with a look that said she knew the answer. Sam fidgeted with his jacket, fighting the urge to bolt.

"No, I, I'm not. I was just—" He glanced at the ground, then back at the woman, as if trying to measure the distance to safety. Her smile widened.

"Figuring out if you wanna come in or not?"

"Something like that." Sam tried a smile of his own, but it faltered. The rain felt colder now, slicing against the back of his neck.

"Well, don't just stand there," she stepped aside, making room in more ways than one, "make your decision out of the rain." Sam nodded and stepped in, relief mingling with a fresh surge of nerves. The space hummed with dim lights and low music, smelling like antiseptic with undertones of leather.

"Rhea." The woman said, shutting the door with a click that sounded like a verdict. She extended her hand, fingers laced with ink.

"Sam." He took her hand quickly, then let go, as if afraid it might bite. Rhea's eyes lingered on Sam's face, taking in every twitch and nuance.

"First time, huh?"

"That obvious?" Sam laughed awkwardly.

"Nah, I just have a knack for spotting a newbie," Rhea leaned against a counter, casual, inviting, "what brings you here?" Sam hesitated, like he were reaching for something just out of sight.

"I have this," he fumbled in his pocket and pulled out a crumpled sheet of paper, "it's probably stupid." Rhea took the paper with interest, her eyes scanning the lines. She tilted her head, and Sam braced for some kind of judgment.

"Flowers?" Rhea looked up, the word wrapped in something more than curiosity. Sam nodded, awkwardness palpable.

"Yeah. I mean, just something small."

"Small." She echoed, but it sounded like she was repeating a different word entirely. Rhea studied the sketch again, as if looking through a window into another world.

"It's dumb, right?" Sam shifted on his feet, suddenly defensive. Rhea handed the paper back, brushing Sam's fingers in the process. "Not at all. Pretty design. You thought about where you want it?"

"I'm not really sure yet." Sam mumbled, more to the floor than to her.

"Maybe I can help with that." Rhea's voice had an edge of challenge now, a soft dare. Sam's cheeks colored, a deepening flush that crept toward his ears. He couldn't quite meet Rhea's eyes.

"I was thinking my wrist. Or maybe, my arm?" He gestured vaguely, as if his own body was uncharted territory. Rhea straightened, coming closer.

"Mind if I take a look?" She reached out, fingers skimming the air near Sam's wrist. The touch was feather-light, but Sam felt it like a pulse in his bones. He swallowed hard, heat rising.

"Yeah, okay."

"Okay." She repeated, softer this time, like a promise. Rhea's grin was confident, knowing.

"Look, I don't know if I'm ready," Sam admitted, the words tumbling out, "I might not—" Rhea cut him off with a nod, her expression never wavering.

"That's cool. I don't pressure my clients. Unless they're into that kind of thing."

"Good to know." Sam laughed again, less awkward now.

"I've seen you around here, you know," her hands were graceful and steady as she stretched and scrutinised Sam's skin, "looking through the window. Walking by and staring at the sketches on the wall. Every few weeks you walk by and—"

"Maybe this was a mistake." Sam withdrew his wrist gingerly. The scent of ink and disinfectant filled the air around them, along with a faint whiff of Rhea's floral perfume.

"I'll tell you what. Why don't we set something up, give you time to think it over?" She picked up a pen, poised above the calendar like a magician preparing for a trick.

"I don't know—"

"When works for you?"

Sam surveyed the parlour, taking in the sketches, rows of tattoo designs, artwork, and glowing neon signs adorning the walls. His gaze landed on Rhea, whose commanding presence was undeniable, even though she was one of the smallest women he had ever encountered. Her skin was a canvas of tattoos. Intricate designs adorned her chest and arms, with a hint of them peeking through the small gap in her midriff. Her fingers were etched with delicate patterns, and even her ankles, visible between her pants and socks, displayed the artistry of her ink.

"Okay," Sam hesitated, nodding, "this weekend?"

"This weekend it is." Rhea said, and Sam felt the weight of the moment settle around him like a new skin. She wrote the date with a flourish, her gaze never leaving Sam's face.

"You'll be here?"

"This is my place," Rhea's satisfaction was like the lingering warmth of a fire, "I'll be here." She opened the door, letting the rain-tinged air slip back inside. Sam nodded again, and the corners of his mouth twitched with a new kind of energy. He stepped out, his heart an echo in his ears, the paper a crumple of hope in his hand. Rhea watched him go, curious and amused.

The space was all shadows and secrets when Sam pushed the door open, rain still clinging to his hair. Every corner felt like a promise wrapped in dim neon and low music. Sam stood still, letting the air settle over him like an aura. The tattoo machines gleamed from across the room. In Rhea's hands, a needle became something almost holy. She glanced up from her preparation, the curve of her smile blurring the line between welcome and want.

"Didn't think you'd show." Rhea's confident grin morphed into a curious and amused expression as she watched Sam hesitate before stepping further into the parlour. Sam hesitated just inside, the edge of anticipation catching in his chest.

"I said I'd be here." His voice wavered, strung tight between nerves and excitement. Rhea gave a soft laugh, a sound that carried its own electricity.

"You were nervous last time."

"I was," Sam's feet were rooted to the floor, caught in a mix of fascination and fear, "I still am."

"Good," Rhea nodded, her attention shifting back to the methodical setup of inks and gloves, "nervous is interesting."

The words wrapped around Sam like the steady thrum of the music. He took a step closer, his shoes squeaking on the polished floor. Rhea's hands moved with a sureness that left Sam breathless, arranging the equipment with a care that bordered on reverence. The air smelled of antiseptic and anticipation. It was an ephemeral thread, thin and malleable, woven into the fabric of possibility and dangling temptingly in front of Rhea's all-knowing gaze.

"You like working here alone?" Sam asked, needing to puncture the silence before it swallowed him. Rhea looked up again, and the sharpness of her eyes was softened by humor.

"I like working," she said, "alone, with others. I'm flexible that way." Sam flushed, the heat creeping back into his cheeks. Rhea's gaze lingered before she turned back to her preparations, letting the hum of the room fill the spaces between them. Sam watched, transfixed by the fluid economy of her movements. Everything about her spoke of intention, the kind that ran deep. He caught himself staring, the lines between artist and art blurring in the dim light.

"You gonna keep standing there, or you wanna get this started?" Rhea's voice cut through Sam's reverie, teasing but edged with something sharper. Sam fumbled, caught off guard by the directness of the question, the pull it had on him.

"I—"

"Last chance to back out, you know." She said, but her tone held a challenge she knew Sam would accept. Sam took another step forward, feeling the thick warmth of the room settle into his skin.

"I'm here, aren't I?"

"You are." Rhea acknowledged, her satisfaction a live wire between them. The atmosphere was thick, a liquid thing that Sam moved through slowly. He took in the sketches on the walls, taped in haphazard rows like dreams in the process of becoming real. Rhea's focus shifted, picking up on Sam's energy, a subtle game of push and pull. Sam finally settled into a chair, the worn leather cool against his back. He watched Rhea with an intensity that surprised even him.

"You really thought I wouldn't show?" He asked, needing to fill the charged silence.

"I thought you'd think about it." Rhea said, her eyes meeting Sam's and holding them in place. Sam nodded, a tight motion that belied the flutter in his chest.

"I did."

"But you're here anyway." It wasn't a question, and Rhea's approval was like a physical touch.

"I guess I am." Sam let out a breath he hadn't realized he was holding.

"Then let's make it worth your while." Rhea said, her voice dipping low. Sam's pulse quickened as he watched her pull on gloves, the latex snapping like a promise. The anticipation was an electric hum beneath his skin.

"I don't know if I'm ready." He admitted, each word a struggle against his own want. Rhea moved closer, her presence wrapping around Sam, soft and insistent.

"You sure about that?" She was close enough that Sam could feel the warmth radiating off her, each movement an invitation, a dare.

"No." Sam said, his voice barely above a whisper. It was the truth, raw and open between them.

"It'll only hurt a little." Rhea held Sam's gaze, the air heavy with more than the scent of ink. Sam nodded, the movement slow, deliberate. He wasn't ready. But he was here. And maybe that was the point.

A shiver shot through Sam's body, ricocheting from skin to bone. Rhea's touch was a jolt of electric clarity in the dim room. The antiseptic cloth ran over Sam's forearm, and he bit back a gasp, unable to hide the reaction. Rhea paused, the corner of her mouth tugging upward, and said nothing. She was a master of seeing, saying only what was needed.

"Aren't you supposed to stencil this on me?" Sam's grip tightened around the crumpled paper, feeling the weight of his decision in his hand.

"No need," the tattoo gun buzzed to life, a promise of hurt and something more, "I can do this from memory." Sam flinched at the first bite of the needle. Rhea's eyes stayed steady on his, the question unspoken. Sam didn't pull away. His hand flexed open and closed, searching for something solid. The sensation was sharper than expected, cutting through the air and into nerve. Rhea stayed silent, letting the experience fill the room. Her hands moved with a precision that was almost sensual. She glanced up briefly, gauging the effect, and the knowing smirk returned.

"Doing okay?" Her voice was low, pitched just above the hum of the machine.

"Yeah." Sam exhaled, not quite convincing.

"Let me know if you need a break." Rhea's dark hair fell in soft waves around her face, framing sharp cheekbones and full lips. Her eyes were a piercing deep hazel, intense and focused as she worked. The pain was vivid, demanding, but the adrenaline that followed was an unexpected rush. It tugged at something deeper, pulling him toward a place he hadn't anticipated. Sam's breath hitched again, more out of surprise than discomfort.

"It's intense."

"Welcome to the club." Rhea said, nodding at her tattoo-covered arms and before her attention dipped back to the task, hands sure and rhythmic. The pulse of the machine matched Sam's heartbeat, a quickening pace that steadied as he grew used to the sensation. Each contact of needle to skin became part of the rhythm. Sam found himself leaning into it, his breathing syncing with Rhea's movements. It hurt, yes, but the kind of hurt that felt strangely necessary. Sam watched Rhea's focus - the intent furrow of her brow, the flick of her tongue against her lip as she concentrated. The intimacy of it was staggering, a level of closeness that snuck up and wrapped itself around Sam before he could push it away.

"Listen to music while you work?" Sam asked, needing a distraction from the layered sensations, needing more than that to keep Rhea's attention.

"Sometimes," Rhea replied, the conversation easy and deliberate, a new kind of tension stretching between them, "depends on my mood. Clients can be interesting." Sam bit back a laugh at the choice of words.

"And this one? How interesting am I?"

"Still figuring that out." Rhea met his eyes again, holding them captive. Her words carried a weight that went beyond their simplicity. Sam let out a shaky breath, letting it mix with the pulse of the room. The initial shock was wearing into something that felt almost good, a wave of endorphins cresting with every touch of the needle. The leather of the chair was cool against his back, but the rest of the world had narrowed to a tunnel of warmth and vibration. He settled in, feeling himself unfurl.

"Favorite movie?" Rhea asked, the question a gentle distraction.

"Depends," Sam said, mimicking Rhea's earlier tease, "Blade Runner if I'm feeling smart. Legally Blonde if I'm not."

"Nice range," Rhea's laughter was a soft, knowing thing, "you must be fun at parties." It drew Sam in further, like she knew exactly how to thread him along.

"If I ever went to any."

"I'll keep that in mind," Rhea's expression shifted, interest piqued, "what's your worst decision?"

"This one might be it." Sam laughed, a sound that felt free and unburdened. He paused, the vulnerability coming easier now. The room pulsed with a new kind of energy, the sting of the tattoo mingling with the sweetness of this unfolding conversation. Each buzz of the machine carved out more than ink, and Sam found himself wanting to stay in this moment longer than planned. Rhea's next words carried a note of playful curiosity.

"Or maybe art school."

"Really?" Rhea's eyebrows lifted, intrigued.

"Dropped out last year." The confession was light but tinged with more than he intended to reveal.

"And here you are. You know I don't give refunds, right?"

"Then I hope you're as good as you say you are," Sam grinned through the building thrill of the experience, "or I'll have to start making better choices from now on." The connection between them stretched taut and personal, every touch of the cloth, every glance, vibrating with significance. Rhea's questions drew Sam out further, each answer feeding the growing intimacy between them. It was more than a tattoo - it was an unveiling, each line exposing layers Sam hadn't known he was ready to share.

"First heartbreak?" Rhea asked, the words carrying a mix of jest and genuine interest. Sam hesitated, then met her gaze with more boldness than he expected.

"Ongoing. Art school." He watched Rhea's reaction, the flicker of something deeper in her eyes. Rhea nodded, and there was an understanding there, one Sam hadn't dared to hope for. Her fingers brushed close to skin again, the weight of her attention both comforting and exhilarating.

"No artist's regret is simple."

"Yours?" Sam challenged back, more daring now, wanting to turn the lens around. Rhea's response was a steady, charged silence. Her hands worked on, her smile teasing, knowing.

Each minute stretched longer, held more meaning. Sam found himself lost in the layers of sensation, the connection that was growing like a vine and winding around them. The shop, the world, faded into the background. All that mattered was here, now. Rhea's touch and voice and presence wrapped around Sam, filling him, making the process feel impossibly intimate.

"We don't have to fill the silence with conversation," Sam's lips were slightly chapped, a mix of flavors between the tobacco and the mint gum he had chewed on earlier while waiting for his appointment, "I mean, if you're trying to concentrate—"

"I like talking to my clients," Rhea replied, a grin ghosting her lips, "but if you'd like I can stop—"

"No." Sam's response was immediate, almost too eager, and he cursed himself for seeming so keen to talk to her.

"Okay then." Over the low hum of the tattoo gun, Rhea's voice was a soothing yet commanding presence. Her lips curled into a smile, almost sinister, almost sensual.

And just like that, time folded in on itself. Sam felt the lines being drawn, the permanence of the ink, but more than that, the mark this moment left on him. It was lasting, it was there to stay. And he didn't want it to end. Rhea's hands were warm and calloused, a result of years of tattooing. As she worked, her fingers glided smoothly over Sam's skin, leaving behind a trail of a stinging sensation. She was like a storm, fierce and powerful, but with a calm eye at her centre that drew him in and held him captive. Her movements were fluid, almost hypnotic, and there was a raw energy emanating from her that was impossible to ignore.

"Let's take five." Rhea's voice cut through the tangle of sensation, grounding Sam with a roughness that matched the hum of the machine. He blinked, awareness rushing back into focus, more piercing than the needle. The sudden absence of touch left him raw and exposed. The room was a silent stage, and Sam felt his movements echo as he reached for a water bottle. Rhea watched from across the space, her eyes an unrelenting presence that dared Sam to speak first. The change was disorienting, from the immediate intensity of the tattoo to the vastness of the shop around them. Sam's pulse was loud in his ears, but the air felt different, expectant. He took a sip of water, trying to quench more than thirst, trying to adjust to the abrupt shift in atmosphere.

"Taking it like a pro." Rhea said, her voice cutting through Sam's thoughts, making him jump just a little. She was leaning against a table, arms crossed, every line of her body an invitation for Sam to engage. Sam laughed, the sound a bit shaky.

"Surprised?"

"Pleasantly." The single word she spoke held a depth that made Sam's breath hitch. Sam rolled the water bottle between his hands, the motion a soothing contrast to the charged air.

"Feels like it's been hours." He said, breaking the quiet that pressed in around them.

"It has." Rhea replied, and there was a note of surprise in her voice, as if time had played the same trick on her.

They sat there, separated by only a few feet but feeling the distance acutely after the closeness of before. The silence stretched, not uncomfortable, but dense, filled with more than just the tattoo. Sam couldn't shake the weight of Rhea's gaze. It wrapped around him, as tangible as the chair he sat in. He searched for something to fill the space, something to bring them back to the unspoken intimacy they'd shared. The question came out before Sam could second guess it.

"What was your first tattoo?"

"Curious?" Rhea uncrossed her arms, surprise flickering in her eyes before humor settled in.

"Very." Sam nodded, too eager to play coy. Rhea straightened, her movement deliberate. She walked toward Sam with a slow confidence, stopping just shy of where the air felt like it would ignite from contact. She lifted the hem of her shirt with an easy grace, exposing a trail of ink along her ribs. Sam's breath caught, his eyes glued to the intricate lines that covered her skin.

"This one." Rhea said, her voice dipping lower, more intimate than before. Sam was aware of everything - the curve of Rhea's body, the roughness of her voice, the tightness in his own chest. He tried to speak, but the words were knotted up, tangled with more than curiosity.

"May I?" Sam lifted his hand gently, and she responded with a simple nod. He grazed the tattoo with the tips of his fingers, tracing the intricate lines and details as if his fingers were a paintbrush.

"Hurt like hell," Rhea continued, letting her shirt fall back into place with a smooth motion that kept Sam's eyes riveted, "but worth it."

"I bet." Sam exhaled, letting out a breath of air he didn't realise he'd been holding. Rhea sat on the edge of the table, still close enough that Sam could feel her presence as a gravitational pull. Her fingers played absently over the fabric of her shirt, and Sam's eyes followed every motion.

"Did it myself."

"Really?" Sam's voice was a whisper, the awe in it unmasked.

"Started the day I turned eighteen," Rhea's smile was wicked, full of mischief and memory, "took a week to finish. Couldn't back out once I started." Sam imagined the scene, the young Rhea with that same fearless determination, and a small thrill ran up his spine.

"No artist's regret, then?"

"Never." The word was a brand, pressing into the space between them, leaving a mark that went beyond skin.

"What's that?" Sam pointed to a tattoo on her bicep, tucked away slightly like a secret, but not enough.

"Another tattoo." She smiled coyly, cocking her head to the side.

"It looks like you're counting something," his eyes grew narrow as he tried to decipher it, "marking something off." The atmosphere buzzed with more than the promise of ink. Sam felt drawn in further, the connection with Rhea wrapping tighter, the intensity of his fascination mirroring that of the tattoo itself. They stayed in that charged moment, Sam's eyes on Rhea, the silence humming with everything he couldn't say.

When Rhea stood to return to the chair, Sam's pulse jumped. The anticipation was sharper, more personal now. Sam knew he should be bracing for the physical part of it, but all he felt was the pull of something deeper, the rush of everything else. The buzz started again, loud in the small space, but not loud enough to drown the tension. Rhea leaned over Sam's arm, the dip of her concentration as focused as any lover's. Sam watched the play of her expression - the narrowed eyes, the way she bit her bottom lip between her teeth. The intimacy of the observation made him dizzy. Sam's stare was as unrelenting as the needle. Rhea smirked without looking up.

"You're staring." She said, her voice a challenge wrapped in velvet. Sam didn't look away. He couldn't.
"So are you." He shot back, the words slipping out with a boldness that startled them both. Rhea's smirk widened, but she didn't break her focus. The sound of the machine was a low hum beneath their voices, a soundtrack to the moment unfolding. Each pass of the needle felt like more than ink - it was an inscription, a shared truth laid bare. Sam's pulse drummed in his veins, every movement of Rhea's hands reverberating with more than physical impact. He followed the shift of her eyes, the slight furrow of her brow, each detail burning itself into memory. Their glances met, held, spoke. The room shrank around them, pulling in close, tighter and more intimate than any brush of skin. The energy was palpable, every line Rhea drew tying them together with invisible thread.

"Relax." Rhea said, and the word held a thousand more, unwritten and unspoken. Her voice was low, intimate, sinking into Sam like the ink itself.

"I'm sorry," Sam let out a breath, slow and measured, a release of more than air, "I'm not very good at conversation, and this seems more intimate than it should be for two strangers." He felt the electric hum between them, more alive than ever. The moment stretched, dense and vibrating with possibility. With each minute, Sam became more aware of Rhea, of the intent in her touch and the warmth in her gaze. The tattoo was almost an afterthought, a surface thing compared to the depth he felt growing between them.

"This isn't a date," Rhea's hands were steady, precise as she spoke, "but tattooing someone is intimate. You're raw, and exposed, and if idle chatting is gonna make you feel better then chat away." But the look in her eyes told Sam she felt it too, that undercurrent that turned the air thick and made every moment linger. The session neared its end, but Sam wasn't ready for it. He felt suspended, caught in a time that didn't tick away in seconds but in heartbeats and glances. Each one more significant than the last.

"Almost done." She said, her voice both a warning and a question. Sam nodded, unwilling to break the spell.
"Take your time." He replied, and the words were an invitation. The machine quieted, but the buzz remained in the air, charged and heavy. Rhea wrapped the tattoo with care, her touch softer than necessary, slower. Sam watched, breath held, already aching for more. The tattoo was finished. But the experience, the connection, the imprint of everything that had passed between them - it was all still there, more vivid than the ink on Sam's skin. Rhea looked at him, really looked, and the seconds dragged out, fat and full.

"Come back if it needs a touch-up." She said, her voice a promise. Sam held her gaze, feeling more marked by that moment than by the design itself.

"I will." He said, knowing it was true in ways Rhea couldn't even guess. The shop felt as small as the silence between them, an airless space thick with more than the scent of antiseptic. Sam clutched the paper, knuckles white, focus split between the words and the way Rhea watched him. He couldn't tell which was more overwhelming - the practical care of the tattoo or the lingering imprint of what had just happened. Sam's pulse was a loud metronome, measuring the moments in a new kind of rhythm. Rhea stayed close, her presence as immediate and tangible as before. Sam's eyes drifted from the instructions to her lips, watching the movement as she spoke.

"Keep it clean, and don't let it dry out." Rhea said, her tone intimate, making every word feel like more than just advice.

"Okay." Sam replied, the word slipping out too fast, too eager, as if it might anchor them to the present.

"Too much sun can mess with the colors," Rhea continued, her smile shaded with knowing, "we wouldn't want it to fade." Sam shook his head, too invested, too affected.

"I won't let it." He promised, and the words carried an edge of something raw and unguarded. Sam stood there, leaning into the doorframe as if it were the only thing keeping him upright, as if moving further away would break the tension that wrapped so tightly around them both. Sam's thoughts were a tangled knot of sensation and uncertainty, each twist pulling him further into Rhea's orbit. Rhea watched, an artist admiring her own handiwork, pleased with the mark she'd left.

"You remember everything I said?" Her question was a direct line into Sam's resolve. Sam nodded, a quick, nervous motion. He felt the pull of the room, of Rhea, like a tide he couldn't resist.

"I do." He said, his voice thin but real. Rhea was as close as ever, her certainty an intoxicating thing. She held the power of the moment, shaping it, stretching it, refusing to let it slip away.

"Then we're good." She said, each word landing like a touch. Sam's hesitation grew, a solid presence in the air, one that neither of them could ignore. He wanted to say something, to break the skin of silence, to find out how deep the ink ran. But the moment was huge and slippery, and Sam was caught inside it, unprepared. Rhea's eyes danced over Sam's face, catching every flicker of emotion, every thought left unspoken. She leaned back against the wall, relaxed and confident, letting the distance close at its own pace. Her satisfaction was clear, a playful energy that lit up the space around her.

"You know where to find me." She said again, letting it linger. Sam opened his mouth, closed it, then opened it again, each movement more tentative than the last. The air held the shape of all the questions they wanted to ask but didn't dare. In the end, the only sound was the soft rasp of the door against the floor as Sam pulled it open. Rhea watched him step out, his reluctance loud and sweet. She felt the same tug, the same need, but savored the anticipation of waiting. She could still feel the connection between them, stretched thin but unbreakable. She knew it would snap back, stronger, pulling them closer than before. As Sam's figure disappeared into the rain-soaked street, the air hummed with a different kind of buzz. It stayed with Rhea long after the door closed, settling into her skin like ink.

Sam couldn't stop touching it. The lines were black and vivid, still raised and tender beneath his fingers. It felt like a secret, one Rhea had written in permanent language, a message that burned its way into his skin and mind. He traced the design, closing his eyes, recalling the warmth of the studio and Rhea's breath on his wrist. Sleep, when it came, was electric, jagged with too-bright dreams. Across town, Rhea's pencil scratched at the paper, but she was drawing more than the flowers she'd tattooed. She was drawing Sam's expression, not the design, sketching from memory that had already marked her in ways she couldn't quite define.

The lines stood out against Sam's skin, a new map to follow, a new story to tell. Every time he traced it, he remembered the pulse of the needle, the closeness of the moment, the depth of Rhea's attention. Sam was wrapped up in it, the whole experience looping through his mind like a song he couldn't stop humming. Sam sat back, exhaling slowly, the rush of emotion as fresh and raw as the ink itself. Each breath was filled with memory, each second spent touching the tattoo pulling him further into a web of desire and intrigue. He saw Rhea's eyes, the play of her smirk, felt the lingering warmth of her hands. It was overwhelming, consuming.

The night stretched long, and Sam was wide awake through all of it. The weight of what he felt was immense, pressing in with a vividness that left no room for sleep. But even that urgency was thrilling, an intensity he had never imagined. When sleep finally came, it was restless and electric, a series of vivid flashes too bright to contain. Sam's dreams were full of ink and eyes, breathless and eager and more real than he could handle.

Across town, Rhea sat hunched over her desk, her pencil moving in quick, deliberate strokes. The soft scratching on paper was a counterpoint to the loud silence that surrounded her, a silence heavy with thoughts she couldn't ignore. She drew the outline of the tattoo, the same design she'd put on Sam's skin. But her pencil veered, tracing more than the flowers, more than the lines. It traced the energy, the expression, the look on Sam's face that had imprinted itself onto her with startling clarity.

The memories came in waves, each one a pulse she couldn't quite catch her breath against. Rhea found herself smiling, the edge of it almost disbelieving. The connection she felt was intense, unexpected, and as deep as any ink she'd ever used. She let herself lean into it, knowing it would take more than sketching to satisfy. Rhea's hand moved with precision, but her mind was a wild, humming thing. Every thought looped back to Sam, to the sudden want that had rooted itself in her and grown tangled in the best kind of way.

Sam woke to the gray light of morning filtering through the blinds, the intensity of the night lingering like the first sharp hit of caffeine. He was raw with the memory of it, a buzz in his veins that nothing but seeing Rhea again could dull. Sam sat up, touching the tattoo once more, feeling the familiar rush. He was awake and alive in ways he hadn't been before, and he needed more. More ink, more Rhea, more of everything they'd barely scratched the surface of. For both of them, the hours stretched and slowed, each minute drawing them back to the point of contact. The connection simmered beneath the surface, waiting to ignite. Neither had expected to be this marked. But both knew it wouldn't be long.

He tried to wait. Three days. Each one felt like forever. Sam couldn't pretend any longer, and it showed in the way he moved, restless and anxious. The first day bled into night, another night of restless sleep, another night of dreams of Rhea. The second day was filled with anxiety and eagerness that morphed into a night of discontentment. The third day he made up an excuse, told himself that he needed aftercare. The parlour door swung open, and Sam's heart stuttered. Rhea didn't even try to hide her surprise.

"That didn't take long." She said, her voice slipping through Sam like smoke. The door closed with a soft click, the anticipation inside already humming. Sam stood there, the sudden heat of the studio washing over him, pooling in his chest.

"I wasn't sure," he said, the words catching on the edges of his breath, "if I should come back so soon."

"But you're here." Rhea pointed out, her smile full of something Sam wanted to drown in.

"I guess I am." Sam's pulse was an urgent beat, every inch of the space between them crackling. Rhea's laughter was low, edged with delight.

"Tattoo holding up?" She asked, her words light but carrying the weight of other questions, unasked but loud. Sam nodded, took a step further in.

"Maybe. Just wanted to be sure."

"Guess I'll have to take a look then." Rhea's eyes flicked to Sam's wrist, then back up to meet his. The look was solid, like hands on skin. They both stood there, the air thick with expectation, each second dragging out into infinity. Sam's head spun, caught in the tug of war between Rhea's pull and the hammering of his own heart. Sam took a breath, steadying himself.

"You didn't think I'd show." He accused, the words more playful than defensive.

"I knew you'd show." Rhea corrected, her confidence a magnetic force that drew Sam even closer. The room felt like it was closing in around them, pulling them together, tighter and more charged than before. Every corner seemed to thrum with the same rhythm as Sam's pulse, a symphony of want and need. Rhea tilted her head, and the loose fall of her hair moved like liquid.

"Sit down," she said, more command than invitation, "let me see." Sam sank into the chair, a rush of relief and anticipation swamping him as he settled in. The distance between them was smaller now, barely existent, the kind of space that begged to be crossed. The conversation turned electric, like the air before a storm. Sam could feel the build-up, the static that made his skin tingle, his breath catch. Rhea stood over him, her presence a blanket of gravity that Sam willingly surrendered to.

"Thought about it for three whole days, huh?" Rhea teased, her voice dipping in and out of a challenge. Sam bit his lip, a smile tugging at the edges.

"I have a confession." The truth slipped out, bolder than he was used to. Rhea leaned closer, every movement deliberate.

"Tell me." Rhea took his wrist in hers as Sam watched, unblinking, her fingers sliding over the skin with a touch that made him shiver. The air was hot with the promise of more, a heat that rose with every breath. As the seconds stretched and thinned, Rhea's attention never left Sam's face. She closed the door slowly, a move as unhurried and full of intent as the first time Sam had stepped into the studio.

"I've been hovering for a while—"

"I know." Rhea's eyes lingered, reading the need Sam didn't bother to hide. The air was intimate and compressed, every particle saturated with a shared urgency.

"I don't think you do." Sam barely glanced at the tattoo. He watched Rhea's mouth, not what it said but what it meant.

"Trust me," she said, the words low, charged, "I *know*." Her fingers brushed Sam's skin, deliberate and slow as Sam's pulse flared. Rhea inspected the wrap, the lines of ink, her breath a soft warmth over Sam's arm. Sam felt each moment stretch out, liquid and heavy. Rhea's attention was a palpable force, like gravity, pulling Sam further in. Every shift of her fingers was a jolt, every touch more electric than the last. She pulled the wrap back with care, her focus a spotlight that Sam willingly basked in. Rhea was close, close enough that Sam could feel the heat coming off her skin, close enough that it felt like too much and not enough at once.

"Looks good," she said, each word soft and intimate, "you heal fast." Sam blinked, struggling to keep his thoughts from unraveling, from losing the thread of what was happening beneath the sheer weight of the moment.

"I've walked past your parlour for weeks." Sam redirected the conversation, the boldness surprising even him.

"I know." Rhea smiled, her eyes catching Sam's with a look that went beyond amusement, a look that was more intent than casual. They sat there, impossibly close, knees almost brushing, the rest of the world narrowing down to this small, charged space between them. Rhea moved a fraction nearer, and Sam's breath stalled in his chest. Every second was saturated with anticipation, so thick that Sam could almost feel it settling into his bones. He didn't dare move, afraid it would shatter the tension, afraid it wouldn't.

"You've been staring at the walls for months," Rhea said, her tone a liquid thing, fluid and full of promise, "walking past every other week. Sometimes in the morning, waiting for me to open. Sometimes at night, watching as I pack up." The words hung in the air, dripping with possibility, with the weight of something that wasn't quite spoken but was definitely felt. Sam stayed silent, letting the anticipation coil tight around them, feeling the burn of it, the thrill. Rhea didn't look away, didn't move away, her focus as steady as her hands had been. It was a hold, it was a bind, and Sam felt it twist deeper than he ever thought it would go.

"It didn't take long for me to decide that I wanted a tattoo." Sam's voice was low and intent.

"I know." Rhea's eyes locked onto Sam's, the intensity binding them closer.

"I decided on it months ago." Sam swallowed, desire pushing the words out. He felt the electricity in each exchange, in the way Rhea looked at him, saw him, the way her voice turned the simplest words into a tangled mesh of want.

"I *know.*"

"I don't think you do—"

"You've been looking at more than the sketches on my walls," her observation carried more than ink, more than casual intent, "I know there was something else you came in here for." It was a dare, a challenge, a promise.

"Did you decide to get a tattoo just to spend some time with me?" Rhea's voice was a quiet lure, the kind of tease that wrapped itself around more than it let go of, light and heavy all at once. It was a comment that somehow felt like a caress, brushing against

Sam's heart in a way that made it skip and race, made it flutter and stumble in his chest. She watched him closely, her eyes a magnet that pulled at more than just words, waiting for him to react. The silence between them grew charged, a balloon stretched to capacity, ready to pop with every possible answer. Sam hesitated, knowing she was baiting him, knowing he had already taken the bait long before he had gathered the courage to walk through the door. But even knowing this, he felt the thrill of it, the playful mock of her question sending another hot rush through his veins.

It undid him, the way she dared him to be honest, mocked him in a way that made him feel more wanted than ridiculous. Every pause, every heartbeat in the thick air around them was loaded with the same jolt of electricity, winding tighter and tighter, the tension of it almost unbearable. Sam didn't known if she'd break the silence this time, if she'd pull words into the small space between them or let it stretch like a taut wire. But Rhea was too bold, too assured, and too aware of Sam to leave it. She watched him closely, her eyes a magnet that pulled at more than just words, drawing him out, waiting for him to react. She already knew the answer, already saw it written on his skin and stitched through every glance.

It undid him, the way she dared him to be honest, mocked him in a way that made him feel more wanted than ridiculous. Every pause, every heartbeat in the thick air around them was loaded with the same jolt of electricity, winding tighter and tighter, the tension of it almost unbearable. Sam didn't want to break it, didn't want to shatter the perfect strain of it, but he couldn't let it choke the breath from his lungs. He opened his mouth to speak, to confess, to give Rhea more of what she wanted. Everything about him was an answer, from the way he leaned in to the way he let the silence splinter with the weight of his intention. Rhea didn't flinch. Her smile was a bright and steady thing, her focus a searing heat that laid him bare. She moved in closer, the shift in distance a beckoning, a command. Sam swallowed hard, feeling every inch of space between them collapse into a nothing that was everything.

"I've never seen, or even met anyone like you," Sam let the admission hang in the air, deep and heavy, "I've watched you for months. Watched the way you work, seen the way you put people at ease." The energy in the room was as thick as smoke, wrapping around them, settling into their skin. Sam was different now, bold and daring, and it showed in the way he moved, in the way he held Rhea's gaze without flinching. Rhea noticed everything. She was sharp, observant, and each detail fed the heat between them. Sam felt exposed, but it was the kind of exposure he craved, the kind that set every nerve alight.

"So you're kind of like my stalker." Rhea touched the tattoo, her fingers gentle and sure, tracing the lines with care. Sam felt each pass like a spark, the heat of it traveling through his body and pooling low, building on itself until it was almost more than he could handle. She shifted, exploring skin beyond the ink, her attention roaming to places they both wanted her to go. Sam shivered again, more intense than before, more intense than they thought possible. The tension was alive, a living thing that wrapped around them and pulled tight. Sam closed his eyes, letting it swallow him whole, letting Rhea's touch do what the needle never could. Rhea's voice broke the charged silence, soft and full of meaning.

"Tell me what you want." She whispered, each word an imprint, each syllable a brand.

"I'm not," he hesitated, swallowing the lump in his throat, "I don't want you to think—"

"Sam—"

"I'm not a stalker. I just don't know many people in the city, and I thought—"

"I don't date." Rhea's response was immediate, the delay between confession and reply nonexistent. She stepped closer, her fingers brushing Sam's face, trailing down like a touch she'd memorized, like a touch Sam had craved. Sam couldn't look away. The line between them was a live thing, vibrant and humming, more immediate than anything else. Every move, every sound was significant, heavy with the weight of shared need.

"I am not the girl you bring home to mummy. I don't date anyone, and I don't have friends," Rhea walked to the front door and turned the lock slowly, the sound loud and deliberate in the charged silence before returning to the chair behind the curtain, "but if there's something else you want, something else you *need*, I can help with that." Sam didn't wait for Rhea's instructions. His shirt was already on the floor, his skin alive and waiting. Rhea's eyes missed nothing, and the air vibrated with the intensity of it all. The machines were silent, but the anticipation was loud. Sam's breath matched the rhythm of Rhea's movements, quick and eager.

Rhea's fingers were already slick with anticipation as she shoved Sam back into the chair, the leather creaking under his weight. Her eyes, dark and predatory, locked onto his as she straddled him, her thighs pressing against his hips like a vice. The tattoo gun in her hand was empty, but the vibrations it emitted were enough to make his skin prickle with electricity. She dragged the buzzing tool down his chest, tracing invisible lines that made his muscles twitch and his breath hitch. Her lips curled into a wicked smile as she felt the heat radiating from his body, the way his cock strained against the fabric of his pants, begging for release.

"You're trembling," she purred, her voice low and dripping with mockery, "never had a woman take control before?" Sam's face flushed, his hands gripping the arms of the chair like he was afraid he might float away. Rhea didn't wait for an answer. She slid off him, her hands moving to his belt with practiced ease. The sound of the buckle coming undone was obscenely loud in the quiet of the tattoo parlor, the air thick with the scent of ink and sweat. She yanked his pants down, followed by his boxers, and his cock sprang free, hard and leaking precum.

"You're a virgin, aren't you?" She teased, her breath hot against his thighs as she grabbed him, squeezing hard. Sam's silence was all the confirmation she needed. She laughed, a low, throaty sound that sent shivers down his spine. Her mouth enveloped him in one swift motion, her tongue swirling around the head of his cock before she took him deeper. Sam's hips bucked involuntarily, a strangled moan escaping his lips. Rhea's hands gripped his thighs, her nails digging into his skin as she bobbed her head, her lips tight and wet around him. The vibrations from the tattoo gun still hummed in her other hand, and she pressed it against his inner thigh, the sensation making him jerk and gasp.

"Fuck," he choked out, his hands tangling in her hair, "I'm gonna—"

"Cum," Rhea commanded, pulling back just enough to let the word hang in the air, "do it." And he did, his release spilling into her mouth with a guttural cry. Rhea swallowed every drop, her tongue lapping at him until he was spent and trembling. She stood, wiping her mouth with the back of her hand, a smirk playing on her lips.

"I'm sorry—"

"Don't apologize," she stepped back, her fingers hooking into the hem of her shirt, "you're just getting started. You'll learn." Slowly, she peeled it off, revealing a canvas of ink that covered every inch of her skin except for the delicate outlines of her black lace bra and panties. The tattoos framed her body like a work of art, the intricate designs drawing the eye to the places she wanted him to focus on. She swayed to the music playing softly in the background, her hips moving in a rhythm that was impossible to ignore.

Sam couldn't stop staring at the vast array of tattoos that decorated Rhea's skin. Every inch of her body told a story, from the colorful sleeves that wound down her arms to the delicate black and grey floral patterns that danced across her stomach. The ink was a riot of colors and shapes, a living mural that drew the eye and teased the imagination. Only the delicate outlines of her black lace bra and panties were unmarked, a deliberate contrast that emphasized more than they hid.

She moved with an easy grace, each motion a seductive invitation, twirling to the music that filtered through the room. The sway of her hips was fluid and mesmerizing, a rhythm impossible to ignore or resist. Sam was transfixed, his eyes following the motion, captivated by the way she seemed to channel the music into every pore, every motion. Her hair swung in time with the beat, a dark fan that added to the allure, to the pull, each breathless second drawing Sam deeper into a haze of desire. It was a dance meant for him, and Sam could feel the intention in every motion, the way she controlled the tempo and tugged at the pulse in his veins.

Wet with heat and anticipation, the air wrapped around them, filling the space with something palpable and more than a little dangerous. Sam's heart pounded in his chest, each beat in sync with the thrust of her hips, with the flow of her limbs, with the rapid tempo of his pulse. She was relentless in her tease, in the way she turned her back to him, the way she tossed a glance over her shoulder, her eyes blazing with challenge and promise. Sam didn't know how much more he could take, how much longer he could resist the lure of her motion, of her inked and shifting skin. He wanted to reach out, to pull her in, to feel those intricate tattoos under his fingers, the warmth of her body against his.

"I've been watching you too," Rhea sensed it all - his need, his capitulation, his raw and unfiltered want, "the way you watched me, the way you wanted me. And you can have me, but just for tonight. Just for now. And I'll show you what you need to know." She knew exactly how to stoke it, how to make it burn hotter without ever touching him. She was an artist, working him like a canvas, and she stepped closer, her body shimmering with the effortlessness of her domination. Sam shivered, and the quiver didn't escape her notice. She knew she had him. She always knew.

"Your turn," she said, her voice a sultry whisper, "stand up."
"Yes." Sam obeyed, his legs shaky as he rose from the chair. Rhea reclined in it now, her legs spread just enough to give him a glimpse

of what lay beneath the lace. She pointed to her ankles.

"Start here." She instructed, and he dropped to his knees, his lips brushing against her skin as he followed her orders. His kisses were tentative at first, but Rhea's sharp intake of breath encouraged him to be bolder. He moved up her calves, his hands gripping her thighs as he reached the sensitive skin behind her knees. He reached the lace underwear, breathing into it as he smelled her. Rhea's fingers tangled in his hair, guiding him higher up to her stomach.

"Skip it," she said, her voice trembling with restraint, "tease it, graze over it, but don't there too quickly. It's a marathon, not a sprint." Sam obeyed, his lips trailing over her stomach, his tongue flicking out to taste the salt on her skin. He moved to her breasts, his mouth closing around one nipple through the lace of her bra. Rhea arched into him, a moan escaping her lips as she tugged at his hair.

"Can I touch you?" He asked softly, almost frightened to make a wrong move, to ruin her pleasure.

"Lightly." Her hand guided his to the waistband of her panties, and he hesitated for only a moment before sliding them down. Rhea's pussy was bare, glistening with arousal, and Sam's breath caught in his throat. Rhea's breath hitched as his fingertips brushed the damp fabric. Sam hesitated, his heart pounding like a war drum, but only for a moment. With a slow, deliberate motion, he slid the panties down her thighs, his fingers trembling as they brushed against her, the heat of her pussy searing his skin.

"Like this?" He asked, his voice rough with desire and intrigue.

"Yes." She breathed, her eyes fluttering closed as he pressed a finger inside her. Her walls clenched around him, hot and tight, and she let out a soft moan that made his body ache.

"Deeper?"

"Deeper," she urged, her hips rocking against his hand, urging him to explore further, "more." He obeyed, sliding another finger into her, the sensation of her gripping him almost too much to bear. Her body was a masterpiece, every inch of her designed to drive him wild. He curled his fingers, searching for that spot that would make her scream, and when he found it, she gasped, her back arching off the bed.

"There," she moaned, her voice trembling with pleasure, "right there. Don't stop." He didn't. He couldn't. His fingers worked her with a rhythm that was both punishing and tender, his thumb circling her clit as he moved his hand. Her moans grew louder, more desperate, her hips bucking against him as she chased her release. Her pussy was a vice, squeezing his fingers so tight he could barely move, but he didn't care. He was lost in her, in the way she writhed beneath him, in the way she cried out his name like a prayer.

"Fuck, Sam," she gasped, her nails digging into his arm, "kiss my neck. Touch me."

"Where?"

"Here." She grabbed his other hand and moved it to her breasts, squeezing his hand underneath hers as her fingers intertwined with his. He leaned in and kissed her neck, biting her ever so slightly that her skin prickled with goosebumps. He pressed his body against her, his hips pushing his hand further into her while he rocked back and forth. As she came, her pussy pulsed around his fingers in waves of ecstasy. He watched her fall apart, her body trembling with the force of her orgasm, and he knew he'd never get enough of her. But she wasn't done. Not yet.

"Again." She demanded, her voice raw with need, her eyes dark with lust. And he obeyed, because he couldn't help himself. She was his goddess, and he was her willing slave. The room was thick with the scent of her arousal, a heady musk that clung to the air like a promise. Rhea sat before him, her body a sinuous curve of temptation, her skin glowing in the dim light like molten gold, her legs spread far apart. Her lips, painted a deep crimson, curled into a smirk that was equal parts challenge and invitation. She slid down the chair, her back pressing against the leather, slick with sweat.

"Kneel." She commanded, her voice a low purr that sent shivers down his spine. He obeyed without hesitation, dropping to his knees before her, his cock already hard and wanting more of her lips around it. But he knew he had to learn, and he wanted her to teach him - he wanted her to *show* him. She slid closer, the skin on her thighs brushing against his face, soft and teasing. He could smell her, the intoxicating scent of her pussy, and it made his mouth water. It wasn't sweet, it wasn't like honey or sugar or anything else he had read or heard. It was sharp and tangy, like vinegar mixed with the sweat of desire, an intoxicating blend that quickened the pulse and lingered in the air with a raw, primal allure. It wasn't as unpleasant as he had pictured, and it made him desire every part of her.

"Good boy," she murmured, her fingers tangling in his hair, pulling him closer, "now, show me how much you want me." He leaned in, his lips brushing against the inside of her thigh, the skin there smooth and warm. He could feel her pulse, rapid and insistent, and it drove him wild. He kissed his way up her leg, his tongue tracing a path towards the apex of her thighs. She let out a soft moan, her grip on his hair tightening, urging him on.

"Lick me," she ordered, her voice breathless with need, "make me come." He didn't need to be told twice. His tongue found her clit, swollen and begging for attention, and he began to lap at it with slow, deliberate strokes. She gasped, her hips bucking against his face, and he could feel her wetness coating his lips, the taste of her driving him to new heights of desire. He slid a finger inside her, feeling her tightness, her heat, and she moaned louder, her body trembling with pleasure.

"Come for me," he growled against her pussy, his voice thick with lust, "let me taste you."

"Fuck," she breathed, her voice a ragged whisper, "just like that. Don't stop."

He obeyed, his tongue and fingers working in tandem, driving her closer and closer to the edge. He could feel her muscles clenching around his finger, her body writhing with pleasure, and he knew she was close. He redoubled his efforts, his tongue flicking over her clit with rapid, insistent strokes, his finger curling inside her, hitting that sweet spot that made her cry out. She screamed as she came, her body convulsing with pleasure. He savoured every drop, his cock throbbing with need. She collapsed against the leather, her body limp and spent, and he held her legs close, his heart pounding in his chest.

"Good boy," she whispered, her voice soft and sated, "now fuck me."

She pushed up onto the chair, her hands roaming over his body, her touch electric. He straddled her, her pussy still wet and glistening, and he could feel the heat of her against his cock. She reached down, guiding him inside her, and he groaned as she pushed up into him, her tightness enveloping him in a velvet vice.

"Jesus, Rhea—"

"Fuck me," she commanded, her voice a low growl, "make me scream." He obeyed, thrusting into her with wild abandon, their bodies moving together in a frenzied rhythm. He rode her hard, her nails digging into his back, her moans filling the room. He could feel her clenching around him, her body tightening as she neared another climax, and he knew he wouldn't last much longer.

"Come with me." She gasped, her voice breaking with pleasure. He tried to delay the inevitable, striving to maintain the sensation of their togetherness for as long as he could, aware that once it ended that would be it. But he couldn't hold it any longer.

"Rhea—" He exploded inside her, his cock pulsing with release, and she screamed as she came again, watching the pleasure on his face, her body shuddering with ecstasy. They collapsed together, their bodies slick with sweat, their breaths coming in ragged gasps. "Good boy," her voice was soft and calm, "you did well." He smiled, his heart still racing, and pulled her close. Leaning in for a kiss, she pressed her finger to his lips and shook her head.

"No," she said softly, "that's too intimate. More intimate than this." They stayed there together, their bodies entwined, the room filled with the scent of their passion. It was a night he would never forget, a night of pure, unadulterated lust. When Sam spoke, the words were raw, an admission and a truth.

"I want more of you."

"You can't have me." Her fingers brushed Sam's face, slow and deliberate. The light was dim, neon casting a haze over everything, tinting the room in colors that felt more sensual than Sam could bear.

"I want—"

"No," her touch was slow and reverent as she ran her fingers along the lines of his new tattoo, then over skin untouched, "don't ruin this. Embrace it for what it was, and never come here again, even if it's for just a tattoo."

As Sam gazed into her eyes, a mixture of desire and sadness clouded his own. She was right, he knew it deep down. This moment, this night, it was something unique, something fleeting and intense. It couldn't be replicated or prolonged. With a heavy heart, he nodded slowly, understanding the gravity of her words. Their bodies slowly disentangled, breaking the connection that had held them so closely together. The room felt emptier now, the absence of their intertwined forms creating a palpable void. Sam stood up, feeling a sense of loss already creeping in.

"I understand." He whispered, his voice barely audible in the dimly lit room. He reached out to touch her one last time, a gesture of farewell and gratitude for the passion they had shared. She caught his hand gently, holding it in her own for a moment before releasing it. Sam lingered for a moment, taking in the weight of her final words, the bittersweet memory of their night together. Then, with a heavy heart but a sense of acceptance, he turned and walked out into the parlour, unlocking the door and walking out into the rain. He knew he would never forget the intensity of that night, the raw connection they had shared, and the fleeting beauty of their encounter.

Rhea locked the door behind him and turned off the lights to the front parlour. She stood, smiling at his retreating figure in the rain.

As he disappeared into the night, she walked back into the other room, sitting on the chair and staring at her body. With delicate fingers, she traced her tattooed arm all the way to her bicep, turning her arm outward and bracing her wrist between her knees. She picked up the tattoo gun, and slowly dragged the needle through her skin, adding another brand to the collection of lines already marked off on her arm. She smiled, that knowing smile she always had, before setting the tattoo gun down to close the store for the night.

The Plus One

The invitation slid from a heap of junk mail. Even his name looked smug in its delicate script. She hadn't bothered with an updated address. It stung more than he let himself admit, a surprise with her unmistakable flourish, paper as smooth as she had been in leaving him behind. He opened it, anticipating his own hollow breath. But it still felt like swallowing a stone. *Please join the future Mr. and Mrs. Watson for their wedding.* The details followed, cold and almost calculated. *St Audries Park. Three and a half hour drive from central London. Accommodation available.*

They had been there once, together, on a quiet country drive. It had rained so heavily that day, they pulled over to escape the torrential downpour and had lunch in the quiet restaurant surrounded by a warm fire and thunder and delicious food. They toured the building as they waited out the storm, and Jason had commented on how it would be perfect for their wedding one day. She had stayed silent, even made an uneasy face at the comment, and he should have known then.

He gazed at the RSVP card, the tick boxes indicating attendance or absence. *Happily Attend* or *Regretfully Decline.* He wondered if he could happily decline, or even angrily decline. He wondered if he could include his own note card informing them that the invitation was a slap in the face, that she had added insult to injury.

But no, he decided, he had to be the bigger person. Then there it was, the smallest addition to the bottom of the card underneath the attendance box. *Names, Jason Billson Plus One* with a space for the name of his date.

It would be one more pity party without a plan. And then, as recklessly as any other mistake, an idea unfurled. Jason tossed the other letters onto the counter, their white corners poking from beneath a glossy real estate advertisement. The house was too quiet, the hum of appliances amplifying the silence she'd left behind. He leaned against the kitchen island, the granite cool and unfriendly. Only last week he'd heard through the grapevine that she was seeing someone else. Now the final twist of the knife had arrived in an embossed envelope asking him to attend the wedding of his ex three months down the line.

He thought about what it would mean to go, the awkward looks, the regretful glances, the melancholy pats on the back. His shoulders ached at the thought. How it would feel walking in alone, his own awkward third wheel at a table of married friends. He pictured himself lifting a solitary glass in a desperate, silent toast. It was all just an invitation to humiliation. But showing up with someone, someone so dazzling that nobody would dare feel sorry for him, that was a different story. If he didn't go, he'd still lose. They would assume he was too crushed to even witness it. But attending, fortified with the right date, he might save some face. He might even convince them he'd moved on as easily as she had. His mind began to work through the possibilities. It was going to take some careful planning. He wondered who he could bring, someone who wasn't somehow connected to her and their past life together.

It had been a year, one whole year since she had left, yet he still felt the sting of her moving on so quickly. He drummed his fingers on the counter, imagining familiar faces and then quickly discarding them. Not his college friends, they were all married or hopeless. Nobody from work either, she knew them all. He stared at the golden letters again, calculating and recalculating the variables. She'd outmaneuvered him once, but not this time. There was really only one option, as absurd and brilliant as it seemed. He couldn't risk just any date. He needed a professional. He smiled to himself, feeling the first relief in days. Someone without emotional baggage, a stranger who wouldn't accidentally befriend his ex over the canapé trays. Yes, someone who knew how to turn an event like this into a success story, not a tragicomedy.

He sank into the leather chair, pulling out his phone, the corners of his mouth twitching. He imagined their faces - his friends, his family - at a stunning stranger on his arm. Suddenly, his self-doubt morphed into boldness. It wasn't reckless if it worked. Maybe he could find an escort whose confidence was contagious enough to make even him believe it. Someone perfect. He keyed in a few search terms, laughing a little at the absurdity. The thought of him paying someone for a date. He had only ever dated one woman, been with one woman, and when he had proposed she left him suddenly to travel the world and had met someone new. This would either be a brilliant save or a legendary failure, but at least it would be on his terms. The first search results were almost enough to change his mind. The images didn't quite match his fantasy. Too desperate. Too obvious. Too fake. He refined the search, honing in on elegance, sophistication, mystery.

He paused, thumb hovering, a flicker of nerves and something close to hope passing through him. Maybe this was crazy. Or maybe it was the best idea he'd ever had. Maybe, just maybe, he could do this. The warmth of his own reckless determination pushed away the chill that had been creeping in since he'd opened the letter. He clicked further down, new faces emerging with every tap, each possibility daring him to commit to this plan. To commit to himself. And he would, no matter the cost. He exhaled, a satisfied release. He was going to that wedding.

He lingered on each face longer than the last. Their eyes were dead giveaways, wanting what they had been paid to want. He sifted through their descriptions - flirtatious, refined, athletic, chic. Words meant to disarm and beguile. It wasn't until he saw her picture that something caught inside his chest. Her glance, as though daring him to underestimate her. He almost felt her voice curl into his ear. She was a little older than the others, she was a little older than him. Intimidating, yet magnetic. Elegant, but far from fragile. There was a confidence there that pierced through his apprehension. Before he could think it through, he sent her a message.

It wasn't just a photo. It was an invitation, an unraveling of everything he thought he wanted from this insane plan. Jason scrolled back to the top, the other faces already erased from memory. Her name - Harper. His thumb hovered, then hesitated. He'd never expected to find someone who'd make him nervous, but now he was. Nervous and excited. It all felt like one step too far and yet too late to stop. Each profile, each caption was a slippery slope of ambition and allure. Just yesterday, the idea of searching like this was pure fiction. He half expected the first click to implode his phone, announcing to everyone how pathetic he'd become. Yet here he was, feeling every inch a voyeur of his own life. He laughed dryly to himself. This would be easier if he could forget the real reason he needed a date.

There was a mad circus of options, the absurdity hitting him every time a new page loaded. Perfect faces, curated confidence. He squinted at one, almost imagining the perfume of desperation in the air. But Harper. There was something else. Not the fake gloss. Not a practiced smile. He enlarged the image, letting it fill the screen, the room, his breath. Dark hair, sharp cheekbones, that smirk. She'd make him look damn good, and the thought of it set his mind spiraling. He wondered how many others were looking at this same photo, thinking the same thing.

Jason tore himself away, back to the top. The impersonal selections, the sterile words. Elegant. Flirtatious. Chic. Empty vessels compared to her. He re-opened her profile, pouring over every detail this time. Confident, poised. Witty. Her smirk all but laughed at his doubts. Before the second thoughts roared back, he typed in her number. He'd only have this one chance. If she said no, he'd have to start all over again. He knew he couldn't bear to go with anyone else now. And then the message itself. He'd crafted hundred-word pitches with less agony than this one line. He wondered what he could say that wouldn't sound ridiculous, too needy, too nonchalant. He gave himself a virtual slap, channeling her imagined voice in his ear - don't overthink this. He breathed in and out, fingers poised above the keys. *Need a date for a wedding. Wanting to make my ex jealous. You're exactly what I'm looking for.*

"Too fucking needy." He cursed aloud and deleted it, rewrote it, stared. Her expression haunted him with its irony. Jason was far too sober to be this rash, but that hadn't stopped him before. A deep breath, a final shot of courage. He pressed send. *Need a plus one for a wedding. Saturday June 14th. Black tie, overnight stay, transport and accommodation included. Separate beds.* And then the waiting. That breathlessness of an uncertain gamble. He wondered if he had been too formal, too professional. But that's what she was, a professional. This wasn't a date, it was a transaction. Minutes passed with the subtle violence of a crashing wave. He wondered what he would do if she replied. What he would do if she didn't. The invitation seemed to smirk at him from the table, but he was too deep in this new plunge to care.

He tapped through her photos again, half expecting them to vanish, half daring himself to dream they might come to life. Every click, every pixel was his fresh undoing. But something had shifted. Maybe just reaching out had done it. He grinned, just a little. For the first time in weeks, Jason felt like he might just get through this after all. And then his phone buzzed. *Free for a drink?* The response was simple, and loaded. It was like she was planning an after hours business meeting, but he supposed that was exactly what it was. It was a weeknight, and Jason wasn't the type to go out when he had to be up early.

"Fuck it." He said, picking up the phone and messaging back. *The Fox & Hounds near Sloane Square, one hour.* He clicked send before grabbing his coat from the rack, heading out into the dark and gloomy London evening. She sat across from him in the corner booth, a slender glass between her fingers. The dim glow from the bar softened her edges, made her seem less distant than he'd imagined. Her smirk remained, an open secret he was dying to be let in on. He stumbled over his words, sure he was blowing it. She tilted her head, amused by his nerves. As she spoke, her voice unfurled around him, answering all the questions he was too afraid to ask.

It was a small bar, more intimate than the online image she had of him - tightly wound, trying too hard. Her curiosity was genuine. Even the location of their meeting, quiet and dim, suggested he wasn't all bravado. She sipped her drink, her presence a beacon against the amber glow. She felt eyes on her, an anomaly in this corner of London that catered to a different crowd, sitting across from the guy in the suit with too much to prove. Harper smiled to herself, spinning his message over in her mind, the mix of confidence and need. It was intriguing, and she wanted to see if he was too.

She had caught sight of him before he saw her. He had hovered near the door, taking a quick, anxious breath. She had raised a hand, watching him register that it was her, the relief washing over his features as he approached. This was going to be interesting. He was tall, clean-cut, that edge of determination hanging from his collar. It was more endearing than she'd expected. And just a little desperate, which she thought amusing.

"So, I need a plus one for a wedding." He laughed, the sound as unsteady as the smile he gave her.

"So you need a date." It was Harper's turn to laugh, a delicate sound that made him feel both at ease and impossibly aware of the space between them.

"I wouldn't call it that—"

"Call it what it is," she sipped casually on her drink, a dark mix in a bold glass with a twist of orange peel, "you need to make an appearance and I assume the guests need to think I'm not paid for. We might as well lean into the parts we're going to play." He sat uneasily, twisting the edge of his coat in his fingers and avoiding eye contact.

"You don't seem the type," she said, her gaze held him in place, unraveling more than he was prepared to give, "to need to pay for a date to a wedding."

"Guess you have me figured out already." He replied, settling into the soft leather and ordering a drink he probably didn't need. Her eyes tracked the motion of his hands, and he realized how much they betrayed him. She liked that. His visible humanity.

"I'm just good at this." She said with a small shrug, as though it was effortless. Maybe it was. But that was what he was paying for. A part of him had hoped it would feel more like a performance. More distant, less engaging.

"Is it the same for every client?" He asked, trying to sound more casual than he felt.

"I'd say you're a special case." She leaned back, her smirk turning his mind inside out. She saw right through him, the tangle of nerves and ambition he carried in with him. He felt caught, but not unwillingly.

"Why?"

"I usually attend royal dinners and plutocratic business events," Harper's deep chestnut brown hair fell in loose waves around her face as she leaned forward to set her empty glass on the table, "wedding's aren't usually my forte."

"Then why did you message back so quickly," Jason's tone was deep and sceptical, with a touch of smoothness that was almost hypnotic, "and want to meet so soon?"

"Curiosity." Her response was quick, polished, the certainty against his growing comfort. Jason felt his defenses slip away, inch by inch, each piece leaving him lighter and somehow bolder.

"You'll have to tell me what kind of impression you want to make," she said, leaning in as though sharing a secret, "sincere, devoted? Bitterly heartbroken?" He was bitterly heartbroken, once, but that wasn't the part he wanted to play.

"Somewhere between madly in love and trying too hard." He quipped.

"Oh, so the real you then." Harper shot back. Her wit was as sharp as her look, but there was a kindness there too, an unspoken assurance that this was all as easy as she made it seem.

"You're okay with this?" He asked, feeling strangely exposed even though he was the one doing the hiring. He needed to hear her say it, needed to know this was as uncomplicated as she made it sound.

"With what?" Her brow arched, genuine interest tinged with playful interrogation.

"With this job," Jason took a sip from his drink, his fingers brushed against the cold glass, sending a shiver down his spine, "with me." She considered him for a moment, her pause less dramatic than deliberate. As if she knew the impact it would have, and she wanted him to sit with it. With himself.

"It's what I do Jason," her voice had the same glide as her look, "you make it sound like such an ordeal." He shook his head, wishing he had more time, more words, more distance between how he'd imagined this going and how it was. She was unfazed by all of it, an immovable object meeting his decidedly resistible force. It was the most fun he'd had in ages. He found himself eager, vulnerable, astonished at how deftly she managed it all.

"This wedding," he was a walking contradiction, with a strong jawline that could cut glass but eyes that revealed a deep vulnerability and need for connection, "it's my ex." Her face held no look of pity, no forlorn gaze which told him that she felt sorry for him. Instead she looked indifferent, with a hint of understanding colouring her green eyes. He filled her in on the details, not more than she needed to know.

"Only a year," she asked, a soft hint of doubt just enough to make him think he might not be in as deep as he already knew he was, "and she's already getting married to someone else?"

"Yeah," he muttered, "she's a piece of work."

"Don't do that," Harper's voice is low and seductive, wrapping around him like a purr, "don't be bitter. If your goal is to attend this wedding as the bigger person, then you're going to have to work on not sounding so hurt." And there it was. She was a master of the game, a chameleon with the power to transform into whatever her clients desired. Her eyes were sharp and calculating, always searching for her next move. But there was a warmth in her smile and a sparkle in her gaze that softened the edges of her facade. She was a mystery, a puzzle that begged to be solved, and he found himself falling deeper into her web with each passing moment.

"You're right," Jason sat up straight, a wave of confidence and determination washing over him, "at least I have three months to work on it." Harper looked at him, smiling at his resolve. His dark hair was styled in a messy yet fashionable way, his jawline sharp and defined. His eyes held a hint of mischief and his lips curved into a small smile. He was charming and attractive, but he didn't know it. "I don't doubt that you'll be perfectly fine come the wedding." Harper leaned forward, placing a gentle hand on his arm. He caught a whiff of it then, her perfume subtle but intoxicating, a blend of jasmine and musk with a hint of vanilla. It added to her allure and made him want to lean in closer.

"What do I tell people leading up to it," he sat forward slightly, his gaze darkening as he spoke, "when they ask who I'm bringing?"

"Tell people you're seeing someone new," she sat back slowly, settling her slender arms on her lap, "someone you met in the dark corner of a dark bar in a dark hole of the city. Someone you wouldn't have met anywhere else if you hadn't walked inside on a cold November evening."

"Very good." His breath caught in his throat, excitement and nerves swirling in a way he hadn't expected. Not just about the wedding, but about seeing her again. Maybe he'd gone into this with a clear plan, but after meeting Harper, the lines were already starting to blur.

"Three months," she confirmed before standing, collecting her handbag and coat from the bench, "we'll talk before then. Get the story ironed out a bit more efficiently. And we should meet again, so that we're more comfortable in each other's presence." As she left the bar, Harper's thoughts lingered on his sincerity, a sincerity she'd almost forgotten existed outside of her work, outside of her usual clients. She hadn't felt this curious in a long time. Maybe she was taking a risk, but she had a feeling it would be worth it. Jason watched her go, her slender body swaying in the dark night, disappearing into the shadows.

The months that followed that first meeting were fast and fluid, the days bleeding into one another in a constant flux of anticipation and excitement, loaded text messages filled the gap between their carefully planned engagements. The messages revealed more of themselves than either had originally intended. Jason found himself waiting for the next notification, seeing her name pop up on his phone as a thrilling distraction from what he thought was his life. They met at the same bar more than once, always sitting closer, always talking with an ease that was both familiar and unnerving. Harper's curiosity grew, fed by his sincerity and the way his vulnerability never quite receded. They started meeting with no particular reason, no immediate plan, the lines blurring even further with every drink shared.

Each time, she would prod at him until his reservations unraveled, all the while catching herself enjoying it more than she should. He wondered if she felt the strange pull too, the way the wedding still hung between them but felt less like a job and more like the promise of something neither could define. Even when she wasn't there, he'd find himself imagining how she'd respond to each unfamiliar situation, how her quick wit and sharp eyes would turn his plans inside out. Then there was her response to his text - surprisingly fast, unexpectedly excited, telling him she'd help him choose the right thing to wear for the wedding. And now, here they were, shopping together, navigating the racks and their growing familiarity mere weeks before the wedding.

The tape measure circled his waist like an accusation. Jason fumbled with the knot of his tie, then abandoned it entirely. This was harder than he'd imagined. Harper's voice curled around the dressing room curtain, an audible smirk in every word. He fought against the surge of relief that followed. They moved between aisles, the fine fabric of his failures stretching behind him. She laughed as he squinted at the price tags, at the daring colors she tossed his way. Her approval meant more than it should. He liked it too much when she called him charming.

"You still alive in there?" She called, amusement weaving through the question. He could picture her leaning against the doorway, arms crossed, delighting in his struggle.

"Depends how you define *alive*," Jason replied, stepping out with exaggerated hesitance, "well?" The tie was askew, the jacket a bit too loose. Harper appraised him like a work of modern art. She smiled, a knowing, deliberate thing.

"It's not bad. If you're going for an underdressed anxiety vibe."

"I was thinking more casual indifference." He looked down, half relieved, half exasperated.

"I'll let you know when you're getting close." She motioned for him to try again, her confidence sweeping him back into the room. This was supposed to be the easy part, but with every shirt he tried, the pressure mounted. She was there, unflappable and waiting, the opinion he suddenly realized mattered more than anyone's. More than his ex's. More than the smug looks he imagined from the wedding crowd. She seemed to know it, and there was power in that knowledge. Another few rounds, and he was ready to concede. But Harper wasn't.

"Let me see." She insisted, pulling back the curtain just enough to slip inside his doubts. Her presence crowded him with ease. He obliged, one last effort at matching her poise, and her expression shifted. Approval, faint and thrilling. It shot through him like an unexpected spark.

"What do you think?"

"Better," she conceded, tugging his sleeve to demonstrate the adjustments needed, "maybe even charming." Her fingers brushed his wrist, a light touch that suggested more than guidance.

"I'll take charming." He said, savoring the word more than he'd planned to. She had him figured out, every misstep anticipated, every insecurity checked with that perfectly measured ease.

"Let's try a different angle." She said, her suggestion ringing with the authority of a carefully controlled coup. He followed her through the store, the fabric of his failures trailing behind. Her attention drifted over jackets and shirts, making him realize he liked this - a fact that should have worried him more than it did. He watched her lift a navy suit from the rack, sleek and a little daring, like her.

"You're kidding, right?"

"You know you can wear navy to a black tie event, right?" Harper shook her head, amused by his skepticism and holding it against him. There was something in the way she said it, as though his future would require it.

"I don't think—"

"Exactly," she interrupted, thrusting it into his arms, "you won't think. You'll trust me." He nodded, aware of how absurd it was to feel this relieved, this delighted by her words. It was only a suit, only a gig. But as he slipped into the clothes, each thread felt woven with her assurance, his image coming together under her guidance. He half expected the sales clerk to swoop in and seal the deal with a pronouncement, but it was Harper who did that.

"Very convincing," she said when he emerged, scrutinizing him with a critical and completely enticing eye, "you might even get away with it."

"With what?"

"With stealing the show." She grinned, her approval the only thing he was looking for. They moved to the accessories, Harper testing him with ties as audacious as the thought of having someone like her at his side. He settled on one that mirrored her taste, his nerves finally calming into something like confidence. She stepped close, aligning the knot with precision and something like affection.

"How do I look?" Jason asked, his voice almost too eager.

"Almost like a new man." She replied. The way she said it left him wondering who exactly she thought he'd been before. They made their way to the counter, Jason glancing once at the price tags, once at her, and he wondered what his performance was truly going to cost him. Outside, Harper paused, turning to him with that familiar challenge in her eyes.

"You ready for this?"

"For the wedding?"

"For me." She replied, the two words loaded with everything unspoken between them. Her smile lingered longer than it needed to. His did too.

"Don't I get to take you dress shopping?"

"No need," her voice was like velvet, smooth and soothing with an alluring hint of mischief, "I purchased my outfit the day after we first met." Jason's eyes scrutinised her, playful and mocking with a hint of curiosity.

"How do you know it will go with my suit?"

"Why do you think I chose the navy one? Trust me, it'll be perfect," her words left a melodic trail, drawing him in with every syllable, "now I must leave. I have a dinner tonight that I need to prepare for." He watched her leave, knowing this had felt like a date. A real date. He wondered if she felt the same. And if she did, whether it scared her as much as it thrilled him.

The long drive was loaded, flirty, the banter between them light and easy. He wondered if this is how he had felt when he had first driven to St Audries Park with *her*, how easy the conversation had been on that quiet Sunday they had nothing better to do. But now, his mind was filled with nothing else but Harper. Nothing else mattered than this idyllic drive through the countryside on this warmer June day.

"Is there anything else we've forgotten?" She mused as she scrolled idly on her phone.

"Favourite colour." He smiled, glancing sideways at her before returning his attention to the road ahead. She continued scrolling, smiling as she did.

"Hmm, let me check." She teased.

"No cheating," he grabbed her phone from her hands and threw it casually to the backseat, "you should know this stuff by heart now."

She turned to face him, her eyes glistening in the late afternoon sun.

"Green," she smiled, "deep green like the captured essence of a surrounding forest, with hues of emerald and jade that shimmer and dance in the sunlight after a heavy rain. Like my eyes. You said that to me once after we caught up for coffee three weeks ago. Trust me, Jason. I know everything by heart. Everything will be okay."

She caught him off guard, an anxiety sweeping through him that he hadn't felt for a long time. They weren't driving to a casual lunch of a weekend getaway, they were headed to his ex's wedding in the country. They would be trapped far from the safety of his home and his routine, and this suddenly set him on edge. She continued to stare at him, a wave of concern washing over her bright face. Her eyes, those deep green dazzling eyes - they were a color that held secrets, an enigmatic hue that seemed to shift with the light, revealing new depths and layers. It was the color of mystery and passion, a shade that could captivate and enchant in equal measure. And for him, it was the color of her eyes that were like a window to her soul and a reflection of his own desires.

"You seem concerned all of a sudden." There was a softness to her voice, almost like a lullaby.

"Just wondering if we'll make it to the dinner on time." His misgiving was etched across his face, the lines in his forehead deepening as his eyebrows furrowed.

"You know we will," her hand reached out to gently touch his arm, "though I am surprised that you wanted to attend the dinner. We could have just gone to the wedding tomorrow and made an early escape on Sunday morning."

"I wanted to show you off," concern manifested in the quiver in his voice, a wavering tremble that revealed his building vulnerability and fear, "I thought the act would be easier to sell if we were there all weekend."

"A cunning ruse," her fingers lightly grazed his skin as she stroked his arm back and forth, "you've become quite the conman."

He could feel the warmth of her touch, the gentle pressure of her hand as if she were trying to comfort him. It was like the beginning stages of a storm, a low rumble in the distance that could turn into a raging tempest at any moment. It crept into his mind and swirled around like a restless breeze, making him feel on edge and vulnerable. They drove the rest of the way in silence, only thirty minutes left, and arrive at the grand estate with an hour to spare. They stood at the entrance, a breath away from crossing the final line. The estate sprawled before them, a gilded monument to everything he wanted to forget. Jason tightened his grip on her arm. If they walked in now, there would be no going back. He braced himself against her presence, against the nerves that made him want to laugh and vomit all at once.

"You check in," she smiled as she collected her bags, "I need to make a few calls."

"A few calls?"

"Yes," there was a hint of concern in her voice, a subtle tremble that betrayed her worries, "just finalising a dinner next weekend. I was messaging in the car but didn't want to bother you with the call. I won't be long. Send me the room details once you have them." And with that she left him, disappearing around a corner, her heels crunching on the gravel as she hurried away. He hadn't been prepared to enter the estate alone, dragging his suitcase and approaching the desk with a new wave of anxiety.

"I have a room booked under Billson." He fumbled with his wallet.

"Let's see," the clerk said, staring over her thick glasses at him, "ahh, yes. We have you in the Lady Lake Suite." Before he could respond, a wave of familiar voices surrounded him, crashing down on him like a tidal wave. They called his name, laughing and jeering at their shock of his arrival.

"Jason!" His mother kissed his cheeks, her nails digging into his shoulders as she held him close.

"Mother." He replied casually, his eyebrows furrowed with a deep crease etching between them while she looked at him with worry in her gaze.

"I didn't think you'd come." Her lips were pressed together in a thin line, a slight downward turn at the corners.

"You were all going to be here," he greeted his brother with a casual and quick hug, "I couldn't be the only one left out." His brother, Carter, stared at him with curiosity.

"We kind of had to come," he said, glancing at his husband, "but I didn't think you'd show."

"Saving appearances, I suppose." Carter's husband, his ex's cousin, appeared at their side.

"Been a while, James," Jason shook his hand casually, "hope you've been well."

"Don't worry," James smiled and pulled him in for a long hug, "we've got your back, but she's still my family."

"I know." Jason nodded, turning back to the clerk who handed him his keys.

"So where is she then?" His mother glanced at his bags, not a hint of a second set of luggage in sight.

"Harper? She's making some work calls," Jason glanced back awkwardly at the door, "she's around somewhere."

"Ditched you already," Carter laughed, approaching the clerk with a casual ease, "well, can't wait to meet her. Or to hear the excuse you concoct of why she isn't here."

"You don't believe she exists?" Jason's voice was low, a guttural response to his brothers mockery.

"Be nice," James placed a gentle hand on Carter's back, "I'm sure she's lovely and we can't wait to meet her."

Jason nodded once, turning to disappear towards his room. He messaged Harper the details, his anxiety causing him to fumble at his phone, the sweat on his palms clawing at his nerves. He would make sure they were ready for the dinner, despite the feeling in his gut, despite the lump that had formed in his throat. And they were. He had recounted the conversation in the lobby, the snide remarks from his brother who always meant his teasing in jest, but it hadn't hurt him any less. She had come up with a plan, a daring entrance that would leave his family and friends reeling. He didn't like it, he knew it would give Carter extra reason to doubt him, but he thought the result would pay off enormously and it was too tempting to pass up.

He was surrounded by them, a flood of people asking him how he was, expressing their surprise at his attendance, his mother in tow to alleviate any anxiety he might feel or to answer any questions he didn't want to. Carter and James stood close by, their support and slight teasing making the situation all the more daring. His grey suit felt tight, almost too tight, and he found himself attempting to loosen his tie. But he told himself, he forced Harper's voice into his mind to stop fiddling, to be calm, and that she would be there when he needed her. And then there *she* was, a picture of angelic presence in a white jumpsuit. Her golden hair cascaded down her back, framed by the low cut and excessive lace trimming.

"Emily!" Carter called her over, his voice a high shrill in the otherwise calm room. It was as if he were almost too excited for them to see each other for the first time, Jason thought, as he silently cursed his brother for being so playful and cruel. Jason quickly removed his phone from his pocket, sending the text he had been waiting to send for what seemed like hours.

"Carter." She smiled, approaching the group with a practised ease.

"Emily." Jason greeted her as he quickly stowed his phone, his palms now coated in sweat.

"Jason," she looked him up and down, a casual sweetness to her tone that bordered on the undignified, "we were so shocked when we received your response. I didn't think you'd come."

"Then you shouldn't have invited me," he said casually before shaking the discourteousness from his head, "I'm sorry. You look lovely."

"Thank you," she looked around the room, waving at a man standing in an all-black suit, "you have to meet my husband." He walked over with an air of authority about him, and something in the way he moved set Jason on edge.

"Future husband," the man smiled, his hand extended prominently between them, "Simon."

"Ex-boyfriend," Jason extended his hand to the man standing in front of him now, conscious of the sweat on his palms, "Jason."

"Well this is awkward," Carter smiled playfully as James elbowed him lightly, "where is this girlfriend of yours anyway. Everyone's been dying to meet her."

"She'll be here soon," Jason glanced toward the stairs, "she was just adding some finishing touches—"

And there she was. Her posture was tall and graceful, standing atop the staircase like a strong and elegant queen. Her dress hugged her body in deep shades of red and dark grey that complemented his attire perfectly. Her hair, a vision of curls, cascaded down one side of her face, framing her features in a soft and alluring way. And those eyes, the deep green capturing the essence of the surrounding greenery outside, enchanting and mesmerising. There was a hint of a smile on her lips, enticing and sweet like a taste of forbidden fruit. The soft click of her heels on the stairs as she descended seemed to echo in the dining room, filling the space with a delicate rhythm. Jason's heart skipped a beat at the sound of her voice, gentle and melodic like a symphony.

"Jason." Walking toward the group, she dared not glance at anyone else though she knew all eyes were on her. The part she had to play, the devoted girlfriend of the jilted ex-boyfriend, meant that she had to see nothing else but him. Before he could speak, she planted a kiss on his lips, delicate and light, like greeting someone you knew all too fondly. Their first kiss, he thought, and he already wanted more. Her lips lingered, just a moment too long, and she smiled before looking toward the rest of the group.

"Who—"

"I'm Harper," she extended her hand to Emily, who was standing in shock at the sudden appearance of this siren, "and you must be the beautiful bride. My, don't you look stunning."

"Emily," her hand gingerly extended outward before she made her excuses, "well, lovely to meet you, and I am sure the story here is compelling but I must greet my other guests." Emily gestured for Simon to follow her, disappearing into the crowd.

The night continued, and Harper made every effort to crush Jason's nerves. She was the perfect symbol of devotion, recounting how they had met and telling stories of Jason's exemplary role as her doting boyfriend. She sold it well. His mother was captivated by her. His brother was so shocked at her existence that he tried to monopolise her time and conversation, wanting every detail of their secret relationship. His father, normally clouded by his usual indifference, eventually warmed to her conversations of politics and fine-dining.

"So what is it that you do?" He asked, his rare laughter flooding the room.

"I dabble," she laughed lightly, "a bit of everything really. I can't seem to settle on something, the only thing I've felt sure about in years is Jason."

"So you're unemployed," Carter mused, "I knew there had to be something wrong with you." She laughed at the jilt, her presence radiating a warm and comforting energy that soothed Jason.

"Last year I did some modelling in Paris," her dress moved with her as she commanded the space, exuding an otherworldly beauty, "and before that I was a stewardess on a yacht in Italy. Sometimes I head to Barcelona to volunteer at Park Guell and one time I assisted some archeologists on the Isle of Skye. So you see, unemployment has its benefits." She was a vision of smoldering embers and storm clouds, rebuffing their doubts with a practised charm.

"But I suppose it's time to settle down in London," she took Jason's arm, gazing into his eyes as he shot her an uneasy glance, "it seems I have something to stay in one place for."

"Quite right," Jason's father said before excusing himself, "I must say hello to Emily's parents. We'll chat more later."

"Looking forward to it," Harper smiled before the group dispersed, her attention turning back to Jason, "what's wrong?"

"I feel sick," he confessed, "I think that's enough for one evening."

"Take me to the corner," she motioned toward the stairs, "take me there for a moment and we'll head back to the room." The hid in the quiet space, her eyes piercing through him as she wrapped her arms around his shoulders and whispered in his ear.

"Pretend you're talking to me."

"We are talking," his voice was uneasy, unsettled in the room full of family and friends who felt like strangers, "how do you know so much about galavanting around Europe."

"Because I have galavanted around Europe," she pulled back, resting her forearms on his shoulders, her fingers delicately intertwined behind his head, "I had a life before I was an escort, you know."

"I'm sure you did." He looked down, her body pressed against him so naturally, relaxed and inviting.

"Don't look so sad," she smiled, glancing down at his lips with a gaze that made his heart flutter, "now kiss me. Kiss me properly. Then whisper something in my ear, take my hand, and lead me away."

Harper's lips were full and slightly parted, beckoning him closer. Her eyes were bright and eager, filled with anticipation. Her hair smelled like lavender and vanilla, a sweet and comforting scent that filled his nostrils as their faces drew closer. Their lips move together in a slow, tender dance. His hand cradled her face, pulling her in closer as their bodies molded together, a perfect fit. In the dimly lit corner, their kiss was illuminated by soft candlelight. They felt eyes on them, prying eyes around the room who had been simultaneously captivated and confused by her. Her lips tasted of peach and honey, sweet and addictive, soft and warm against his. Her arms wrapped around him in a comforting embrace as his fingers gently stroked the back of her neck, relishing in the feeling of her silky hair between his fingertips. And then they disappeared into the hallways, saying goodbye to no one.

"That was perfect." Jason breathed a sigh of relief as he closed the door behind him, feeling a sense of ease wash over him as they were finally alone in their room. Jason didn't know whether to laugh or cringe at how easily she played the part. All he knew was that he didn't want this to end. Not tonight, not soon, maybe not ever. Harper wrapped him in this comfort, this game, and for the first time in months, he could breathe without catching on his own failures.

"Am I worth every penny?" She squeezed his arm, a physical promise as convincing as the facade she had put on for show. They had moved like conspirators among the oblivious. She was everything he'd hoped and nothing he could have expected. Her role was more than an act - it was the lifeline he'd never had the sense to ask for.

"And then some." Jason admitted, an attempt at humor that cracked against the reality of what they had just accomplished.

"Do you think Emily was jealous?"

"I thought this wasn't about making her jealous," Harper said, an undercurrent of genuine concern in the statement, "I thought this was about showing *everyone* that you had moved on."

"Still," Jason retorted, his pride all too evident, "the added sting would be a bonus."

"Don't be like that, Jason. Not when you've come so far." Harper whispered, leaning in, her breath warm against his neck.

"I can't help who I am." Jason said, turning to face her, noticing how close they were in this private space, the first time he had been alone with her.

"We're both here to play a part," Harper said, reaching up to run a finger along his jawline, "try to pretend to not be jilted, just for the weekend." Her touch, so gentle and soft, sent shivers down his spine.

The air between them crackled like a live wire, thick with unspoken desire and the kind of tension that could make a saint sin. Harper's eyes locked onto his, and it wasn't just a look - it was a dare, a challenge. He didn't hesitate. His hand shot out, fingers tangling in the silken strands of her hair, yanking her head back just enough to expose the delicate curve of her throat. His lips crashed into hers, not a kiss but a conquest, all teeth and tongue and raw, unrelenting hunger. She moaned into his mouth, a sound that went straight to his stomach, and he pressed her body flush against his. His other hand roamed down her back, fingers digging into the curve of her hips, pulling her even closer until there wasn't a breath of space between them. The fabric of her dress was a nuisance, and he tugged at it impatiently, desperate to feel her skin against his. But then she stopped him, her hand clamping down on his wrist with surprising strength.

"We're not in public anymore," she said, her voice low and husky, but with an edge that made him pause, "you can stop pretending." He froze, his breath coming in ragged gasps as he stared down at her.

"Who's pretending?" He whispered, his voice rough with need. She smirked, a wicked little curve of her lips that made his blood boil.

"I am." She said, and before he could react, she slipped out of his grasp and walked away, her hips swaying with deliberate provocation. He watched, his heart throbbing painfully, as she disappeared into the bathroom and locked the door behind her. The sound of the shower turning on was like a taunt, and he clenched his fists, his entire body vibrating with frustration and lust.

He leaned against the door, his forehead pressed to the cool wood, and listened to the sound of water hitting tile. His mind raced with images of her naked body, water sluicing over her skin, her hands sliding over her curves, touching herself in ways he ached to do. He could almost see it - her nipples hardening under the spray, her fingers slipping between her legs, teasing herself until she was wetter than the water cascading down her body.

"Harper," he growled, his voice low and dangerous, "open the door." There was a pause, and then her voice came through, soft and mocking.

"Go to bed, Jason."

"What are you here for?" He slammed his fist against the door, the sound echoing through the room. She laughed, a low, throaty sound that sent shivers down his spine.

"I'm here to make you look good," she said, "now go to bed. We have a big day tomorrow." He growled again, his body aching so much that it was painful. He could feel the heat of her through the door, could almost taste her on his tongue. He wanted to break the door down, wanted to pin her against the wall, but he knew better. Harper wasn't the kind of woman who could be commanded - she had to be seduced, had to be made to want it as much as he did.

Pale fingers of dawn reached across the room, touched the curtains, and split the shadows in two. The early light crept in, tentative at first, but then bolder, painting the walls in soft hues of pink and gold. It caught the edges of the bed, the curl of the sheets, and finally Jason. He lay there, eyes half-open, still hazy from the dreams that had pulled him under. He could almost hear her laugh, still warm and wicked in his ears, feel her fingers, soft and sure as they trailed across his skin and unspooled him. Even now, her presence was a ghost that haunted his senses. The remnants of last night danced around him - the jilt of her touch, the tease in her smile, the way she'd let him get so close only to slip from his grasp, leaving him desperate and alive in a way that he hadn't been for a long, long time. He thought of the day ahead, of playing his part, of the game they had started and how he didn't want it to end, ever.

"Morning." Harper whispered, setting a cup of tea next to the bed. "Harper," Jason rubbed his eyes, sitting up against the headboard, "I'm sorry about last night. I wasn't—"
"It's okay," she placed a gentle hand on his cheek, "you're not the first man to want something more." He was suddenly pulled back into reality, into the fabric of the world that made him realise that she was still someone who he had paid to be his plus one to a wedding.

"Have you—"

"Yes," her reply was instant, not letting him finish the question, "the ones who pay for it." He didn't know how to respond, not when the last time he'd felt this alive was before he had been spurned.

"I'll tell you what," she placed her teacup gently on her bedside table, "why don't we go for a walk before breakfast? It might make you feel—"

"No." Jason interjected, his body tense and reeling.

"What?"

"No," he grabbed her arm, gazing into her eyes, "how much?"

"Jason—"

"How much?" Jason's eyes narrowed as he stared at Harper, a determined glint in them as he repeated his question. There was a metallic tang in Jason's mouth from biting down on his cheek, his jaw clenched in determination. Harper's lips parted slightly, the hint of a bitter taste of unspoken words and emotions hanging in the air. The room filled with their heavy breathing, the only sounds in the tense moment.

"That's not something I'm prepared to offer," she said slowly, used to the aggression and demands of men in the past, "not when you're like this." His grip on her arm tightened, his fingers digging into her skin, sending a sharp pain through her body. Then he let go, sinking into the bed and staring out the window.

"I'm sorry."

"You're upset," Harper interjected, shifting the focus with such finesse that even the awkwardness became something like grace, "why don't you take a shower and I'll have them bring breakfast to the room. We can talk about it then."

Jason nodded, his body a coiled spring of tension, and he stumbled toward the bathroom on unsteady feet. Her words echoed in his head, wrapping around his mind like barbed wire as she offered him a lifeline he couldn't bring himself to take, and he punished himself for being the kind of man who even made the offer necessary. He closed the door behind him, feeling the silence like a weight pressing down on his chest. Turning on the shower, he stared into the mirror, at the eyes staring back at him. Eyes he didn't recognise. They reflected a stranger, a man he never thought he would become, someone desperate and pathetically needy. It wasn't who he was, it wasn't who he wanted to be. A tear fell down his cheek before he wiped it away in frustration. He inhaled sharply, like a dying man taking his last breath.

Stepping into the cascading water, he let it scald his skin, hoping the heat would burn away the shame that clung to him like a second skin. Images of her swirled in his mind, tormenting him with what he had lost and would never have. Her laughter, the reckless abandon with which she'd thrown herself into the role, the touch of her fingers that felt so real, the tease in her smile that made him feel alive again, all played through his mind like the same film on repeat. She was what he needed and everything he couldn't keep.

This wasn't him. Not anymore. Not since Emily had left him raw and exposed, since he'd hired Harper to fill an emptiness he thought he could never name. He wanted to be better, to be more, to be enough. But Harper's dismissive words showed him exactly who he was. Her indifference was a mirror he couldn't bear to look into. He was losing his grip, on himself, on the illusion, on her. This is what he had been reduced to - renting someone to care, to fill the spaces between the broken pieces of his life. He stood there, letting the water fall like tears he refused to shed, wondering if he would recognise himself once she was gone. He reappeared in the bedroom, a towel wrapped around him casually.

"Are you feeling better?" Harper's voice was a gentle murmur, barely disturbing the air as she crossed the room and placed a soft hand on his arm. Her calm presence was jarring against the chaos inside him, and Jason froze, paralysed by the kindness she offered so effortlessly, even after the way he'd treated her. They paused, each heartbeat dragging the moment out, a quiet tension enfolding them like a cocoon. And then it cracked, his composure shattering like glass against concrete. He began to cry, fat tears he couldn't stop and didn't want to admit, a response to her words that shook him to his core. His shoulders heaved, and he dropped his face into his hands, ashamed and exposed in front of her. She was so composed, like she belonged here more than he did, like she had always known exactly what this weekend would mean to him. She filled the void between them, taking him in her arms and pressing his head against her shoulder.

"I'm so fucking sorry." He wailed into her skin, as if she would absorb all of his problems with her existence. She let him cry, not saying a word, not needing to. She was enough. Her being there for him was enough. And then she kissed him, full and unexpected. His body tensed with anticipation, his mind racing with filthy fantasies.

"Three fifty." She whispered.

"What?"

"Three hundred and fifty pounds." She said again, her voice

softer this time. There was another pause, and then the sounds surrounding them stopped The voices in the hallway disappeared, the birds chirping outside vanished. His heart pounded in his chest as he hesitated, every second feeling like an eternity. He didn't waste any more time, his hands grabbed her waist and pulled her against him. His lips crashed into hers, and this time there was no hesitation, no pretense. It was pure, unadulterated lust, a fire that burned hotter with every touch, every kiss. His hands roamed over her body, exploring every inch of her skin, and she moaned into his mouth, her hands tangling in his hair.

He lifted her up, her legs wrapping around his waist as he carried her to the bed. He laid her down gently, his eyes drinking in the sight of her spread out before him. She was perfect, every curve and dip designed to drive him wild. He kissed his way down her body, his lips trailing over her collarbone, her breasts, her stomach. When he reached the apex of her thighs, he paused, his breath hot against her.

"You're so fucking beautiful." He murmured, his voice thick with desire. She moaned, her hips lifting off the bed as he buried his face between her legs. His tongue flicked over her clit, teasing and tasting until she was writhing beneath him. He could feel her trembling, could hear the way her breath hitched with every stroke of his tongue. He didn't stop until she was begging for release, her hands clutching at the sheets as she came undone.

"What if someone hears us?"

"Let them," he stepped back, admiring her as if she were the perfect piece of artwork, "it will add to the mystery." The air was heavy like a storm about to break. Jason stood there, his towel pooled at his feet, his cock already hard and throbbing.

She lay on the bed, her body a canvas of soft curves and flushed skin, her nipples pebbled and begging for his mouth. Her legs parted slightly, a silent invitation, and he didn't need words to know what she wanted. He moved toward her, his steps deliberate, his eyes dark with need. When he reached the edge of the bed, he knelt, his hands sliding up her thighs, feeling the heat of her skin beneath his palms. She shivered, her breath hitching as his fingers traced the delicate lace of her panties. He hooked his fingers into the fabric and pulled them down slowly, his eyes never leaving hers, watching as her cheeks flushed and her lips parted in anticipation.

"You're beautiful," he murmured, his voice low and rough, like gravel dragged over silk, "fucking perfect." She reached for him, her fingers tangling in his hair as he leaned down, his mouth finding the soft, wet heat between her legs. He licked her slowly, savoring the taste of her, the way she gasped and arched into him. His tongue circled her clit, teasing and coaxing, until she was writhing beneath him once again, her moans filling the room.

"Jason," she breathed, her voice trembling, "I need you." He didn't make her wait. He rose above her, his cock pressing against her thigh, the tip slick. He pushed into her slowly, inch by inch, feeling her envelop him, her walls clenching around him as he filled her. She gasped, her nails digging into his shoulders, and he paused, letting her adjust to him, his breath ragged against her neck.

"You feel so good." He whispered, his lips brushing against her skin. He began to move, his hips rocking against hers in a slow, steady rhythm. Each thrust was deliberate, each stroke designed to draw out every ounce of pleasure. He could feel her body responding, her hips rising to meet his, her moans growing louder with every movement. Her hands roamed over his back, leaving trails of fire in their wake, and he buried his face in the crook of her neck, breathing in the scent of her.

"Jason—"

"Tell me," he whispered, his voice thick with need, "tell me you want this."

"I want you," she gasped, her voice breaking on a moan, "I need you." Her words sent a jolt of heat through him, and he fucked her harder, his pace quickening as he chased the pleasure that was building between them. Her legs wrapped around his waist, pulling him deeper, and he groaned, the sound raw and primal. He could feel her tightening around him, her body trembling as she neared the edge, and he reached between them, his fingers finding her clit and rubbing in tight, desperate circles.

His cock was buried to the hilt inside her, thick and unrelenting, stretching her in ways that made her gasp, her walls clenching around him like a velvet vice. Sweat dripped down her thighs, slicking the sheets beneath them. He moved with a slow, deliberate rhythm, each thrust a promise, each withdrawal a tease that left her whimpering. His hands gripped her hips, fingers digging into her soft flesh, leaving marks that would bruise beautifully by midday. Their lips met in a kiss that was anything but gentle. It was raw, hungry, devouring. His tongue plunged into her mouth, claiming her, tasting her, as if he could consume her whole. She moaned into him, her hands tangling in his hair, pulling him closer, deeper. Their breaths mingled, hot and desperate, as their bodies moved in perfect, filthy harmony. He pulled back just enough to look into her eyes, his gaze dark and intense, burning with a need that mirrored her own. She felt tears prick at the corners of her eyes, not from pain, but from the overwhelming intensity of it all.

"I wanted this," she whispered, her voice trembling, raw with emotion, "I wanted you." He didn't respond with words. Instead, he kissed her again, deeper this time, his tongue sliding against hers in a slow, sensual dance. His hips snapped forward, driving his cock even deeper, hitting a sweet spot inside her that made her cry out. She could feel every inch of him, every ridge, every pulse of him as he fucked her with a rhythm that was both punishing and tender. Her nails raked down his back, leaving angry red trails in their wake. He groaned, the sound low and guttural, and she could feel the way his cock twitched inside her, as if it was begging for release. But he held back, drawing out the pleasure, making her beg for it.

"Please," she gasped, her voice breaking, "please, don't stop." He didn't. His thrusts became harder, faster, each one driving her closer to the edge. She could feel the heat building in her core, a tight coil of pleasure that was ready to snap. Her pussy clenched around him, and he let out a growl that sent shivers down her spine. Their eyes locked again, and she could see the raw need in his gaze, the way he was just as lost in this as she was. He leaned down, capturing her lips in another searing kiss. She could taste herself on his lips, could feel the way his body was trembling with the effort of holding back. And then it hit her - a wave of pleasure so intense that it stole her breath.

"Come for me," he demanded, his voice rough and commanding, "let go." Her body convulsed around him, her pussy clamping down on his cock as she came hard, her cries muffled by his mouth. He followed her over the edge, his hips stuttering as he buried himself deep inside her. She cried out, her body arching off the bed as she clenched his thighs together in waves of ecstasy. He followed her over the edge, his own release crashing over him like a tidal wave, his cock pulsing inside her as he spilled himself deep within her. He collapsed onto the bed beside her, his chest heaving, his body slick with sweat. They stayed like that for a moment, their bodies still touching, their breaths ragged. He leaned over and kissed her again, softer this time, a gentle contrast to the raw intensity of what had just happened.

The rest of the day disappeared into the void, a blur of hours that passed unnoticed, every second bleeding into the next until time had all but ceased to exist. Harper was the perfect date - poised and confident, projecting an air of control that suggested the morning had meant nothing. She laughed easily, the sound like music, and accepted compliments as if they were her due. She didn't look at Jason, didn't need to. It was enough that he was there, and she was playing her part. Jason was a mess, but nothing different to the night before, just for different reasons. Distracted and distant, he tried to focus on the rehearsed conversations but found it difficult to form coherent sentences, his mind replaying the morning in vivid detail. They commented on his beautiful navy suit, the way it complemented her stunning blue dress, but he heard none of it.

He heard their voices almost as if from a great distance, the congratulatory remarks fading into an indistinct blur. And then the weekend was gone, faded into just another memory, closing the chapter on Emily but opening one with Harper. He hadn't imagined this, hadn't allowed himself to believe it could be more than an act, but there they were, alive and untethered, everything they shouldn't be and exactly what they were. It was more than he'd dared to hope. More than she'd promised. It was exactly what neither had expected. The drive back to the city was mostly silent, occasional mentions of the weather and idle talk of the music and food. But Jason was distracted, and Harper knew it.

"So what now?" Harper's voice was steady, but Jason could hear the myriad of unspoken questions that lingered beneath her words. Her eyes, those piercing green eyes that had always seen through him even when he wore his best mask, bore deep into his soul. She was searching for answers that neither of them had, answers that seemed to hide just out of reach, tantalizing and elusive. The air between them felt heavy with possibility and uncertainty, charged like a wire waiting to spark. It was dangerous, electric, the unplanned and unmapped course of everything they had never expected to be. He hesitated, his fingers tapping against the steering wheel, as if the rhythm might offer some kind of clarity.

He was uncharacteristically silent, forgoing the calculated words that usually came so easily. But the truth was, there was no clarity. Nothing had changed. Everything had changed. It hung between them, raw and inevitable, as real and as precarious as the moment that would follow this one. Jason felt the stirrings of something reckless and unfamiliar, something that defied the control he was used to having, as certain as the weight of the story that was just beginning.

Sweat & Secrets

The gym still slept when she arrived, light slipping in through the wide glass doors and falling softly across the polished floors. There was a strange peace to Core Elite being empty, as if the space itself held its breath, waiting for the day to begin. Tasha breathed it in, the hint of eucalyptus, the promise of solitude. Here, she could work. Here, she could be alone. She crossed the floor with purpose, her towel trailing her like a banner. No one saw Tasha without a plan. Her life was a meticulously arranged itinerary, a world of schedules and goals that she had built with relentless precision. The silence of the gym surrounded her, a reminder that she was always the first to arrive, the last to leave. She cherished these hours before the world intruded, when she could focus, control her surroundings, and bend them to her will.

Her steps were silent on the smooth floor, the high-end machines standing like sculptures in the low-lit expanse. She set her bag down next to the row of weights, claiming her territory with a swift, practiced motion. She wore her dedication like armor, her focus a shield against anything that dared distract her. It had taken her years to carve out this life, to become indispensable in a world that demanded success without offering any in return. Fitness was more than a hobby or a diversion - it was another rung on the ladder she climbed every day, a way to hone not just her body but her resolve. She wasn't here to play.

Core Elite felt like an extension of herself, all clean lines and luxury, a place that understood the seriousness of her intent. It wasn't a gym so much as a sanctuary, a sleek haven for people like her who wanted the best and wouldn't settle for less. Its exclusivity suited her just fine. Tasha moved through her routine with the ease of a dancer executing a well-rehearsed choreography. She dropped her towel onto a bench and adjusted the angle of a mat with a nudge of her foot, everything in its place, everything in order. She liked things that way - organized, efficient, no room for error.

The hush of the gym was a constant, comforting presence. It enveloped her like a cocoon, reminding her of what she could achieve when she put her mind to it. Her high-powered job demanded nothing less. She was as disciplined in her career as she was in her workouts, a force of nature who knew exactly what she wanted and how to get it. There were no excuses, no half-measures, no compromises. She pulled her hair into a tighter ponytail, dark braids catching the ambient light as she secured them with a practiced flick. Her gaze was intent, her muscles already thrumming with anticipation. The weights lined up before her like a challenge she couldn't wait to meet.

She reveled in the clarity these mornings gave her, a sharpness that carried over into the rest of her day, pushing her further, higher. She was the kind of woman who set records and then broke them. No one got in her way. Tasha began her warm-up, the slow stretch of limbs and the steady rhythm of breath. There was a confidence to her movements, a certainty that came from years of discipline and determination. She didn't doubt herself. She didn't second-guess. Everything about her was intentional.

As she eased into the familiar routine, she thought about the new trainer she'd been assigned. Another man who thought he'd seen it all, no doubt. They were all the same, until they weren't. A smile almost touched her lips at the thought. She knew how to deal with men like that. Businesslike, distant. She kept her eye on the goal, and she always came out on top. The weights felt light in her hands, her muscles a finely tuned instrument ready to play. She didn't need anyone to tell her how to perform. She was already at her peak, but that wouldn't stop her from pushing harder, reaching further.

Her world was under control, a carefully balanced equation. But beneath the surface, something shifted, a ripple of uncertainty she was quick to tamp down. It was too quiet here. That wouldn't last long. The light changed, the sound of the city waking beyond the walls a distant hum. She paused, listening to the silence around her, knowing it wouldn't be empty for much longer. She had the sense of standing at the edge of something she couldn't quite define. It thrilled her, that hint of the unknown. She let herself feel it for a moment before brushing it aside. Her intensity, her focus, her drive - they were all she needed. She didn't let herself wonder if there might be more.

Micah's first impression of Tasha was her determination. She was a study in focus, in that single-minded need he had seen so often before. It usually meant trouble. But it also meant she was interesting. He watched her lift weights like a sculptor chipping away at stone, relentless and methodical. Clients like her were not unusual at Core Elite, their intensity filling the space as palpably as the machines and mats. Micah was used to it, used to high-powered individuals with expectations as lofty as their bank accounts. They wanted miracles, or at the very least, results they could show off. He gave them both, more often than not.

He'd seen her kind before - obsessed, ambitious, unwilling to accept anything less than perfection. It was the same drive that had propelled him through a career in pro football, until the injuries caught up and the glamour faded. The kind that made people push themselves too hard and then blame the world when it all fell apart. He wondered how far she'd let it take her. Micah worked the edge of a towel between his fingers, feeling the soft weave as he watched Tasha move through her warm-up. She was all business, as he'd suspected, and that suited him. He respected clients who knew what they wanted and went after it. It was the ones who came in with a thousand excuses that tested his patience.

He'd been the top of his game once, used to the roar of stadiums and the crush of adoring fans. Now, his field was quieter, the stakes more personal, but the rush of transforming a body, a life, still fed something deep in him. It wasn't fame, but it was close. The front desk manager handed him the schedule, Tasha's name in bold print at the top. He studied it for a moment before tucking it into his pocket, a faint smile on his lips. This would be interesting. He'd developed a reputation for getting the best out of his clients, for results that bordered on the miraculous. But Tasha seemed different. He sensed that what she needed wasn't just a regimen or routine. She was the kind of challenge he liked.

The gym felt quiet despite the hum of activity from a few early risers. The low lighting cast long shadows across the room, and the machines gleamed like unused promises. It was upscale and discreet, more akin to a spa for the ambitious than a place to sweat and grunt. He knew these types - the driven, the determined. He knew them because he'd been one. He'd come out the other side, maybe a little wiser, certainly less willing to sacrifice everything for the sake of winning. Watching her, he wondered what her story was, what she thought she could conquer.

As he observed her, he noticed the subtleties in her demeanor, the things she probably thought invisible. The way she glanced at her watch, as if timing herself down to the second. The way her muscles coiled and uncoiled with such precision that it seemed rehearsed. She would be a demanding client, but she would also be rewarding. Tasha paused for water, eyes sweeping over the gym as if taking stock of potential competition. Micah caught her glance and held it for a second longer than necessary. Her expression didn't change, but he didn't expect it to. The morning stretched ahead of him like a blank slate. He liked that, the anticipation of what could be filled in, the slow burn of tension that could ignite if he let it. But he'd been down that road before, and he wasn't sure he wanted to travel it again.

Micah adjusted the sleeve of his polo, feeling the familiar stretch over his biceps. His tattoos peeked from beneath the hem, whispers of a past life he no longer wore so openly. Tasha would probably see them, see him, and sum him up in an instant. He looked forward to proving her wrong. The sound of weights clinking together and the steady rhythm of treadmills filled the air, a symphony of effort and determination. It was a place that felt like home to him now, a second act that had become more than just an encore. It was his life, and it was good. He made his way over to her, weaving through the carefully arranged equipment, his step confident and sure. He didn't have to call her name to get her attention. She'd known he was coming long before he got there.

"I'm gonna be training you today." He said, already knowing what her response would be.

"I told you last time that I didn't like your style," she met his eyes with a level stare, unblinking, assessing, "which is why I've been seeing Kyle for the last few months." He didn't miss the way her eyes lingered on him for a fraction longer than they needed to. A challenge, he thought. This was going to be fun. He could tell that she didn't want to like him, that she had already made up her mind about him. That was the first thing he noticed when he had met her, her cool detachment a barrier she erected between them like an iron gate. Micah found himself wondering if he could get through it, if he even wanted to try.

"Kyle's had an emergency this morning," he said, maintaining a professionalism that mirrored hers, "it was very last minute. I had to come and fill in for him on my day off. Unless you'd prefer to reschedule—"

"Reschedule to when? I have him booked every morning, five days a week." She replied, her tone clipped. Micah nodded, resisting the urge to smile at her lack of pretense. He respected it.

"So what have you two been working on?" He said, holding her gaze.

"Strength and endurance mostly."

"Anything else you want to work on today?

"Just those," Tasha's response was a small nod, a barely perceptible acknowledgement, "for now."

"We'll push your limits, then. But safely." He sensed the effort it took for her to hand over even this small measure of control.

They moved into the warm-up, and Micah watched her closely. Her movements were efficient, her form immaculate. He'd expected nothing less. He caught the briefest flicker of a glance when she thought he wasn't looking, a spark of awareness that pleased him more than it should. Tasha's focus was unwavering, but she felt the subtle tug of his presence. It annoyed her, that she was even slightly aware of him beyond his role as a trainer. He was good, she couldn't deny that. His knowledge and technique were apparent in every suggestion, every correction. But it was more than that, something she couldn't quite define and didn't want to. He stayed close but not too close, always mindful of her space, her need for distance. Yet she felt him there, a constant in her periphery. She forced herself to concentrate on the routine, on the demands she set for herself.

"Your form is already solid," Micah said, offering a rare compliment as she worked the weights, "you're serious about this."

"You sound surprised." She shot back, a hint of defensiveness creeping in. He laughed softly, the sound rich and warm.

"I'm not." His ease disarmed her, made her irritation seem almost petty. Tasha gritted her teeth and pushed through another set, determined to ignore him. Micah observed her, taking in the tension in her shoulders, the way she breathed through the exertion with controlled precision. He noted the defiance in her stance, the way she seemed to brace herself against him as if daring him to break through. He liked it. They continued, the session proceeding with clockwork efficiency. His adjustments were minor but impactful, a testament to his experience and intuition. She couldn't deny how effective he was, even as she tried to keep their interactions strictly professional.

"So what was it about me that turned you off?" Micah asked, his tone half teasing, half sincere.

"You were too aggressive." Tasha didn't bother looking at him as she replied. Her candor was refreshing, a change from the cautious, guarded approach of so many others. Micah found himself wanting to crack that exterior, to see what lay beneath the polished surface. But he knew better than to push too hard too soon, especially with her.

"Aggressive?"

"You're intense," she remarked as she finished another set, "but you already know that." She kept her gaze averted, focusing on the machines, the mats, anything but the intensity of his presence. Yet, in the mirrors, she watched him as he moved around her, the deliberate pace of his steps, the calm confidence that radiated off him. It was distracting. It was infuriating.

"When you walked in here six months ago, you were a fragile presence in want of help."

"Exactly," she paused, her expression a perfect mask of indifference, "I needed help, and I had no idea what I was doing, and you just wanted to push." He liked that. He liked the way she matched him for confidence, the way she seemed almost to challenge him with her restraint. It was the opposite of how people usually responded to him, and he found it surprisingly compelling.

"Some people need to be pushed."

"Well I needed to be lead." Tasha shot him a dry look, one of mild anger and disappointment.

"I'm sorry I didn't listen to you," his apology seemed sincere, but Tasha still had her walls up, "they paired you with me because they thought I would be the best fit for your goals. I guess we had no idea you needed coddling."

"Well Kyle was the better fit, and he got me where I needed to be," Tasha compelled herself to concentrate on her set, "I don't need coddling anymore, just training." As the session wound down, Tasha felt the familiar burn in her muscles, the satisfaction of having pushed herself hard. But there was something else there too, a twinge of frustration that wasn't entirely physical. She hated it, that she couldn't just shut it off.

"I guess I'll scc you tomorrow then," Micah handed her a towel, his smile knowing, "if Kyle is still out." She nodded, already turning away, already planning the rest of her day in a desperate attempt to clear her mind of him.

"Yes." She said, not trusting herself to say more.

"Good." He replied, watching her leave with an expression that was part amusement, part anticipation. The air outside was cool, and Tasha let it wash over her, tried to let it calm the heat she couldn't quite ignore. He was different than she'd expected. Dangerous, in a way that had nothing to do with strength and everything to do with control. Micah watched her go, felt the slight tremor in the world she left behind. She was different now. This was going to be fun.

Tasha entered the gym, bright and eager to once again begin her day with the routine she had become accustomed to. Looking around, she saw no sign of Kyle. Only the leering presence of Micah and the distinct smell of his cologne. It was sweet, and oddly alluring. The smell of confidence and refinery. She had smelled it the day before, she had smelled it six months ago, and it reminded her of the pent up rage and tension she had felt for him then, the way she felt about him now.

"No Kyle again today." Micah stood tall and confident, his dark eyes seemed to hold a mischievous glint. His strong jawline was shadowed with stubble, giving him a rugged and alluring look. She shook her head in protest, dismissing the same disruption two days in a row from her mind.

"Let's get stuck into it." The taste of adrenaline and determination lingered on her tongue, and she wouldn't let the absence of her preferred trainer disrupt her day. She was determined to get the session over with, and emerge the other side the bigger person. Micah reached out to correct her form, his hand a whisper against her skin. He felt her stiffen, saw the way her breath caught on an exhale. For a moment, neither of them moved. The world around them held its breath.

"Your form's off." He said, his tone casual, almost nonchalant. But he knew the effect he had, knew the charge of electricity that crackled in the space between them. He'd felt it the second he got close enough to touch. They had been working through weights, Tasha's focus an almost tangible thing, something that pressed against him like a physical force. He admired her intensity, the way she attacked each exercise with precision. But he noticed the small things too, the slight shifts in posture, the tension in her shoulders that hinted at imperfection. His approach was careful, calculated.

He wanted to see what she would do, how she would react when he crossed the line between professional and personal. He didn't expect the jolt that shot through him at the moment of contact, the way his own breath caught and held, mirroring hers.

It should have been nothing. Just the lightest touch, the kind of adjustment he made every day, dozens of times. But with Tasha, it was different. He could feel the thrum of her pulse under his fingertips, the way her body went rigid but refused to retreat. The defiance in it thrilled him. Tasha was aware of him in a way she had tried so hard not to be. That brief moment when his hand brushed her waist sent a shock through her system, one she couldn't ignore no matter how hard she tried. She was used to control, to reigning in her responses with military precision. This was something else.

They remained frozen, an eternal second where the air seemed to shimmer with something unspeakable, something she wasn't sure she wanted to define. She felt the burn of her muscles, the sweat on her skin, but mostly, she felt him. Micah stepped back sooner than necessary, granting her space she didn't ask for but somehow needed. He met her eyes with a calm he didn't quite feel, gauging the reaction there, the flicker of uncertainty and the iron resolve beneath it. She watched him retreat, a few steps that seemed like miles, and the breath she'd been holding came out in a rush. It left her unsettled, more so than the toughest workout, more than any challenge she'd faced in recent memory. She wasn't used to this.

"Better." He said, his voice a rumble that seemed to echo in the quiet of the gym. She didn't trust herself to answer, instead nodding curtly and resuming her reps with renewed vigor. The weights felt heavier now, her form less certain. His touch lingered on her skin, a phantom sensation that refused to be dismissed. For a while, they said nothing, the clink of weights and their mingled breath the only sounds. But there was a dialogue happening in the silence, a conversation made up of glances and proximity and the awareness that buzzed like static. Tasha forced herself to focus, to channel her surprise and frustration into the familiar rhythm of the workout. She was all business, all purpose, refusing to let him derail her. But underneath, a current of something she couldn't name threatened to pull her under.

The session continued, each rep a punctuation in the story they began to write. Micah kept his distance, but not enough to give her the illusion of control. He knew what he was doing, knew the effect it had. And he suspected she did too. They didn't mention it, didn't acknowledge the moment that hung between them like a suspended note. But it was there, a promise or a threat, and neither of them quite knew which. As the session came to an end, Tasha felt a sense of accomplishment mingled with a sense of loss. She'd pushed herself hard, but it wasn't just the physical exertion that left her breathless. The awareness of him was a new challenge, one she hadn't prepared for.

Micah stood by as she gathered her things, his expression unreadable but his eyes alight with something she couldn't ignore. She felt it in her core, the undeniable truth that things had changed. She left without saying more than a swift goodbye, her steps quicker than usual, a sign of her inner turmoil. She needed to think, needed to plan, needed to figure out how to handle the unexpected complication of him. But as she exited the gym, she realized it was more than she thought. She realized that this was the start of something, and that terrified her as much as it thrilled her.

She pushed harder than ever, as if distance and speed could erase the memory of the uncertainty from the last few days. Her footsteps echoed in the quiet gym, each one a refusal, a challenge, a silent scream against the chaos he'd introduced into her life. The rhythmic pounding of her feet was a familiar comfort, a reminder of the things she could control. Tasha increased the pace on the treadmill, ignoring the burn in her lungs and the voice in her head that whispered of things she wasn't ready to admit. She was competitive, even in isolation, and right now, she was competing against herself, against him, against the memory of that touch.

Her focus was razor-sharp, the intensity of her run a testament to her determination. But try as she might, she couldn't completely drown out the awareness that gnawed at the edges of her mind. Micah's touch had been brief, inconsequential, but the effect lingered, a ghost of a feeling that refused to fade. She pushed through it, drove herself harder, trying to bury the distraction in sweat and speed. Her heart pounded in her chest, but even as her body cried out in protest, she didn't let up. She wasn't the kind to back down, especially not from something that felt this important.

"You're going to break a record." Micah called out, his voice cutting through her thoughts like a knife through butter. Tasha pretended not to hear, her gaze fixed straight ahead, her focus unyielding. The sound of her own breath was loud in her ears, a cadence she clung to with desperation. She wasn't ready to let him disrupt it again. He stood there, arms folded across his chest, watching her with that maddening half-smile. She saw him out of the corner of her eye, and even though she tried to ignore it, she felt his presence like a weight on her skin, heavy and inescapable.

"Pushing yourself harder doesn't always mean better results." He continued, his tone light, teasing. She clenched her jaw, her annoyance with him almost as palpable as the treadmill's whir beneath her feet. She didn't slow down, didn't give him the satisfaction of a response. Not yet. But her mind circled back to the day before, to the way his hand had brushed against her with such casual confidence, to the way she'd frozen, exposed and uncertain. She hated that it haunted her, that it chased her with the same relentlessness she now displayed. She wanted to be done with it, with him, but she knew it wasn't that simple. Micah moved closer, a lazy, confident stride that contrasted with the fervor of her effort.

"I'm impressed," he said, "most people stop after mile ten." His mock admiration and the glint of amusement in his eyes made something in her snap, but not in the way she expected. She felt her resolve cracking, and before she knew it, she was smiling - a quick, unguarded flash that was more real than anything she had shown him before. The expression surprised her as much as it did him. She had no intention of letting him see that side of her, of letting him think he was getting under her skin. But in that brief moment, something shifted, and she realized with a start that she didn't entirely mind.

The treadmill slowed, the pace finally decreasing as her willpower gave in. She could feel her face still flushed, partly from exertion, partly from the disarming, unexpected smile. She wiped the sweat from her brow, the memory of his touch replaced by the new challenge of what to make of her own reaction. Micah caught the smile and stored it away like a secret, a triumph he hadn't been sure he'd see this soon. It was just as he thought - beneath the controlled, professional exterior was someone he could reach, someone he could engage with more than just in training.

"See," he said, taking a step back as if to give her space to decide what to do next, "you can let up a little and still survive." She shot him a look that was equal parts exasperation and something she wouldn't call affection. It was dangerous territory, but she felt the pull and didn't immediately resist. Maybe he wasn't as dangerous as she feared. Or maybe he was more so.

"I wanted to warm up before my session," Tasha took a moment to catch her breath, the cooldown as much for her emotions as for her heart rate, "so I let myself in before hours with my keycard. I assume Kyle won't be in again today?" She wondered if the brief, real smile meant she was losing ground or gaining it. Either way, she couldn't deny the spark of something that felt dangerously close to interest.

"I'll be with you in ten. Just need to finish my set first." Micah left her to her thoughts, the smile a victory, a promise, or perhaps a challenge. As Tasha watched him go, she realized it might be all three. She watched him train as she sat with the weights, his muscles rippling beneath his fitted shirt. Micah's cologne filled the air around him, its sweet and alluring scent making it hard for Tasha to focus on anything else. It was a scent of control and power, seemingly able to pull her towards him against her will. His presence was like a simmering storm, all coiled power and quiet intensity. His structure alone was enough to create a charged atmosphere, drawing everyone's attention towards him like a magnet. And with every move he made, he seemed to effortlessly exude an air of danger and control that left Tasha both intrigued and unsettled.

"Ready to begin?" Micah's voice was deep and smooth, with a slight hint of amusement and anticipation which broke her from her reverie.

"Oh," her laugh was quick, almost reluctant, but it was there, "yes. Let's start." Micah heard it as he helped her re-rack the weights, an unexpected sound that seemed to startle her as much as it did him. They had a rhythm now, and it was one he intended to break.

"You can pretend you didn't enjoy that, but I heard you," he teased, that familiar glint in his eyes, "I heard you laugh." Tasha rolled her eyes, but her smile lingered just long enough to give her away.

"Don't get used to it." She replied, but the edge in her voice was softer than before.

They moved through the sets with a new ease, the playful banter slipping between the reps like an unspoken agreement. Micah joked about her intensity, about her refusal to accept anything less than the best, and she pretended not to care. But he saw through it, saw the way her defenses lowered, if only just. Tasha felt it too, the shifting dynamic, the way she couldn't maintain her distance no matter how hard she tried. It should have annoyed her, this failure to keep him at arm's length, but instead she found herself enjoying it more than she wanted to admit.

"You know," Micah said, taking a seat beside her on a bench as she caught her breath, "there's no extra credit for running yourself into the ground." She shot him a sharp glance, but her heart wasn't in it.

"You'd like that, wouldn't you? Slacking off?"

"I knew you had a sense of humor in there somewhere." He laughed, a rich, warm sound that filled the space between them. The ease with which he said it, the genuine amusement in his voice, made something inside her crack. She was used to men backing off, intimidated or uninterested in the challenge she posed. Micah was different. He leaned in, refusing to be shaken, and it made her want to let him get closer.

Their words were layered, each exchange carrying more than its surface meaning. They both knew it, and that knowledge hummed in the air around them, as loud as any declaration but left unsaid. He began to see the subtleties in her reactions, the things she left unspoken but nonetheless clear. Tasha was careful, even in the way she opened up. She gave little away, but when she did, it was intentional and precise, a calculated risk. He liked that, liked the challenge she posed and the slow reveal of the person underneath the polished surface. Each time he made her smile or crack a joke, it felt like a small victory, a glimpse into something she didn't show the world.

"Just admit it," he said as they transitioned to a new exercise, his tone teasing but with an undercurrent of sincerity, "you're starting to enjoy this." She hesitated, and he caught it, that split-second pause that said more than any words could.

"Maybe a little." She conceded, the admission both honest and defiant. Micah found himself more intrigued by the minute, his curiosity about her morphing into something deeper, something that felt dangerously like desire. It was a slippery slope, one he was more than willing to slide down. Tasha felt herself slipping too, despite her best efforts to hold on to her detachment. There was a freedom in letting go, in letting someone in, and though it scared her it also thrilled her in a way she hadn't expected. He threw out another quip, something about her needing to schedule fun into her calendar, and she almost laughed, a sound she caught and swallowed at the last moment. He saw it, though, saw the crack in her composure, and his satisfaction was evident.

"You're impossible." She said, shaking her head but unable to hide the smile.

"That's what makes me interesting." He replied, helping her to her feet with a touch that was professional but lingered just a second too long to be strictly so. Their session wound down, and Tasha felt the weight of something unspoken settle between them. It wasn't the heaviness she was used to - this was lighter, tinged with promise and potential. She was almost reluctant to leave, a first for her and something she wasn't entirely sure how to handle. They stood by the door, the end of their time together a palpable thing that neither wanted to acknowledge just yet.

"Kyle's out for the rest of the week," Micah said, his tone casual but his eyes anything but, "just so you know, in case you want to cancel tomorrow and Friday."

"Why would I do that?" She asked, her voice softening in a way that surprised her.

"So you admit it then."

"Admit what?"

"You're starting to enjoy your sessions with me." A smirk crept across his face. Micah's cologne was a mixture of musk and wood, a scent that was simultaneously overpowering and alluring. It reminded her of a forest after a rainstorm, fresh and invigorating. The smell overwhelmed her, and sent a shiver down her spine.

"I don't want to disrupt my training by taking a few days off," her piercing blue eyes sparkled with determination and a hint of frustration, "even you don't put me off that much." Micah's lips curled upwards, forming a smug and knowing smile. His eyes glinted mischievously as he gazed at her.

Tasha felt a warm tingle spread through her body at the sight of his expression, her skin almost prickling with anticipation.

"Tomorrow then." It was a barely contained explosion of confidence, a crooked grin that oozed smug satisfaction.

"Tomorrow." The goodbye was loaded, a promise of more, an admission of interest, an agreement that neither of them voiced but both understood. Tasha left, the silence of the gym echoing with the words they didn't say. She knew she was giving in, and that thought should have frightened her. Instead, it left her eager for more.

Micah suggested the assisted stretching session with a casual air, expecting her to dismiss it as unnecessary. But now, as they unrolled the mats and set up in the quiet corner of the gym, he realized this was more dangerous than he'd anticipated. He didn't mind. He guided her into position, the warmth of his hands against her skin a preview of what was to come. He was careful, deliberate, the gentleness in his touch belying the tension that simmered beneath.

"Just relax." He said, the hint of a smile on his lips. It was a command and a wish, one he wasn't sure either of them could follow. Tasha feigned a confidence she didn't entirely feel. The promise of intimacy, of contact that crossed the line between professional and personal, made her pulse race. But she wouldn't back down, wouldn't let him see the turmoil inside her.

"I'm always relaxed." She replied, even as her heartbeat betrayed her. The first stretch felt like a revelation. His hands cradled her shoulders, and her breath hitched in response, a soft exhale that filled the space between them. They were close, closer than she'd let anyone get in a long time, and the intimacy of it nearly overwhelmed her.

Micah's focus was absolute, each movement considered and precise. He could feel her body respond, feel the struggle for composure that matched his own. It affected him more than he'd expected, the immediacy of her, the challenge she presented just by being there. They moved through the routine like dancers learning a new choreography, unsure but in perfect sync. The stretching was both an exercise and a seduction, a delicate balance between too much and not enough. Tasha felt the tremor of his presence in every muscle, every fiber of her being. The heat of his touch seeped into her, blurring the line she was desperate to maintain. She had expected the session to test her physically, but it was the emotional strain that left her breathless.

Her eyes fluttered closed as he leaned her back into a deeper stretch, his touch a constant, grounding her even as it threatened to undo her. The trust it required, the vulnerability it demanded, was something she wasn't sure she could give, but there she was, giving it anyway. The silence around them was deafening, filled with all the words they couldn't say, all the desires they didn't dare voice.

Tasha felt it like a weight, pressing against her, pulling her toward him in ways she couldn't resist.

Micah was no less affected, his determination to keep it professional slipping with each second they remained entangled. He marveled at the pull she had on him, the raw, consuming need that built inside him despite his best efforts to keep it at bay. They continued, the stretches an excuse to remain close, the contact as much an embrace as any he could imagine. He knew they were crossing a line, that they'd already crossed it, but the inevitability of it only fueled his desire. Their bodies moved in tandem, the moment stretching out like the tension in her limbs, neither of them ready to let go. The connection between them was visceral, undeniable, and the effort to hold back felt like a losing battle.

Micah shifted, pulling her gently into a new position, but his composure was as tenuous as the breath she drew with effort. The awareness of her, the intimacy of the session, left him dizzy, unmoored. He was about to say something, anything to diffuse the intensity, but the words died on his lips. Her eyes opened and met his, and the look they exchanged said more than words ever could. It was all there - want and hesitation, need and restraint, the promise of what they could be if they let themselves. But for now, they kept it unspoken, kept it on the edge of control. They knew what they were risking, what they stood to lose or gain. They knew it wasn't just stretching. Not by a long shot. Her breath was ragged, her composure slipping, but she still held on. Micah watched her as they moved through the last stretch, the fine line between control and surrender playing out in each exhale, each tremor of her pulse.

His hand was at her back, steadying her, guiding her, but the touch felt like more than support. It felt like a declaration, one she wasn't sure she was ready to accept. Tasha was unshielded and exposed, the vulnerability thrilling her as much as it scared her. Her heart raced, the beat of it visible at her throat, and she wondered if he noticed, if he knew what he was doing to her. The proximity was more than she had prepared for, the contact more intimate than she'd ever let it be before. Micah leaned her into the final stretch, and she felt the resolve she clung to waver, felt it slip as her eyes fluttered closed under the weight of everything unsaid.

Micah watched her carefully, the precision of his touch belying the chaos inside him. He knew she was close to letting go, that this last exercise was more than just physical. He felt the struggle in her, the push and pull between control and surrender, and it mirrored his own. The world outside their moment ceased to exist, the gym fading into nothingness as they became each other's entire focus. Her breath, his touch, the charged air around them - everything was heightened, electric, and he marveled at the effect she had, at how quickly he was losing himself to it.

He shifted his grip, fingers firm but careful, and he felt the heat of her, the tension that sang through her muscles as she fought for composure. It left him raw, stripped of any pretense, and the urge to pull her in, to let them both go, was almost too much to resist. Tasha felt her heart pound in response to every touch, every careful adjustment he made. The firm press of his hands was more than she had expected, and the intensity of her own reaction caught her off guard. She felt exposed but exhilarated, on the brink of something she couldn't quite define but desperately wanted to.

It was a moment suspended in time, both of them hyper-aware of how close they were, how close they wanted to be. She held her breath, waiting for the inevitable, wondering if he knew just how thin the line was that they walked. Micah sensed the shift in her, saw the surrender beneath her struggle, and it made his own resolve slip dangerously close to the edge. She was right there, in his hands and in his thoughts, and the knowledge of it fuelled a desire that threatened to undo them both. Their closeness was almost overwhelming, almost more than either of them could take. He felt it like a physical thing, a gravity that pulled him toward her and promised everything if he just let it happen.

They hovered on the brink, the tension a live wire between them, the connection undeniable and consuming. Micah knew he should pull back, knew they were seconds from crossing into territory that would change everything. He wasn't sure he cared. But then he saw the flicker of uncertainty on her face, the brief crack in her composure, and it gave him pause. He exhaled, the decision made in a heartbeat that felt like forever. With a reluctant shift, he eased her out of the stretch and back to reality, the sudden distance both a relief and a disappointment. Tasha opened her eyes, the world returning in a rush that left her breathless in more ways than one. She met his gaze, searching for something she couldn't quite name, and saw in it a pledge left hanging, a moment unresolved but promising.

"Thanks." She said, her voice a little too even, a little too controlled. "Anytime." Micah replied, his expression a mix of emotions that made her pulse quicken all over again. They lingered, the weight of the moment still heavy between them, still unfinished. It would be easy to fall back in, easy to pick up where they left off. Too easy. As Tasha gathered herself, she wondered how long they could keep pretending, how long before the distance they'd forced shattered completely. She left, not quite sure whether she was grateful or frustrated, but certain of one thing - this wasn't the end. Not by a long shot.

Tasha stared at her phone for a long time before pressing send, her finger hovering over the screen as if a single word might undo her. *Thanks for the stretch*, she typed, *might need that again tomorrow.* She watched the message stare back at her, feeling the reckless intimacy of it settle in her chest like a small, fluttering bird. The decision to reach out was one she agonized over, knowing full well the implications of a text that seemed so simple, so casual. But it was more than that. It was an admission, an acknowledgment that what had happened between them was too significant to ignore.

She erased it, sitting on the edge of her bed, the room dark except for the glow of the screen, and felt the weight of her uncertainty like a presence in the room. She was used to control, used to knowing exactly how things would play out. But this, this was something different. The internal debate raged, each argument clashing with the next until she wasn't sure which side was winning. She wanted to talk to him, to break the silence that had lingered after the session, but the idea of being the first to reach out, of making herself vulnerable, was terrifying.

A part of her said to let it go, to wait and see if he would make the first move. But a stronger, more reckless part wanted to act, to seize the moment before it slipped away. It was that part she listened to, that part she couldn't quite silence. Her reluctance was palpable, a tension in her body that wouldn't ease. She hated feeling out of control, hated the idea of giving him even the slightest indication that he was getting under her skin. But she also hated the thought of losing the connection they'd started to build. And then she wanted none of it.

Something came up at work today, she typed quickly, her fingers frenzied on the screen, *I have to be in early tomorrow so I won't be able to make it. Sorry.* With a deep breath, she crafted the message, trying to strike a balance between interest and indifference. Before she sent it, she erased the apology - she was a client, he was paid by her for training. She wasn't sorry she couldn't make it, she was sorry she had let it get this far. Before she could even put the phone down, it buzzed in her hand.

No worries. The words stared back at her, taunting and daring. She hesitated, a long moment of indecision that felt like standing at the edge of a cliff, looking down and wondering if she had made the right decision. Tasha put the phone down, unable to look at it, as if avoiding the screen would lessen the sting she felt from the simple two word response. And just like that, he had the upper hand. Her thoughts circled back to him, to what they had started and where it might have lead. She breathed deeply, trying to calm the fluttering that danced in her chest.

The suspense was unbearable, the not-knowing gnawing at her insides with relentless insistence. She stared at the phone, unable to resist the pull of it, wanting to send another message. Opening her phone, she stared at the keyboard, her thumbs dancing over the screen until something caught in the corner of her eye. A flicker of dots indicated that he had begun typing something else before they disappeared. And just like *that*, it was once again an even playing field.

She walked in like nothing had changed, as if the text was merely a throwaway gesture, but Micah knew better. He knew because his own pulse quickened at the sight of her, because they couldn't make it through a single exercise without the air between them crackling with potential. The moment she stepped into the gym, he felt it - a shift in the atmosphere, a charge that hadn't been there before. She was different, but pretending she wasn't, and he found the act as compelling as the truth underneath. Her eyes met his briefly, a flicker of something that matched the beat of his heart, and then she was all business again.

"What are you doing here so late?" He moved toward her, and even before she answered he felt the familiar tug, the inevitable draw that pulled him into her orbit.

"I had to miss this morning," she said casually, "so I wanted to get a workout in before the weekend."

"You know I'm off in twenty minutes." A hint of a smile played on his lips as he straightened his stance.

"I don't need a session," she replied, but her mind kept circling back to the text, "I know you're busy. So I thought I'd just get a workout in myself. You don't need to coddle me." With that, she pushed past him, a confidence in her stride that he hadn't seen before, even when she was at her peak. Something had changed, something was different, and he needed to find out.

Tasha was a burst of energy, her movements sharp and purposeful as she glided through the gym, her body taut and strong. And yet, there was something else about her, a tension and frustration that simmered just beneath the surface, giving her an edge of vulnerability. She was a paradox, both fierce and delicate, a force to be reckoned with. Tasha continued her warm-up, her mind focused on nothing more than pushing herself to her limits. She ran and ran on the treadmill, feeling the breeze from the fans above, the music pumping loud in her ears. And then she smelled it, his cologne somehow a mix of both something sweet and masculine. He appeared before her - Micah's eyes were the color of a stormy sea, dark and swirling with emotions she couldn't quite decipher. His dark hair brushed against his forehead, perfect strands that seemed to defy the laws of gravity.

Tasha felt the touch like a jolt to her system as his arm grazed against hers, her breath catching despite her resolve to stay composed. She pretended it didn't affect her, just as she pretended the text was casual, meaningless. But her body betrayed her as she stumbled, catching herself on the arms of the treadmill. Micah was at her side almost instantly, ripping the emergency chord from the machine as he held her up. Her ankle twisted slightly, and her knees buckled under her as he swept her up and pulled her back.

She could feel every hard plane of his chest against hers, their proximity creating an electric tension that crackled between them. They were close - too close for comfort and yet not nearly close enough. His warm breath fanned across her face, and she was painfully aware of how his sweatpants hugged his powerful thighs just perfectly right. The air between them was heavy with sexual tension - an intoxicating mix of panic, adrenaline and desire that had Tasha's heart pounding in sync with Micah's steady heartbeat. It was in this very moment that she realized just how drawn she was to him – not just physically but something deeper and far more dangerous.

"Thank you." Tasha felt her control slipping with every touch, every lingering moment where he was closer than necessary. It was exhilarating and terrifying, the reckless desire to be near him warring with her instinct to hold back. But the holding back was a losing battle, and she knew it. Micah knew they were close, knew they were at the edge of something neither could walk away from, and the certainty of it thrilled him. It thrilled her too, and he saw it in the way she didn't immediately turn to leave, in the way she lingered, hopeful and exposed.

"Are you okay?"

"My ankle—" Before she could even form a proper response, Micah swept her up off her feet, carrying her to the stretching mats in the corner of the gym. He placed her gently on the ground, his restraint and resolve barely bucking at the weight of her as he knelt down and let her go from his arms.

"I'll get you some ice." He was gone before she could protest, barely noticing the way he had clenched his hands at his sides, his body alive and electric from the feeling of her pressed against him. "Perhaps I should stick to stretching for the rest of the night." She laughed awkwardly, the walls around her crumbling down as she spoke.

"Here," Micah said, moving toward her feet, "let me look." He removed her sneaker carefully, flexing her ankle as she winced slightly.

"It doesn't feel broken," she placed the ice on the ground gingerly, "just a sprain."

"Let's try walking on it." He stood slowly, pulling her to her feet. His grip lingered, the contact brief but loaded with everything they weren't saying.

"It's fine," she replied, her voice breathy and charged, "I'm just gonna stretch before I head home."

"I wouldn't be doing my due diligence if I didn't assist you," he said, the words more than a statement, more than a promise, "especially after an injury."

Every stretch was an opportunity, every adjustment an excuse. He watched her closely, saw the way her eyes darkened when he got near, the way she refused to pull away even when she could. It thrilled him, the knowledge that she wanted this as much as he did. The session was a dance, a carefully choreographed routine where each step, each breath, each glance was part of a larger whole. She didn't mention the text, didn't need to. It hovered between them, unspoken but undeniable, a reminder of what they were edging toward.

Micah saw the way she responded, the way she softened under his touch and let herself get lost in the moment. Her skin tingled where he brushed against her, a heat that spread through her body and settled like a challenge she was finally willing to accept. She looked at him, and in that look, he saw the shift, the realization that she wasn't going to keep pretending, that she was done pretending. His own desire flared, a match to her fire, and he knew it was just a matter of time. The tension between them built, each movement, each extent adding to the pressure, the need. Micah was aware of it, aware of her, and the way she leaned into him left no doubt about what she wanted, what they both wanted.

Tasha's thoughts were a tangled mess of anticipation and hope, of fear and longing. She couldn't keep the distance, couldn't maintain the facade, and she didn't want to. She wanted more, wanted him. It was everything that came after, everything they were edging closer to. The session wound down, but the energy between them didn't. If anything, it increased, a live wire that sparked and hissed and refused to be contained. They moved together, as in sync as if they'd planned it, but this was something they couldn't plan, couldn't organize or control. It was raw and consuming, and they both knew it.

Micah's touch was more than she could take, more than a suggestion of what could be if they let it, and as he pulled back at the end of the session, Tasha felt the weight of what they had left unsaid, unfinished. She looked at him, eyes meeting with an intensity that neither could mask, and the world around them seemed to fade into nothing. The gym was empty, but it felt like they were more alone than ever, more isolated in their desire. It was like waking up in a familiar room only to find the furniture rearranged. The gym was the same, but the silence stretched like a blank canvas, daring them to paint outside the lines, to make the first stroke that would turn possibility into certainty.

"So." He said, watching for her reaction, knowing what he'd see.
"So." She echoed, the word a universe of possibility, a testament to how far they'd come and how close they were to finishing what they'd started. Neither moved, neither ready to break the tension

that pulsed around them like a heartbeat. The silence was no longer empty - it was full of promise, full of certainty. He hesitated, the question hanging in the air between them like an echo of the distance they'd worked so hard to maintain. It was the first time they'd risked the truth, the first time they'd let themselves be more than desire and determination. They were alone, the gym their private world, and the air was thick with anticipation.

"You coming?" Tasha walked toward the locker rooms, her question an attempt to regain control over the room. He looked at her, the weight of her gaze matching the weight of the question. It was a test, a gamble, and the trust inherent in it left him exposed in ways he hadn't anticipated. But there she was, waiting, the curiosity and need for honesty in her eyes a reflection of his own. Micah breathed deeply, the decision made in that same moment of hesitation.

The air in the locker room was thick with the scent of sweat, steam, and something else - something electric, something dangerous. Core Elite had an image, an image that would work to her advantage. The sleek mahogany panelling and marbled features adorned the stylish space. Gold-gilded hooks and taps glistened from the overhead lighting, and the faint scent of cedar and vanilla filled the air. It was perfect, she thought, perfect for a seductive rendezvous. Tasha's sneakers squeaked against the marble-tiled floor, each step a deliberate provocation, a challenge. She didn't look back, but she didn't need to. Micah was already following, his presence a shadow that clung to her like a second skin. The door swung shut behind them with a soft, final click, sealing them in a world of their own.

Tasha's fingers moved to the rim of her pants, the sound of the lycra sliding down her legs like a whisper of fabric against skin. She let them pool at her feet as she kicked off her shoes, revealing the curve of her hips, the swell of her ass barely contained by the lace of her thong. Her dark skin glowed under the dim lights, a canvas of soft curves and hard edges. She turned her head slightly, just enough to catch Micah's gaze in the mirror. Her lips curved into a smirk, a silent dare. Micah's breath hitched, his cock already straining against the confines of his sweatpants. He stepped closer, his eyes raking over her body with a hunger that bordered on violence.

"You always this forward?" He asked, his voice low, rough, like gravel dragged over silk. Tasha laughed, a sound that was all throat and no humor.

"Only when I'm winning," she purred, her fingers trailing down her sides, "I have to stay ahead." She removed her top and teased the edge of her bra, unhooking it with a practiced ease and letting it fall to the floor. Her breasts were perfect - full, round, the kind of breasts that made men forget their own names. Her nipples were already hard, pebbled against the cool air. Micah's hands clenched at his sides, his control slipping with every second she stood there, naked and unashamed. He wanted to touch her, to claim her, to make her scream his name until she forgot hers. But he knew better. This was a game, and Tasha was a player who didn't lose. She turned to face him fully now, her eyes dark with challenge.

"Your move." She said, her voice a sultry promise. Micah didn't hesitate. He closed the distance between them in two long strides, his hands gripping her waist, pulling her against him. Their bodies collided with a force that was almost painful, the heat between them igniting like a wildfire. His lips crashed down on hers, hard and demanding, his tongue forcing its way into her mouth. Tasha moaned into the kiss, her hands tangling in his hair, pulling him closer. Their kiss was a battle, a clash of wills and desires. Tasha bit down on his lower lip, drawing blood, and Micah growled, his hands sliding down to grip her ass, lifting her off the ground.

She wrapped her legs around his waist, her pussy grinding against the hard length of his cock through his pants. The friction was maddening, and Micah knew he was losing control. He carried her to the nearest bench, setting her down roughly before stepping back to strip off his clothes. His shirt was off in one fluid motion, revealing a chest that was all muscle and sinew. His pants followed, and then he was standing there, fully erect, his cock thick and heavy between his legs. Tasha's eyes widened for a fraction of a second before she regained her composure, her smirk returning.

"Impressive," she said, her voice dripping with mockery, "but can you use it?"

"Why don't you fucking find out." Micah grabbed her by the ankles, pulling her to the edge of the bench and spreading her legs wide. Her pussy was already wet, glistening in the light, and he couldn't resist tasting her. He dropped to his knees, his tongue licking a slow, torturous path up her thighs. Tasha's breath caught in her throat, her hands gripping the edge of the bench as Micah's tongue delved deeper, exploring every inch of her. He teased her clit with the tip of his tongue, flicking it back and forth until she was writhing beneath him. Her moans filled the room, a symphony of pleasure and desperation. But Tasha wasn't one to be outdone. She reached down, tangling her fingers in his hair and pulling him up to meet her gaze.

Tasha's breath hitched as she dropped off the bench to her knees, pushing Micah to the floor, her hands sliding up his thighs with a practiced ease. Her lips parted, a wicked grin spreading across her face as she leaned in, her tongue flicking out to taste the salty pre-cum already beading at the tip of his cock. She didn't waste time teasing - she took him deep, her throat opening up to swallow him whole, her cheeks hollowing as she sucked with a hunger that bordered on feral. He groaned, his head thudding back against the cold floor, his fingers tangling in her hair as she worked him over. Her mouth was a wet, hot vice, her tongue swirling around him, her lips tight and demanding. She could feel him twitching against her tongue, the way his hips bucked involuntarily, desperate for more. But she wasn't done yet. She pulled back, her lips popping off his cock with a lewd sound, her eyes locking with his as she licked her lips, savoring the taste of him.

"Fuck." He growled, his voice rough with need. He grabbed her by the shoulders, yanking her to her feet and spinning her around, her breasts slamming against the lockers. His hand snaked between her legs, fingers finding her soaked pussy with ease.

"Micah." She gasped as he pushed two fingers inside her, curling them just right to make her legs tremble.

"I'm gonna make you cum first." His thumb circled her clit, his breath hot against her neck as he whispered in her ear. But Tasha wasn't one to be dominated for long.

"Not if I have anything to say about it." She pushed him back, her ass pressing against his cock as she ground against him, her hand reaching back to grip his thigh and push him against the lockers opposite them. She turned, her eyes dark with lust as she started to touch herself, her fingers sliding through her slick lips, her other hand cupping her breast, pinching her nipple until it hardened under her touch.

She watched him as she played with herself, her breath coming in short, sharp gasps, her body trembling with need. He moved toward her, but she was already gone, slipping away with a laugh that sent shivers down his spine. She disappeared into the shower room, the sound of her footsteps echoing off the tiled walls. He followed, his cock throbbing with every step, his need for her burning hotter than ever. She was waiting for him, her back against the cold marble of the shower wall, her eyes gleaming with mischief. As soon as he stepped inside, she was on him, her hands pushing him back against the benchtops, her mouth descending on his cock once more.

She sucked him hard and fast, her head bobbing up and down, her tongue working him over with a skill that left him breathless. He grabbed her hair, pulling her head back so he could see her face, her lips swollen and glistening with spit and pre-cum. He thrust into her mouth with a brutal rhythm that had her gagging and moaning at the same time. He stopped suddenly, his hand wrapping around her throat as he pulled her to her feet. She smiled up at him, her eyes half-lidded with pleasure, her body trembling with anticipation. He pushed her against the shower wall, the cold tile biting into her skin as he pinned her there, his cock pressing against her soaked pussy.

She hit her head lightly against the wall, but she didn't care - the pain only added to the pleasure, the sharp sting making her clench around nothing. He reached over and turned on the water, the cold spray hitting them both and making her gasp. But it didn't cool the heat between them - if anything, it only made it burn hotter. He pressed his body against hers, his cock sliding between her thighs, the tip brushing against her clit as he ground against her. She moaned, her hands gripping his shoulders as she arched into him, desperate for more.

"You're mine." He growled, his voice low and dangerous as he pushed inside her, his cock stretching her open in one brutal thrust. She cried out, her nails digging into his skin as he fucked her hard and fast, the sound of their bodies slapping together echoing off the tiled walls. The water ran down their bodies, mixing with their sweat and the slickness between her thighs, making everything wet and slippery and perfect. He fucked her like he owned her, like he wanted to ruin her for anyone else. And she loved it - every thrust, every grunt, every time he pulled her hair or squeezed her throat.

The steam from the shower curled around them like a lover's embrace, thick and suffocating, clinging to their skin as if it didn't want to let go. Tasha's curves were slick with water, her nipples hard and begging for attention under the cascade. She pushed him back with a force that was both commanding and desperate, her hands firm on his chest, her nails digging in just enough to leave marks. He stumbled, his ass hitting the cold, wet bench with a slap, his cock already throbbing, thick and heavy against his stomach.

She didn't wait. She didn't ask. She straddled him in one fluid motion, her pussy already dripping, her thighs trembling as she sank down onto him. He groaned, his head falling back against the tile, his hands instinctively gripping her hips. She was tight, so fucking tight, and wetter than he'd ever felt her before. The water ran down her stomach, pooling between them, making every movement slick and obscene.

"Fuck." He hissed, his voice ragged, his fingers digging into her flesh as she started to move. She rode him like she was born for it, her hips rolling in slow, deliberate circles, her pussy gripping him like a vice. He could feel every inch of her, every pulse, every twitch, and it was driving him insane.

"Come for me." She demanded, her tone low and husky, her voice echoing off the walls. Her hands were on his shoulders, her nails scraping down his chest as she leaned in closer, her tits brushing against his skin.

"No." His voice was strained, his hands tightening on her hips as he tried to slow her down. But she wasn't having it. She reached behind her, her fingers wrapping around his balls, squeezing just enough to make him gasp. She slid her hand lower, her fingers teasing his perineum, pressing and stroking in a way that had him seeing stars.

"Come for me." She commanded again, her voice dripping with sin. He shook his head, his jaw clenched, his body trembling with the effort to hold back. But she didn't stop. She kept riding him, her pussy milking him with every thrust, her fingers working him in ways that made it impossible to think. She leaned down, her hand wrapping around his throat, squeezing just enough to make his vision blur. She grabbed his hand, forcing it to her breast, her nipple hard against his palm.

"You're so fucking big," she breathed, her voice a low purr, "I wanna see you come. I wanna watch your face when you realise you've lost."

"Fuck, Tasha." He couldn't hold back anymore. His body betrayed him, his cock pulsing as he came, his release spilling into her with a force that left him shaking. His face was a mix of relief and frustration, his breath coming in ragged gasps as he realized she'd won. She smiled, a wicked smile that made his cock twitch again despite himself. She leaned in, her lips brushing against his ear.

"I win." She whispered, her voice dripping with satisfaction. But he wasn't done. Not even close. He grabbed her, flipping her onto the floor under the stream of the shower with a growl. Her back hit the cold tile, her legs instinctively wrapping around his waist as he positioned himself between her thighs. He grabbed her ankles, holding them up as he thrust into her again, his cock still hard, still demanding.

"Was winning fun for you?" He growled, his voice low and dangerous as he fucked her, his thumb finding her clit and pressing down on it, just enough to make it hurt a little bit. She gasped, her back arching off the floor, her hands grabbing onto his arms.

"Fuck." She moaned, her voice breaking as slapped her thigh so hard it made her wince. He didn't let up, his thrusts hard and relentless, his thumb back on her clit with a precision that had her screaming.

"Say my name," he demanded, his voice loud and controlling, "scream like you're gonna crack the fucking tiles."

"Micah." Her scream echoed off the walls, raw and primal as she came around him, her pussy clenching so tight it was almost painful. He didn't stop, not until she was trembling beneath him, her body spent and shaking with the force of her orgasm. She came hard, her body convulsed around him as he continued pounding into her. The sound of skin slapping against skin echoed through the locker room, mingling with their moans and grunts. Tasha tried to free her legs but his grip was firm, his other hand pushing down on her stomach as he grunted.

"I'm gonna come again." Tasha cried out, her nails digging into his arms as he pounded into her with a ferocity that left them both gasping for air.

"Do it," Micah groaned, his pace faltering as he felt her body shaking, "come for me." Tasha's response was a guttural moan as she came undone beneath him, her body convulsing with pleasure. They stayed like that for a while, their bodies still joined, their breaths coming in ragged gasps as the water continued to cascade over them. Then Tasha pushed him away, a sly smile playing on her lips as she lay on the floor, clenching her thighs together while she sat up.

"Not bad," she said, her voice teasing, "but I think I still won." Micah laughed, a deep, throaty sound that sent shivers down her spine.

"How? I made you come twice." He said, his eyes dark with promise as he sat on the bench.

"Then I guess we need a rematch." Their eyes locked, and in that instant, everything was clear. It was all there, the unspoken finally spoken, the need and the want and the undeniable truth of them. The hesitation that had once held them back was gone, dissolved into the steam, leaving only the raw, consuming need that pulsed like a second heartbeat.

"One condition." Micah stood and walked over, kneeling down and leaning over her, his hand finding her thigh and clamping down on it.

"Name it."

"Your mine," he growled, "tell Kyle you're moving your sessions to me."

"No," she smirked as her hands slid up his arms, pushing him onto his back and straddling him, "I'll tell Kyle that you're my personal trainer from now on, but I'll never yield to being *yours*."

"Then I guess we're at a standstill." He leaned up and kissed her, the first proper kiss. Something in it was different, and it made her weak for a moment before she pressed him down once more, her hand flat against his chest.

"Nice try," she stood, turning off the tap and grabbing a towel from the racks, "I'll see you Monday morning. Now get the fuck out of the women's locker room."

"Yes ma'am." He said, surrendering to her before gathering his clothes and leaving. As he exited the locker room, a sly grin played on his lips. The encounter with her left him wanting more, craving the challenge she presented. He would let her win this round.

Office Hours

When Lily stayed late in the office, the night enveloped her in the way a novel did - an indigo quiet punctuated by breaths and paper, both touched by thoughts and ink. She imagined this was what he heard, that this was what kept him lingering in spaces that might otherwise have folded into sleep. Her fingertips skimmed across the spines lined up like ribs in the shelf, and the room became a library of beating hearts. She was often alone there, an afterthought in an office meant for daytime precision. The muted desk lamp pooled around her, making an island of light where she sifted through the pages of her thesis.

The Modernist Self: Fragmentation and Desire. A promising title, according to him. The empty hallway hummed with the memory of footstepped, and her own tapping was the only echo now. Her dark auburn hair fell forward, unkempt, over the glasses that framed her face as she scribbled notes in the margins. The smell of old paper and faint coffee stained the air, as familiar as the oversized sweater hugging her shoulders. Each movement was an extension of the solitude she thrived in. She should go home. There's no reason to stay this late, she told herself, but she knew the reasons existed, piled up like drafts on her desk.

She paused, the pen resting against her lip. professor Julian Reyes. His name rose in her thoughts with the same clarity and persistence as his critiques. She knew his presence even when he's not here, the weight of his words as tangible as his watchful eyes. The faculty, her fellow grad students - they all talked about him, this well-respected academic whose lectures were an exercise in gravitational pull. Tall and lean, a charisma that was both inviting and inscrutable, he was the kind of man who commanded a room without trying. And her. She was embarrassed by how he seemed to command her thoughts.

For all her intellect, she felt like a child when he was around. Not because he treated her as one - no, he treated her with a respect that left her breathless. It was her own reaction, the way her ambition crumbled into awareness of him. He was in his early forties, the lines at the edges of his eyes mapped decades of inquiry. But to her, he was everything in the present tense. She tried to remain professional, focusing on the work, on the push toward completing her thesis, but his face haunted her paragraphs. Lily pushed back from her desk, a shiver working through her despite the heat in her cheeks. It was too quiet now, the kind of quiet that reflected the loudness of her thoughts. She began to gather her things, stuffing notebooks into a satchel, as if retreating from her own distractions. She was convincing herself to call it a night when there was a light knock at the doorframe. The room absorbed her breath.

"Still at it, I see." professor Reyes stood in the threshold, tall and composed. His sleeves were rolled to the elbows, as usual, and the fitted dress shirt was taut with the day's wear. He seemed as if he had always been here, the hum of the office adjusting to accommodate his presence. Lily hesitated, feeling the scramble of her heartbeat like a secret trying to escape.
"You know how it is," she smiled at him too quickly, "it never quite

lets you go.”

“Let me guess,” he stepped into the office, “you’re circling back to Yeats again.”

“The man doesn’t make it easy to move on.” She laughed softly, the tension unfurling in her chest. He leaned against the desk, his nearness drawing her into an orbit she’d fought to resist.

“And neither does Joyce, or so I’ve heard.” His tone was teasing, a playfulness she had come to expect but never anticipated.

“Guilty,” she nodded toward her scattered pages, “I might need an intervention.”

“Or a breakthrough,” his eyes were steady, meeting hers in a way that seemed to take root while the moment hung there like a word at the tip of the tongue, “what were you stuck on?” Lily faltered, the room collapsing inward to the space between them. She thought of every time she had gone over this, alone and with him, the pointed she wanted to make colliding with the subtext she was afraid of exposing.

“It’s the identity stuff. Whether it’s fluid or just lost.” Her words came out haltingly, almost an admission. Reyes regarded her with an imperceptible pause before he replied.

“Fragmented doesn’t mean lost, you know. Maybe it just needs to be seen from a different angle.” She heard the double-meaning, the way his voice wrapped around the words like a touch.

“A different angle,” she repeated, swallowing the breath that caught on the way out, “I’ll try to remember that.” He straightened, adjusting his glasses with a careful hand.

“Don’t work too late, Lily. We can always revisit tomorrow.” The offer sat between them, open and charged.

"I won't," she lied, already feeling the absence as he moved to the door, "goodnight, professor."

"Julian." He corrected with a warmth that lingered like an echo. Then he was gone, the office resettling into its paper-dust quiet. Lily watched the doorway as if it might still contain him, then sank back into her chair, pulse fluttering beneath her skin like wings. Her eyes drifted to her notes, to the stack of books that promised solace in their density, but she found no anchor there.

Instead, she stared at the words she had scrawled across the margins - desire and fear, one tangled with the other. She closed her eyes, trying to summon the will to be only a student, only a researcher. He wanted her best work, he wanted to be impressed. He wanted - she wouldn't finished that thought. She pressed her fingers to her temples, imagining she could force herself into coherence. What did it mean to be whole, she wondered. She was there and not there, like the Modernist figures she studied. It should have made her feel at home, but it only made her want. The shadows stretched longer as the evening bled toward night. And still Lily sat there, a single presence adrift in the empty office. There was time yet to make sense of the fragments.

The noise of the corridor wrapped around her, swallowing the footstepped that hurried to claim his time, his attention. Lily waited. It was a waiting that required all her energy - the clenching of her fingers around the stack of papers, the stillness of her breath as it knotted and unknotted inside her chest. She watched the office door, trying to appear as though she wasn't. This was a routine she knew well. These Monday office hours where her anxiety competed with the noisy hustle of students vying for a piece of him. The papers trembled in her handed, whispering with a life she wished she could still.

Yeats: An Obsession. He would find humour in that title. Her auburn hair slipped from its neat ponytail, and she tucked it back with a fidgeting impatience. She had fifteen minutes at best, time enough to discuss her paper if she could keep her thoughts from scattering the way they did whenever she was alone with him. Whenever he looked at her. The seconds frayed like her nerves, and she steeled herself, preparing to fight through both crowds and feelings. One student left the office, another slipped in. She adjusted her glasses and glanced at the clock, pretending to calculate her schedule but really counting down the minutes until it was her turn. She knew she should be going over her pointed, rehearding her questions, but her mind was elsewhere. On him, as always.

The office door swung open again. This time, a timid first-year was lost in her phone, and the oblivious shuffle allowed an opening Lily couldn't ignore. Her pulse quickened in response, anticipation binding her breath to the corridors and thesis that held it. She crossed the threshold with a confidence she doesn't quite feel, like an actress slipping into character.

"Professor Reyes?" Her voice was controlled, measured against the trembling excitement in her chest. He looked up, his glasses perched on his nose, an expression of focus yielding to recognition. "Lily." The way he said her name was a welcome, an invitation that carried her across the room. The office was cluttered with the weight of ideas - books stacked like neglected lovers, papers splayed in urgent disarray. A small table held two coffee mugs, evidence of a recent meeting. The walls were lined with framed academic achievements, their edges collecting shadows as if even they competed for his attention. She inhaled the scent of old paper and cool, sunless air, and suddenly felt as if they were sharing a secret.

"Come in," he stood to clear space among the academic debris, "I'm glad you could make it." He sounded as if it was a pleasure, and she was momentarily dizzy from the thought.

"I wasn't sure if you'd have time," she forced herself into the chair, the proximity rendering her rehearsed questions useless, "before either of us left for the night."

"Always. What has Yeats done to earn your ire this time?" He leaned back, as comfortable in his presence as she was uneasy in hers. Lily smiled, aware that it was too broad, too full of something she hoped he couldn't see.

"Just the usual," she shrugged, "shattered identities, unrequited passions, the works." She offered him the papers, conscious of how close he was as he reached for them. He glanced at the title and laughed, a soft sound that matched the easy curl of his posture.

"Obsession," he lifted an eyebrow, teasing, "should I be concerned?" Her heart tripped over itself, scrambling to recover with humour.

"I think it's safe. I'm not obsessed with him. He was obsessed with things in his life. Remember? You taught us that."

"Of course," he flipped through the pages, nodding to himself, "this looks promising, Lily." The sound of her name, unadorned and warm, ignited a spark beneath her skin.

"I hope so." She said, and it came out like a wish. They fell into a rhythm, a back-and-forth that began with minor revisions, structural notes. Reyes made commented in the margins with swift, elegant marks, the efficiency of his critique both unnerving and reassuring. Lily watched him as he read, noting the way he adjusted his glasses, the deliberate pauses before he spoke, like someone arranging flowered to create maximum effect. She found herself leaning forward, matching his focus.

"I think this part on artistic autonomy could be stronger," he said, pointing to a section in the third paragraph, "try expanding on the personal versus the universal." She nodded, grateful that he couldn't see the flutter of her pulse.

"So more theory, less poetry?"

"More of both, ideally," his smile reached across the desk, "I want to see the same energy here that you have when you're discussing it in class." His tone was earnest, a softness beneath the authority.

"Easy for you to say," she teased, but it was a tentative teasing, the kind that hinted at what neither of them would mention, "you've got the energy of half the faculty combined." He considered this, head tilted, gaze steady.

"I doubt that," the pause stretched between them like a sigh, and his eyes meet hers with an intensity that she felt in the pit of her stomach, "though you do make it sound appealing."

"You've got the energy of half the faculty combined," she looked away, tucking a strand of hair behind her ear to hide the redness she knew has spread there, "and the attention of every student in the school. Even the ones not in your classes."

"If you applied that energy into your writing," he gazed at her with a curious expression that seemed to penetrate to the depths of her soul, "that wit and provocative manner would do wonders for you."

"I'll do my best." She flushed with color, gulping nervously as she glanced at the papers he held.

"Do," he leaned forward as if to close the space she had created, "I'm counting on it." His voice was low, meant only for her, and she felt the familiar imbalance - his calm against her chaos, his impact against her resolve.

They moved through more pages, more questions, the dialogue flowing as naturally as her unsteady breathing would allow. She marvelled at his grasp of her ideas, the way he elevated them without dismissing her initial instincts. He was everything she wanted to be, and the thought both inspired and immobilized her. As they finished, the air hung heavy with the silence of all that was unsaid. She reached for the draft, their handed brushing, and even that accidental contact sent a jolt she couldn't dismiss. It was all she could do to hold his gaze.

"Thank you professor." The formality was a thin shield, and she knew it.

"Julian."

"Julian," she repeated, savoring the sound of it, "I appreciate your time. I know you're busy."

"Never too busy for this," the words slipped out like an afterthought, like they weren't loaded, "you're doing good work Lily." His focus returned to her, just shy of the intensity that would expose everything. She stood, her movements sudden and graceless against the tide of his composure.

"Thanks to you." It was more truth than modesty, and she hoped he didn't notice the imbalance in her voice. His eyes followed her to the door, a weight she felt but couldn't acknowledge.

"Let me know if you need anything else." He sounded as if he knew she would.

She stepped out, the corridor swallowing her in a rush of noise and other people's haste. Her heart raced in time with the distance, a dizzy pulse that resisted settling. All the reasons she came here had merged, tangled with the tension and impossibility that always accompanied her back into the hallway. He made it impossible to think straight. He made her feel capable of anything. Lily hugged the draft to her chest as if it could quiet the noise within her. There was a long week ahead before their next formal meeting. There was an impossibly long week.

The office held its breath around them, a quiet charged with what neither would acknowledge. The hallway noise was distant, a low murmur that served to make the space between them feel even closer. Lily was all too aware of the narrowed gap, how every tilt of his head, every rustle of paper resonated within her. The session was supposed to be professional, focused, but her heart had never been one to obey. Reyes was studying a section of her thesis, intent and absorbed, and Lily watched him read her words. His sleeves were rolled to the elbows, familiar and arresting, a casual intimacy in the gesture that set her pulse in motion. He didn't need to say much for her to hear everything she was afraid of.

"This part, here," he said, his finger paused to underline a phrase, "I like how you approach identity as both presence and absence. There's something sharp about it." He glanced up, and she felt the full weight of his observation.

"Thanks." She managed, though it was a threadbare word for

the enormity of what she wanted to convey. He leaned back, considering her with an ease she envied.

"Your writing style is distinct," he added, and though it was an offhand remark it pierced her composure, "almost as distinct as your presence in class." Her breath caught, a brief imprisonment that gave way to rapid release. She lowered her eyes to the page, forcing herself to focus on the text when all she could feel was him. Reyes tapped the paper lightly, drawing her attention back.

"I'm serious, Lily. You have a way of getting to the heart of things." His gaze lingered, and in that lingering she sensed both recognition and a gentle teasing that made her heart unsteady.

"Maybe I'm just overthinking it." She said, attempting a levity she didn't feel.

"Or maybe you're exactly right." There was a pause, a moment too long, and she knew they were not just talking about the thesis. The conversation spiraled outward from there, a dance of theory and analysis that couldn't quite disguise the tension. She tried to absorb his feedback, to remember the pointed he was making, but the current beneath their words was a force she couldn't ignore. She felt it in the tightening of her throat, the warmth spreading from her cheeks to her fingertips.

He shifted in his chair, moving slightly closer, and it sent her senses into disarray. The office shrunk around them, a confessional without the barrier of secrecy. Lily's mind flitted to the compliment, the way it sounded almost tender. She imagined the boundary dissolving and then steeled herself against the foolishness of the thought. The air grew dense, like an unspoken confession weighing it down. She knew she should speak, say something to puncture the moment, but the words were impossible in her throat. Instead she watched him, this man who was both a map and an unreadable text to her, and her gaze was helplessly full.

"Are you alright?" He asked, the concern in his voice an invitation and a taunt.

"Yes," she lied, aware that the breathless quality of her reply betrayed her, "just a lot to process." His smile was gentle, conspiratorial.

"I hope you mean the theory, not my commented."

"Both, I guess." She said, and it was more honest than she intended. They continued to speak, though she hardly heard what was said. Each word felt laden with a subtext that defied their shared commitment to professionalism. She knew she was imagining most of it, but the lingering looks and charged silences told her otherwise. Finally, as the session wound down, he handed back the thesis with an approving nod.

"Keep going in this direction," he advised, "I'm curious to see where it leads." His choice of words ignited a fresh surge of confusion, and she clutched the pages with a trembling grip.

"I'll try." She promised, her voice caught somewhere between confidence and hope. He stood as she gathered her things, and she felt his gaze like a hand at her back, propelling her toward the door, toward her frantic need to decipher all that just happened. The room expanded with each step she took, the exit both a relief and a loss.

"Let me know if you need to meet again before next week." He said, and she heard it for the invitation it might be. She nodded, trying to maintain a semblance of control.

"I will." It was as much a question as an answer, and the double-meaning ached between them.

Lily exited into the hallway, the commotion swallowing her like surf swallowing a breathless swimmer. She kept moving, determined not to look back, to not reveal the desperation she felt curling in her chest. Outside, the air was crisp, cutting, and she told herself it would help clear her mind. She thought of the compliment, his lingering gaze, the way the air between them refused to thin. It was all too much. It was all too much and not enough. As she walked, Lily tried to convince herself that it was nothing, that her imagination was running away with her. But the trembling of her hand, the flush on her cheeks, suggested a truth she wasn't ready to face. Not yet. Not while the line between them was still drawn, however faintly.

The office was evening-lit, shadows dissolving into the quiet certainty of dusk, and with each session, the certainty that it was more than her imagination dissolving as well. She saw it in the way he watched her, an attention so direct it became almost corporeal. She told herself not to overthink it, but the urge to understand him, to understand herself, rendered that impossible. They sat across from each other, separated only by the thin barrier of papers and intentions. The office seemed to draw inward, wrapping their sessions in a cocoon of silence where every whisper of pen and thought hung heavy with implication. Lily felt the heat of it, the gravity of his focus, and her resolve was like wet ink - impossible to hold.

"The chapter on Eliot," he began, his voice an anchor in the drifting air, "it's becoming a centre of gravity for the whole argument." His words were as careful as his eyes, each carrying a weight that she struggled to support.

"I hope that's a good thing." She wanted it to sound like an academic inquiry, not the anxious plea it became.

"It is," he assured, leaning forward in a way that closed the space between them more than physically, "it's like you're mapping out the fractures, showing where the light gets in." His choice of words was deliberate, and she felt the swell of meaning beyond their surface. Lily nodded, but the simple motion belied the complexity of what coursed through her. She was the sum of wants and fears, balanced precariously on the thin line of his gaze.

"I've been trying to stay true to the themes."

"I can see that," he said, and his eyes lingered on her in a way that shifted the weight of the room, "you bring a clarity that's rare." The compliment threaded itself through her, a taut and trembling wire. She knew that she should look away, return to the words on the page, but the intensity pulled her in like a force of nature.

"Thank you." She replied, though it was not enough for the gratitude and confusion he evoked. He leaned back, allowing the space to expand with all that was unsaid.

"I mean it, Lily. Your perspective, your *voice*. It's unique." Each pause felt deliberate, a gift and a challenge in its ambiguity. Her cheeks were hot, her heart racing to meet the urgency of the moment. She glanced at her notes, tried to tether herself to the ink instead of his presence, but it was futile. Every comment was a constellation she couldn't help but navigate toward, drawing a map of things she wasn't sure was even there.

"I wonder sometimes if it's too obvious." She ventured, hoping to deflect the attention but instead inviting more of it.

"Not at all," his response was immediate, almost too much so, "the best arguments often are." They continued the session, but Lily heard only the subtext - the thread that bound their conversation into a narrative she didn't intend to write. He spoke of her work with a passion that set the air humming, his words enlivened by the punctuation of glances that never quite left her. She listened, half-disbelieving, half-hopeful, the fear of misinterpretation clawing at the edges of her composure. It was impossible to tell if this was real or if she had crafted it from desire and fragments. The session became a blur, a montage of emotion and analysis that blended into a whole she couldn't yet define.

"Your instincts are sharp. Trust them." He told her as they neared the end, and Lily felt the flutter of validation in places she couldn't admit. He didn't look away as he said it, and she was dizzy from the recognition that she was both the thesis and the researcher, the centre and the observer.

"I'll try." She managed, though it was a promise that reached far beyond the academic. They fell into a moment of silence, the kind that shattered noise into confetti. His gaze was steady, and she swore it touched more than her face, reaching toward the quickened beat of her heart.

"Don't second-guess yourself," he continued, almost a whisper in the fading light, "you're closer than you think." It was unclear if he meant the work or something else, something more. The ambiguity was a spark that could ignite or consume. Lily rose, the effort of maintaining her calm exhausting and incomplete. She gathered her notes with unsteady hands, aware of how they trembled under the pressure of being seen, really seen. He stood as she reached the door, the gesture a quiet insistence on decorum or a signal of something she couldn't yet translate.

"Same time next week?" The question hovered in the charged air. "Yes," she said, breathless and full of the space between panic and desire, "I'll be ready." She hoped it was true. She left the office, the door closing softly but reverberating through her like a crash. The hallway was busy with the indifference of others' lives, and Lily tried to anchor herself in the external chaos. It failed. Her own chaos was too loud, too persistent. Every step away from him was a step toward a greater confusion.

She replayed the session in her head, his words looping in her mind like a record she couldn't stop spinning. Unique, distinct, closer than you think. They circled her thoughts like a flock, never landing. Lily walked faster, trying to outpace the whirlwind of longing and fear. She couldn't shake the feeling that everything was about to change, that she was on the brink of something vast and uncharted. She couldn't shake the feeling that, despite her best intentions, she wanted it to.

Every session felt like a new frontier, a strange land where desire and discretion waged their daily wars, and Lily was the mapmaker without a compass. She chartered each encounter, drawing lines and arrows, but Reyes's eyes created new territories she wasn't sure what to name. The office was dimmer today, its atmosphere almost conspiratorial. She felt the weight of its silence pressing against her ribcage, compressing the air she tried to breathe. Every corner seemed softer, more forgiving, as if to remind her how sharp her edges were in his presence.

"Back to the labyrinth." He said as she settled into the chair, the words punctuated by a quick, promising smile.

"Seems I can't escape it." She easily matched his tone but failed to emulate his ease. They dove into the session, but the work became secondary, background noise to the conversation unfolding in glances. Reyes was more focused than ever, and it felt like his focus was not just on the thesis, but on her. Lily found herself lost in his attention, a wilderness of thoughts that tangled and spread completely unchecked. She was hyper-aware of each look, each pause, each implication that suspended itself in the air between them.

"Your perspective on Woolf, it's an interesting shift." He held her gaze a fraction too long.

"Interesting how?" She asked, though her heart was in the question, not the answer.

"Unconventional," his word landed heavily, an anchor with the potential to become something else, "but insightful." Her skin felt electric under his scrutiny, and she wondered if he could see the effect he had on her, the way her thoughts scattered in his presence. Each time his eyes meet hers, it was as though he was redrawing the maps she clung to, pushing her toward uncharted territories. They moved through the text, but every word was an echo of something louder. She tried to stay focused, but the awareness was a current she couldn't resist. He was so close, she thought, not just physically but in a way that made her fear the erosion of boundaries she struggled to maintain.

"You're pulling away from traditional readings and making them your own." There was a weight to his words, and she felt them sinking into the parts of her she couldn't hide.

"Is that good?" She meant academically, but there was an urgency that made it more. His gaze softened, an impossible warmth.

"It's exactly what you should be doing." He didn't look away, and she felt her breath stall, caught in the space he created by watching her so intensely. Each moment became a testament to the gravity between them, a gravity she was powerless to ignore. Lily heard her pulse like a distant drum, an echo of the emotions she tried to suppress. She watched his eyes drift, unbidden, to her mouth, and her thoughts erupted in a wildfire of possibility and dread. It was a quick glance, easily denied, but it branded

The session stretched out, a landscape of growing tension and shortening silences. She struggled to stay composed, aware of every movement, every glance that pulled her deeper into the confusion of what he meant, what she imagined, and what might be real. Reyes leaned closer, his focus more intent, and she was swept up in the enormity of what it could signify. She tried to anchor herself in academia, in the safety of ink and text, but the effort was futile when everything blurred into the wanting. He stood as they finished, an implicit reminder of formality in a room charged with its opposite.

"Keep exploring these paths," his smile was intimate, and the room shrunk around it, "you're onto something." She didn't know how she managed the words, but they left her mouth like a secret slipping into the world.

"Thanks professor. I hope so." She felt like she's promising more than she understood.

"Julian, please." The way he looked at her as she gathered her things was an invitation and a denial, a loop she couldn't break or understand. Lily moved toward the door, fighting the urge to let her confusion speak louder than she wanted it to.

"Next week, then."

"Yes." She answered, too quickly, the need and apprehension wrestling in her voice. The corridor's noise was a relief, a way to drown out the rush of thoughts that jostled for dominance in her mind. She walked through the campus with an urgency she couldn't quite define, the echo of his attention replaying itself with each step. Each meeting felt like a promise half-made, a territory claimed but not yet named. Her longing was as sharp as her fear, both leaving her breathless and undone. She played back the session in fragments - the looks, the silences, the words he chose so carefully. Lily was aware that every possibility lead to something irrevocable, and the weight of it filled her with a terrifying, exhilarating anticipation.

She looked for an excuse to see him, any excuse to see him, and requested a meeting in the middle of the week. It felt unnatural this time, as if she had disturbed a ritual he had become so accustomed to. His eyes were dark and heavy, his tone leaving a bitter taste in her mouth. He picked up a book and rested it between them, not quite facing either of them. She glanced at it slowly, then back at him. He had not taken his eyes off her, every movement he made was slow and graceful, but he looked at nothing except her.

"Tell me what you see." He said slowly, his breathing quiet and his body relaxed. She leaned forward slowly, looking at the cover before glancing back at him.

"There's nothing on the cover."

"Exactly," he stood up suddenly, forcing his chair back in a way that made her jump, "so many unknown authors, unread books, unseen words written by people who could have been so great but never applied themselves."

"I don't understand—"

"Why are you here so soon after out last meeting, Lily?" He turned to face her, peering down as she looked at him with wide eyes.

"Professor—"

"Why?" His question lingered in the air like smoke, curling around her uncertainty and filling the space between them.

She stood slowly, his presence so dominating that she could almost feel the heat radiating from his body though he was a few feet from her. She wondered if the words meant more than the sum of their parts, if they were a challenge or an invitation, and whether her answer would alter their precarious balance. Her hands hovered idly at her side, then moved like she might reach for the book and all that lay beneath its cover. Then her body shifted. She stood tall and sure of herself, seeking the words in her mind that her mouth seemed to refuse to speak aloud. The lie that had brought her to him so soon in the week.

"I needed some guidance," her tone was demanding, much more than she had intended, but she needed to sell the lie, "I wanted some advice."

"Why?"

"Because you're my professor, and I am here to learn." She turned to face him fully, holding his gaze with a fire she hadn't known she possessed. He watched her carefully, as though trying to see behind the facade she had built so carefully.

"You'll have to do better than that," he said slowly, his voice like velvet wrapped around steel, "I can see you're passionate about the subject, and I can feel your desire to prove yourself. But why are you here?" She took a breath, her mind racing as she tried to think of another lie that would satisfy him.

"You're becoming obsessed with the subject," his tone was even now, but there was an intensity behind it that made her shiver, "just like Yeats."

"'Yeats was obsessed with his muse." She argued, finding it difficult to hide her offense to his implication.

"And in turn became enamored with his work." He leaned forward slowly, bracing himself with his hand on the desk, his eyes never leaving hers.

"Well, I'm not Yeats. I'm not nearly as talented," she swallowed hard, trying to find the courage to step onto this new path she had carved for herself, "nor am I as *obsessed*." There was a moment of stretched silence that seemed to last for an eternity. She bit her lip and took in a deep breath, the heat of the argument just as fiery as the tension in the room.

"You said I could come to you before our meetings if I needed."

"You're right," he said slowly, his voice like velvet wrapped around steel, "I can see you're passionate about this subject, and I can feel your desire to prove yourself."

"I'm applying myself by wanting extra help from my professor, my teacher, who I admired a lot more up until this moment." Her words stung him as if they had been a physical slap. He stood straight, adjusting his jacket and glancing down at the book.

"I'm sorry, Lily," he swallowed hard, a remorseful expression adorning his face, "I don't know what came over me. I thought some tough love might make you see how *good* you are. But if you're in need of a lesson then of course my door is always open."

"Well then," she held her chin up, attempting to maintain the control that she had gained, "shall we continue?"

It happened like a slip in gravity, an imperceptible shift that pulled them into collision. One moment she was standing, reaching for the book, and the next his hand was brushing against hers - brief, electric, everything. They froze, caught in the charge of the contact. Time spilled itself into fractions of seconds that stretched like eternities, and Lily felt the shockwave before she registered it. He pulled away first, his hand lingering in the air uncertain of where to go. She mirrored his retreat, both of them retracting as if the distance might disguise the inevitability of their orbit.

"I—," Reyes' voice caught in his throat, less sure than she had ever heard it, "sorry."

"No, I'm sorry." Lily felt the absurdity of the apology, the weightlessness it tried to excuse. The book sat between them, an unclaimed artifact of the moment, and they stood like statues, neither wanting to be the first to break its spell. Lily was acutely aware of her skin, of every cell firing with the aftershock. She wanted to speak, to acknowledge the enormity of what had happened, but the words collapsed before forming. He recovered first, offering a tight smile that bordered on pained.

"Got a little too involved there."

"Just a little." She echoed, the word falling flat against the vaulted space of her longing.

They returned to their chairs, both avoiding the closeness that was so briefly, overwhelmingly shared. The room felt like it was learning how to breathe again, each inhale charged with what they both felt in that suspended second. Lily stared at her notes, the words dissolving into meaningless shapes. She tried to concentrate on anything but the lingering sensation, but it was impossible. The touch replayed itself in her mind, a looping filmstrip that caught and released her breath. She wanted to believe it wasn't just a reflex, that the surprise in his eyes held more than shock. Her heart stuttered at the thought, an erratic percussion against the soft drum of his voice as he attempted to steer them back to the relative safety of analysis.

"Right, where were we when we left off last week?" He asked, the calm surface barely disguising the tension below.

"Middle of Pound, I think." She managed, though she wasn't sure if the reference was to poetry or something more fundamental.

"Yes, right." His composure was fractured, visible only in the way his hand trembled slightly as he shuffled the pages. His eyes lifted to hers, a connection that rekindled the flicker in her chest. It was meant to be reassuring, but it sent a fresh rush of uncertainty through her. The session continued, though it was clear that neither could fully shake the disruption. They talked theory, literature, the distance across the desk both a comfort and a regret.

Lily noticed the new tension in his posture, the way he leaned forward but never too close. She wondered if he could see the effect of the moment written on her face, in the tremor of her fingers as they twisted around her pen. Each minute that passed felt suspended, like a truth hovering just out of reach. As the clock pushed them toward the session's end, the awkwardness shifted into something more familiar, yet just as charged. She stood, aware of the infinitesimal distance between them, the empty air now fuller than when they began.

"Friday?" His question was soft, almost tentative, and she heard the same hesitation in his voice that had taken root in her chest.

"As always." She replied, breathless with the effort of staying composed. Lily moved toward the door, a retreat she forced into a deliberate walk. The intensity of the touch, the brief, accidental truth of it replayed over and over in her mind. It was real. She felt it. Maybe he did too. She stepped out into the hallway, the clamor of other lives a dull hum compared to the tumult inside her. Every step echoed with what they shared and didn't share, what the silence left hanging like a promise, a threat, a possibility she couldn't yet fathom. Her pulse was a rapid, ecstatic thing. The encounter - a slip in gravity - propelled her, and she was helplessly, wonderfully at its mercy.

He appeared in her doorway like a thought she hadn't meant to speak aloud. The office was already tight with her urgency, and his presence pressed against the remaining space, an inevitability she should have foreseen but didn't. Lily looked up from her notes, the clutter of drafts and highlighters spilled across the desk. Her surprise barely masked the flush that warmed her cheeks, and she tucked a loose strand of hair behind her ear with fingers that didn't quite steady.

"Professor Reyes." The way she said his name was an exhale, more relief than greeting.

"I'm not sure how many times I have to tell you," he smiled, "please call me Julian. I'm surprised to see you here so late." The warmth in his voice made the observation less fact and more a gentle tease. She smiled, nervous and bright.

"I could say the same. Working late?"

"Perhaps. Or avoiding work. Sometimes it's hard to tell." He stepped into the room, and the walls seem to draw back to accommodate his easy confidence.

"I wanted to go over some notes before tomorrow night. I was unsure if I had time tomorrow so I wanted to—"

"You're making me look bad, Lily." His voice was steady, yet there was an underlying intensity that sent a shiver down her spine. Her pulse quickened, the simplicity of her name on his lips too intimate for the hour and too long anticipated to be real.

"I guess I'm trying to impress you." She admitted, a hint of humor in her tone to disguise the truth beneath it.

"It's working," he took the chair next to hers, uninvited but welcome, "need a fresh set of eyes?" She nodded, trying not to overplay her eagerness.

"If you don't mind. The Eliot section."

"I had a feeling." He leaned in, his shoulder brushing hers as he scanned the pages. It was casual, and her reaction was anything but. The small contact sent a shiver through her, and she was grateful that he was too absorbed in her work to notice her unsteady breath. Lily shifted slightly, aware of every inch that separated them, and every inch that didn't.

The atmosphere was different this night, softer, as if they had stepped outside the boundaries that usually fenced them in. His nearness was a comfort and a terror, a familiar unknown that she couldn't resist. They discussed the paper, and she found herself swept into the current of his insights. The conversation flowed with an ease that mirrored the undercurrent she felt between them. Each comment was a ripple, and the water rose as they spoke. Reyes pointed out a passage, his hand grazing her fingers. It was a gesture as light as air, but it landed heavily, the echo of it vibrating in her bones. She wondered if he felt the spark that ignited in her, the fire that spread to her cheeks and beyond.

"I've always thought this argument needed a little more urgency." He said, shifting his gaze from the paper to her.

"Urgency?" Her voice caught on the word, the double meaning searing through her. She hoped he didn't hear the way her heart amplified it.

"More immediacy, maybe." He smiled, and the room felt as if it was exhaling with them. Lily laughed, a sound she hardly recognized as hers.

"You think?"

"Only if you want to make an impression."

She tried to focus, but the academic distance she had worked so hard to maintain slipped like water through a sieve. The reality of his presence, his touch, his voice so close to hers, made her feel as if she was standing on the precipice of something vast and consuming. Their discussion became less about the paper and more about the spaces between words, the subtext she heard beneath his calm and confident guidance. His attention was intoxicating, and she was at once afraid and in desperate need of more. Reyes seemed more relaxed than ever, an openness in his demeanor that bordered on playful.

"Have you been holding out on me?" He asked, referring to the argument she had circled in red pen. She shook her head, trying to sound casual and failing.

"Just a work in progress."

"Feels finished to me." His eyes lingered on hers, and Lily felt the precarious balance of hope and fear shifting beneath her feet. The clock moved without their notice, and the world beyond the office felt irrelevant, an afterthought in the charged intimacy of the moment. He stood as they wrapped up, and she mirrored the motion, feeling the weight of the evening settling in her chest.

"Are you sure I'm wasn't keeping you?" She asked, though she dreaded his answer. He paused, considering her in a way that stole her breath.

"I don't mind." It was a simple statement, yet it expanded in the room like a promise. Lily gathered her papers, the effort futile against the scattered state of her mind. She didn't know how to leave, didn't know how to stay. Her hesitation filled the air, and she sensed he was waiting, watching.

"I'll let you escape, then." She attempted a smile, but it carried the heaviness of what she didn't want to end.

"I'll be here a while still. Plenty of work to grade. I was just taking a break when I saw you were still here."

"You should get back to it then." She smiled slowly, gesturing toward the door.

"Lily." He said as he turned, and the hesitation she heard in his voice made her heart leap and sink all at once.

"Yes?"

"Don't overthink it," he smiled over his shoulder, "the paper, I mean." She nodded, though it was clear to both of them that she was thinking of much more than that.

"Thanks, professor."

"Julian." It was less a correction than a plea, and she swallowed against the tightness it left in her throat.

"Julian." She echoed, savoring the closeness of his name, the proximity it implied. She watched him leave, and he felt the gravity of her gaze all the way to the door. Each step was a calculation, a countdown, a refusal to let her heart set the pace.

Lily heard the thunder rumble as she shut her laptop and headed for her car. Outside, the night air was sharp and bracing, but it did nothing to cool the fever that rose in her. She replayed the evening like a film with no clear ending, every moment an unfinished script she longed to revive. The storm had arrived without warning, a crash of light and noise that engulfed the campus and everything inside it. Lily watched the rain streak the window of the glass doors, frantic and alive, and she knew that leaving was no longer an option.

Her phone beeped with an emergency warning. Flooding, power lines down, roads unsafe. The warning urged for everyone to stay indoors. She listened for life within the building, but the sounds outside drowned out her other senses and she stepped backward, retreating further into the building. She walked past offices, study rooms, classrooms, and the grand lectures halls - all without signs of life. But she knew she wasn't alone. She knew that someone else had been trapped with her inside the building.

She could have walked back to her office to continue her own work, but she found herself walking the opposite way to Reyes' door. She knocked lightly, and he startled at the noise. He stood suddenly, caught off guard by the violent transformation outside.

One moment the sky was indifferent, the next it was a furious blur, a wet chaos that blanketed the view and beat against the glass. It echoed the pounding of her heart, a tempest she both dreaded and craved.

"I'm surprised my small knock startled you," she teased as she took a few small steps into his small office, "considering what's going on outside."

"I was so caught up in my reading that I hadn't even noticed," Reyes said, a mix of resignation and something else in his voice that she couldn't quite place, "looks like we're stuck here." Lily nodded, the breathlessness of the last session still a tight coil in her chest.

"I didn't even know it was supposed to rain." The words were hollow against the dense air, the atmosphere thicker than the storm that contained them. Reyes glanced at the window, then back at her, and the pause was its own kind of weather - an electrified silence charged with all they hadn't said.

"Not exactly a light drizzle." He observed, but his eyes suggested he was talking about more than the weather. She swallowed hard, aware of the inevitability that wrapped around them like the night. The rain poured down, isolating them in a cocoon of sound, a private world where nothing could intrude. The thought was thrilling and terrifying, the close quarters an invitation she wasn't sure how to accept.

"What were you reading that captivated you so obsessively that you didn't even hear the thunder and rain outside?" She teased, sitting down at the chair in front of his desk.

"I was going over your work," he stared at her, his face deep in thought and clearly still lost in the pages, "interesting that you chose the word *obsessively* to ask your question."

"I was teasing." She shrunk in her chair, her mind alight with the thought of being so forward that she flushed with embarrassment.
"We might as well wait it out." He suggested, though there was no proposition in the way his voice held her.
"Right. Not much choice." She agreed, and it came out a whisper, an echo of the longing that churned inside her. The conversation was stilted at first, a series of half-formed attempts to ignore the tension that was almost a third presence in the room. They spoke of the storm, the unpredictability of it, but beneath the surface the dialogue looped back to them, to the impossibility of keeping the charge contained.

The rain grew heavier, a curtain that cut them off from the world. It left them alone with each other and the mounting intensity of their silence. The office shrunk, enclosing them in its dim light and unresolved tension. Lily felt the press of it, the weight of their unsaid thoughts gathering like thunderheads. Her mind raced with the knowledge that they were truly alone, that there was nothing to stop the moment from escalating to its inevitable conclusion. Reyes leaned against the desk, arms crossed, a stance that belied the storm she knew must mirror her own.

"Quite the weather." He finally said, but the triviality was undone by the look in his eyes.
"Yes." She replied, unable to look away from the intensity that rooted her to the spot. Lily's thoughts spiralled, caught between fear and the raw, exhilarating pull of the moment. She was acutely

aware of him, of herself, of the thin veneer of control that threatened to shatter under the weight of the storm and their proximity.

"I guess we have nowhere to be." He added, and the casualness was too thin to disguise the truth beneath it. She shivered, though the room was warm, though everything between them was edging toward combustion. The fear of being exposed fought with her desperate need for confirmation, and the resulting chaos left her dizzy, unmoored.

The lights flickered, and for a heartbeat they were cast into darkness, into the rawness that had defined every moment between them. The sudden lack of light was both terrifying and relieving, as if now there was less to hide. Reyes moved closer, and in the dim glow of the storm, she saw the question on his face, the same question that had been her constant companion. The same question that the past weeks had asked in glances and silences and touches.

"Lily." The way he said her name was both everything and not enough.

"Yes?" She barely breathed the word, the anticipation knotting her insides. The power flickered again, leaving them in near-darkness once more. The effect was electric, and Lily knew that neither the storm nor their connection could be contained much longer. They had nowhere to go, nowhere to run. The silence grew as loud as the rain, and the certainty of it pressed down, enveloping them like the sky itself. The rain was relentless, a torrent that swallowed hesitation and filled the silence with its roar. In the dim and flickering light, Lily felt her heart's pace quicken, an urgent tempo that matched the chaos outside and inside.

"This is intense." He said, but his eyes never left her, and Lily knew he wasn't just talking about the weather.

"It is." Her voice was thin, stretched over the enormity of the moment. She felt exposed, caught in the light and the dark, in the rush of emotion that fought its way to the surface. The last session, the hesitation, the look of desperation - each thought collided with the next, and the resulting confusion was a beautiful, terrifying mess. Lily's breath stuttered, and she knew she should respond further, knew the risk of saying too much, but the intensity left her mute.

"You have no idea." He said, and there was wonder in his voice, a newness that broke through the tension. The rain crescendoed, a symphony that drowned the world outside but left the interior notes clear and unmissable. He looked at her, and Lily was caught in the immediacy of his focus, the raw truth that vibrated between them.

"I wasn't expecting," he paused, and the silence swelled with the pounding rain, "I didn't mean to—" The frustration and need were naked in his voice. She was on the edge of everything - of asking him, of telling him, but the fear knotted her tongue.

"Professor—"

"Lily I've been distracted." He stepped closer, and the proximity was a shock to her system. The honesty was like a jolt, and her heart exploded in a cacophony of hope and panic.

"Distracted." She echoed, her pulse a drumline beneath the single word. Reyes ran a hand through his hair, a gesture of frustration or longing, she couldn't be sure.

"By you." He admitted, and it was both everything and too little to hold. A sudden crash sent her reeling forward, and the sound echoed through the hallways. She found herself in his arms, her heart pounding so intensely that it made her knees feel weak.

"Stay here." His voice was soft, calming, a stark contrast to the storm brewing outside. Racing down the hallway, Reyes checked every office until he found the culprit - a tree branch had forced its way through a window creating a tangled mess of twigs and leaves and rain and chaos. He returned to office to find Lily shivering, and in an instant he was at her side.

"What happened?"

"A tree crashed through a window." He placed his hand gingerly on her arm. The space between them was a chasm and a breath. She didn't know how to cross it, but she knew she had to try. She raised her hand and placed it gently on top of his.

"Are you frightened?" His other hand found her back, his thumb gently rubbing circles on her blouse.

"I'm," her words stuttered into being, the fear and need coalescing into one reckless truth, "I've been distracted too." He was still, so still, as if her admission had stopped time. The silence surged around them, full of possibility, of fear, of the things that were always there and never said. Reyes began to speak, the relief and disbelief a tender mix on his features.

"I didn't know if—"

"Neither did I." She confessed, a rapid, breathless volley of sound and emotion. The honesty was a hurricane - a sudden, brilliant upheaval that shifted everything.

She felt the exhilarating spin of it, the way it whirled them into a new configuration, and the disorientation was thrilling, a high wind she was more than willing to ride. The office was a small, urgent world where only they existed. The storm's fury receded in the face of what they had unleashed, the tumult inside more pressing, more profound. The truth of it hung between them, a bright and unexpected tether. She felt its pull, the way it had already begun to rewrite everything she thought she knew.

"Is there anything in particular you'd like to do to pass the time?" He moved closer, so close she could feel his breath, warm and real, a counterpoint to the chill of rain and uncertainty. Lily took a small step back, sitting slightly on the desk and bracing herself on either side with her hands, her nails digging into the wood as if she could break off the edges. The storm raged on, outside and in, but they were in the eye of it now. For the first time, Lily didn't feel lost. She felt found. He stared at her lips as they quivered, though from the adrenaline or the cold air, he couldn't tell. She slowly brought her hands to her shirt, unbuttoning gradually from the top down. The gap reached her bra, and Reyes could see the distinct outline of the lace, teasing him with its inviting patterns.

"Lily—" His voice was barely above a whisper. His fists tightened at his sides, his pulse hammering in his veins so forcefully it made his entire body tremble with raw desire.

"It's just you and me," her eyes reflected the the mix of trust and fear that fuelled her, "and the storm." She slowly unclasped her bra strap, letting it fall to her wrists. It made a soft thud on the desk, and she let out a long breath as if relieved. Naked from the waist up, she picked up the loose wrapping of her shirt and threw it towards him. For a moment he just stared at where it landed on his desk, then looked back at her. She was so exposed, yet so certain.

As if on cue, the lights flickered off again. The office was dimmer now, more intimate, charged with everything that had passed between them. They stood there for a moment, taking in the atmosphere that had created a perfect storm. Reyes' heart thundered against his chest like drums in a parade band, loud and impossible to ignore. He took a slow step towards her, his hands tracing the contours of her body like he was memorising her by touch. The silence hung between them like mist over a river that had finally found its way home.

His fingers traced over her skin, leaving goosebumps in their wake. Reyes' hands moved like a thief in the night, slow and deliberate, as if he were stealing her secrets one touch at a time. His fingers brushed against her skin with a tenderness that betrayed the hunger burning in his veins. He started at her collarbone, tracing the delicate curve with the pad of his thumb, feeling the way her breath hitched as he dragged it down to the swell of her breasts. Her nipples were already hard, pebbled under his touch, and he circled one with his index finger, teasing until she shivered. He didn't rush, didn't give her the satisfaction of his urgency, and he studied her body in the same way he studied her thesis.

His hand slid down her stomach, mapping every inch of her like he was committing her to memory. He lingered at her belly button, dipping his finger inside just enough to make her squirm, before moving lower. Her pants were tight, hugging her hips like they were made for him to peel off. He unbuttoned them slowly, the sound of the zipper coming undone echoing in the dim room like a symphony. He hooked his fingers into the waistband and tugged, letting the fabric slide down her thighs inch by torturous inch. Her skin was smooth, warm, and he couldn't resist running his hands over her legs as he knelt before her, pulling the pants down to her ankles. She stepped out of them, and he let them fall to the floor, his hands already moving back up her calves, her knees, her thighs.

Her panties were next, a flimsy scrap of lace that did nothing to hide the wetness already soaking through. He hooked his thumbs into the sides and dragged them down, his breath hot against her skin as he exposed her to the cool air. He spread her legs wider, his hands gripping her thighs as he leaned in, his tongue flicking out to taste her. She was sweet, divine, and he licked her slowly, savoring every drop as he worked her with the tip of his tongue. He didn't rush, didn't give her the release she was begging for with every whimper and moan. He took his time, exploring every fold, every inch of her until she was trembling, her hands gripping the edge of the desk like it was the only thing keeping her upright.

The storm outside howled like a beast in heat, its fury a perfect mirror to the tempest raging inside the dimly lit room. Her moans were swallowed by the thunder, but the way she clawed at his hair, pulling him deeper into her, spoke volumes. His tongue was an artist, painting her with broad, wet strokes that made her back arch off the desk. He lapped at her like it was the last drop of water in the desert, his lips sealing around to suck and tease until she was writhing, her thighs clamping around his head like a vice. His fingers, thick and relentless, plunged into her, curling and stroking that sweet spot inside her with a precision that had her gasping his name.

"Julian." She whimpered, her voice trembling with need. Just as she teetered on the edge of ecstasy, he pulled back, leaving her panting and desperate. He stood, unbuttoning his pants and sliding them down his thighs with urgency as his cock sprang free, thick and throbbing, the tip glistening. She stared at it like it was the answer to every prayer she'd ever whispered, her lips parting in awe. Without a word, she spread her legs wider. He didn't make her wait. Gripping her hips, he slid into her in one slow, deliberate thrust, the heat of her enveloping him like a velvet glove. She gasped, her nails digging into his shoulders as he bottomed out, his cock stretching her to the limit. He paused, savoring the way she clenched around him, then began to move, his hips rolling in a rhythm that was both punishing and tender.

"Julian." Her moans grew louder, mingling with the storm as he fucked her with a relentless intensity. He kissed her neck, his teeth grazing her skin as he whispered into her ear.

"Call me professor." He growled, his voice rough with desire. He grabbed her hair, pulling her head back to expose her throat as he pounded into her with a force that had her screaming.

"Professor." She obeyed, her voice trembling as she repeated the word, her body shaking with the force of her impending orgasm. The desk creaked beneath them, the sound lost in the cacophony of their passion. She was a masterpiece of desperation, her body writhing, her thighs trembling as they clamped around his hips. Her thighs were soaked, dripping with need as her back arched off the desk, her breasts bouncing with every shuddering breath, her nipples hard as diamonds and begging for attention.

"Professor, professor—" She chanted over and over which only seemed to make him somehow harder inside her. Her voice broke and her body tightened like a coiled spring. She was so close, so close, and then it hit her - a wave of pleasure so intense it felt like her soul was being ripped from her body. Her orgasm crashed over her, her entire body convulsing as she came harder than she ever had in her life. The thunder raged on outside, so loud is seemed to fill the room and break her from her reverie.

"Lily," he paused as his other hand found her back, his thumb gently rubbing circles on her blouse, "are you okay?"
"I'm, I—"
"You're shaking, and you're covered in sweat. Are you frightened?" The look of concern on his face made him take a small step back. Her words stuttered into being, the fear and need coalescing into one reckless truth.
"I'm sorry," she whispered, shaking her head, "I'm perfectly fine. I don't know what came over me."
"Let's find something to distract you," he moved closer, so close she could feel his breath, warm and real, a counterpoint to the chill of rain and uncertainty, "is there anything in particular you'd like to do to pass the time? We could go over your thesis—"

"No," she interrupted, her hands steady and her voice a swell of confidence and wanting, "no, there's something else I'd like to do." He stared at her lips as they spoke, mesmerised by this new persona she had taken on - confident and demanding and assertive. Lily took a small step back, sitting slightly on the desk and bracing herself on either side with her hands, her nails digging into the wood as if she could break off the edges. A smile played across her lips as she slowly reached for the top button of her shirt.

Writer's Block

Cassie's screen glared at her, bright and damning. She tugged her sweater sleeves over her knuckles, shifting her glasses as if the problem were the view. But the problem was her. She glared back, as if stubbornness alone could will the words to life, then looked away, resisting the blank page with the same skill she used to resist emotional intimacy. Her toes curled against the hardwood, grounding her. She considered how many drafts her agent expected, probably by yesterday, and she couldn't even get a first one to cooperate. Finally, she typed. *Desmond's lips were fire against Charlotte's*. She stopped, sighed, hit delete until it was gone. A glance to her notebook and its mess of incoherent scrawl, phrases that hadn't sparked anything but doubt. The cursor blinked again. Blank. Tempting, she thought bitterly, to leave it just like that. Her agent's voice rang in her memory. Sharp, relentless.

"I want the new one even hotter, Cassie. The last book was practically chaste," and then, like a thorn in her side, "you're not losing your touch, are you?" She had promised the manuscript was almost there, an optimistic understatement. She hadn't expected the words to dry up like a southern summer. Yet here she was. As flat as yesterday's soda. Maybe she'd switch to another genre. Murder mysteries, perhaps. That was what this draft felt like - an agonizingly slow death. The chaotic post -its on her desk stared at her next, equally judgmental. *MORE HEAT*, one shouted in purple ink. *Cliché??* Another demanded. It was the extra question marks that got to her, like even the criticism wasn't quite sure where it was going.

She considered a drink. Coffee was the rational choice. Vodka, the honest one. Her fingers drummed against the desk in staccato indecision. The apartment, her so -called creative sanctuary, had turned on her. She watched rain stripe the window, each line a reminder of words unspooling on a page, except hers wouldn't. She tucked her feet beneath her on the chair, huddling into herself. At least she had writer's block down to a science, she thought with grim humor. First, she avoided. Then, she rationalised. Finally, she despaired. It should be simple. She knew the tropes, could execute them with her eyes closed. That was part of the problem - execution without execution. She needed something raw and real, but the thought of facing that truth, stripping down to vulnerability, terrified her more than the deadline itself.

She fiddled with the neck of her sweater, restless, trapped. Maybe she should just write it like the agent suggested. Add a few perfunctory moans and groans. Pretend it wasn't going to drive her insane. A plan. More lines on the screen, only to be purged in another fit of deletion. Even the keys clicked their impatience at her. She yanked off her glasses, tossed them on the desk. This was getting childish. The loft's stillness screamed at her as loudly as any doubt. Her agent had already extended the deadline once, and Cassie had nothing to show but excuses. Maybe this time she really had lost it. Her head sank into her hands, the page stark and unflinching. And for the first time in her career, she truly believed it might beat her.

She typed a sentence. *Desmond pulled Charlotte onto the bed, his hands gripping her thighs.* Her fingers flew over the keyboard, punctuated by occasional grunts of satisfaction or groans of frustration as she fought with herself to get each word perfect. *Charlotte moaned into his ear, soft and careless and deep.* Desmond and Charlotte's story unfolded before her eyes, their passion spilling onto the page in a way that left her breathless. Except that every word was trash, and she knew it. She had done it before, successfully. She had described passion in a way that had left her readers wanting more, more of Desmond and Charlotte, a sequel to her successful first novel. But she couldn't do it.

Online, the answers should have come easier, should have at least come. But Cassie surfed through forums and advice columns, as lost as if she were offline. She stared at the screen until her eyes ached, her own reflection pale and blurry behind the glare. Even after the long day of frustration, the spectre of tomorrow's blank page haunted her. Desperation flared into a click of the mouse. *Writer's Block Help,* she typed into the search bar, barely believing she was back here again. Her mouth twisted into a wry smile. Maybe that's what she should call her next book. With a stretch and a sigh, she pushed away from the desk, pacing the loft with feet that knew the path too well. Five steps to the kitchen, three back to the window. She caught a glimpse of herself in the dark glass - barefoot, oversized sweater, auburn curls an unruly mass. Cassie Monroe, chaos in progress. The keyboard called her back like a habit.

Overcome Block in 5 Steps, and *Finding Your Creative Spark!* It was a comedy routine, almost, if it weren't so fucking sad. She had tried them all, a smorgasbord of the inane and ineffectual. Nothing. She should just quit and take up pottery, she thought, as she scanned another useless blog post. The cursor blinked. The time blinked. Her inbox blinked, reminding her of the agent's last email. Just thinking about it made her coffee feel bitter. She skimmed through personal stories of miraculous breakthroughs, each one another twist of envy in her gut. A novelist who found inspiration while climbing Everest. Another who had her epiphany underwater. Cassie, in her typical way, had over -thought even the metaphors, and now they lay dead on the page.

Find a muse, said one post. Look beyond yourself, suggested another. Have an affair, a cheeky comment advised. She bit her lip, remembering the last time she'd tried for intimacy. The scars still smarted. Her hand moved to close the laptop, to abandon this useless search. As if summoned by her resignation, a new link appeared. *Looking for a Creative Muse?* The question mocked her, almost daring her to click. She hesitated. It took her to a site she didn't expect. A high -end escort service. Heat rushed to her cheeks, followed by the absurdity of it. She couldn't, wouldn't. She clicked out, back to the safety of failure.

But it was already too late. Curiosity, fierce and dangerous, bloomed in the pit of her stomach. She clicked back in, holding her breath. She scrolled the profiles with the detached interest of someone on the edge of insanity, ready to be appalled, not quite expecting to be intrigued. She could hardly believe herself. Could hardly believe them. Then one stopped her. Logan. The first picture - casual, half-smiling, tousled dark hair and a white shirt. The second more intense, full of brooding heat. Tattoos peeking out beneath the sleeves. His bio was even worse. *Actor. Improv skills. Open-minded.*

Her heart picked up speed, ridiculous and insistent. This was impossible. It was outrageous. But she couldn't tear her eyes away. Ideas swirled, dangerously tempting. She needed something hot, she needed inspiration. And there it was, on her screen, written in the reckless script of a woman at her wit's end. It was just a matter of deciding if she dared. Cassie didn't blush often, but just dialing the number brought heat to her cheeks. She nearly hung up, even after she heard his voice. Especially after she heard it.

"Logan here." There was no trace of self-consciousness. Not a hint of irony. Cassie's tongue stuck to the roof of her mouth as she sat at her desk, heart pounding like a nervous sixteen-year-old on her first date.

"Hi, um, this is—" she trailed off, wondering if she could hang up and never show her face in public again, but desperation was a cruel mistress, "I'm Cassie." The silence on the line felt like it spanned entire universes.

"Cassie," he spoke again, low and warm, "how can I help you?" She wanted to say 'you can't' and get it over with. She wanted to say 'I have no idea' because it was true. She forced herself to breathe. Focus. She tried to imagine he was one of her characters, scripted, fictional. Not a devastatingly real voice in her ear.

"Are you still there?" He didn't sound annoyed. He sounded amused. Her stomach flipped.

"Yes," she blurted out, "yes, I'm here."

"Good. So what can I do for you?" His words rolled like they had no idea she was breaking out in a sweat. A thousand responses flared and died. This was absurd. Impossible. And yet, a dangerous thrill shot through her. She told herself it was inspiration, not nerves. Or maybe a fatal mix of both.

"I wanted to see about." She hesitated, unable to say it all at once. She had never been this bad at getting to the point.

"About meeting. To talk."

"Sure. When and where?" He paused, and her heart lodged in her throat. That was it. One simple answer, and her whole world tilted. They arranged a time, a place. Cassie dropped the phone onto her bed, shaky with relief. Shaky with what felt suspiciously like anticipation. She wondered what the hell she was getting into. When the day came, she half expected she wouldn't have the nerve to show. Half expected he wouldn't, either. The café was busy, chaotic. She took a deep breath, adjusting her glasses, scanning for his face. For once, she hoped he wasn't as advertised. Hoped this would be the kind of disaster she could handle, a straightforward failure.

Then she saw him. She almost wished she hadn't. He was there, looking entirely comfortable. Like he was waiting for a friend, not an ambivalent, blocked writer with dubious intentions. He spotted her before she could consider bolting and stood to greet her, a slight grin playing on his lips. The smile didn't help her nerves one bit.

"Cassie?" He asked, though there wasn't a doubt in his mind it was her.

"Logan." She replied, unsure if she should extend a hand, a hug, or a sudden excuse to leave. He seemed to read the uncertainty in her face.

"Thanks for meeting," he said easily, waving off her awkwardness, "grab a seat?" She did, stiff and cautious, as if the chair might collapse beneath her. Logan leaned forward, his attention disarmingly direct. He wasn't just good-looking. He was charming, sincere, interested. The worst kind of combination for a woman like her.

"I've got to be honest," she began, steeling herself, "this is new territory for me."

"That's okay," he nodded, unfazed, "I like new territory." She stared, thrown by how simple he made it sound. As if people came to him with strange requests all the time. As if they probably did. Her hands twisted in her lap.

"I'm working on a book," she started, the words gaining momentum as she realized she wasn't turning back now, "and I'm stuck. Creatively."

"Right." He followed, patient, even curious.

"I thought maybe," she hesitated, every instinct warning her away, every nerve keeping her there, "if we could act out a few scenes, just for research." She bit the inside of her cheek. Waited for him to laugh or walk away. To find the whole thing ridiculous. Logan leaned back, contemplative, his eyes never leaving hers. She found herself holding her breath.

"Research." He repeated. Not a question. Not a mockery. His interest surprised her.

"It's a bit unconventional, I know."

"Unconventional is my specialty." He smiled then, a full one that spread slow and genuine. The relief was like a burst dam, but it flooded her with something else, too. Excitement. She barely registered the rest of their conversation, a flurry of details, schedules, agreements. She nodded at all the right times, or at least she hoped they were right. Before she knew it, she was back outside, wind on her face, head spinning. They had agreed to a trial session, and Logan seemed undaunted, maybe even intrigued by her proposal. But Cassie was less sure than ever. She wondered if she was making the biggest mistake of her career, or the most brilliant decision of her life.

Cassie rearranged the loft as if it were a stranger's, but even in her obsessive disarray, she couldn't figure out where he'd sit. Her heart knocked erratically, betraying the calm she tried to impose on her surroundings. A stack of books on the coffee table, shifted three inches to the left. Two identical mugs, just in case he drank coffee. The café table she'd set up seemed absurdly small in the wide, open space, but not as absurd as the prospect of him walking through the door. She'd almost called to cancel three times. She'd almost called a fourth when the doorbell rang.

She froze. It could have been anyone. It could have been a miracle. It could have been a nightmare. But it was Logan, and if he heard the way her heart pounded against her ribs, he didn't mention it. She answered the door with what she hoped passed for composure. He stood there with his easy smile, tousled hair, and eyes that seemed to know far too much. More tattoos than she remembered, and much tighter jeans.

"Hi." He said. One word and she almost forgot how to reply. Before she could compose a coherent sentence, she found herself blurting out the first thing that came to mind.
"Coffee."

"Excuse me?" A smile crept across his face, amused by her anxiety and awkwardness.

"Coffee," she repeated, trying to cling to coherence, "I made a fresh pot. Um, please come in." It was surreal. He moved through the space like he'd been there before, while she lingered by the door, unsure of what to do with her hands or her nerves. She shut it quickly, trapping them in together. The apartment shrank, her world along with it.

"This is great." He said, gesturing to the loft, the view, the life she pretended was organized.

"Oh, thanks." She didn't know why she was so flustered. She'd invited him. She'd started this whole ridiculous venture. He watched her, waiting, an amused curve to his lips.

"It's usually more of a mess," she continued, her hands fluttering like nervous birds, "I mean, more of a different mess."

"Glad I'm not the only one." He gave her a look that made her stomach flip.

"Yes, right." She wondered if it was a line. It was hard to tell. They stood there, an awkward silence stretching between them, each second threatening to snap her resolve. The weight of expectation was almost too much, until he picked up the thread again.

"So, what's the plan?"

"The plan," she repeated it like a lifeline, "right, the plan."

"We could, um, start with the café scene?" She gestured to the setup she'd obsessed over. Logan nodded, completely unfazed, more composed than she would ever be.

"Just tell me what you need." He stood close, smelling of warm, musky cologne, a hint of freshly cut wood, and a faint trace of cigarette smoke. *Tell me what you need*. She wondered how she was supposed to do that when she didn't even know.

"We're strangers," she explained, every word feeling like an apology, "meeting in a café. I thought it might be good to, you know, start simple." He grinned.

"Simple's good," his gaze locked onto hers, a challenge and a promise, "ready when you are." She was never going to be ready, but she nodded anyway, her mouth suddenly dry.

"Let's, uh—" It was ridiculous. She felt like an impostor in her own loft. He moved to the small table, pulling out a chair. The scrape of it against the floor set her nerves jangling. She followed, taking a seat across from him. It was intimate. It was terrifying.

"You can stop me anytime." He offered, reading her mind. No, she couldn't. Not after he'd agreed to this. Not after he'd shown up. Logan leaned forward, slipping effortlessly into character, slipping effortlessly into her thoughts.

"Hi." He whispered, tilting his head like he'd known her forever, like he hadn't just met her. Cassie blinked.

"Hi," she whispered, finding it hard to maintain her minute semblance of composure, "can I help you with something?"

"I saw you from outside," he continued, his voice a perfect blend of curiosity and intrigue, "I couldn't help but come in to talk to you." His intensity caught her off guard. She almost broke, almost laughed, but his sincerity held her in place. This wasn't a game. It was a scene. A scene she needed.

"Really," she managed, finding the line somewhere inside herself, "do you do this a lot?"

"Only when I can't help it." He smiled, genuine and infuriatingly attractive. Cassie's heart skipped, though she told herself it was only the dialogue.

"You look like the kind of woman who doesn't need to be noticed," Logan said, "and like the kind who hates that she was." She'd written the line. She'd forgotten she'd written it. Hearing him say it did strange things to her, made her breath catch, made her face flush.

"Is that your way of asking me out?" She asked, more breathless than intended.

"Depends," his eyes locked onto hers, unflinching, undoing, "are you going to say yes?" Cassie's world slipped away for a moment. The loft, the agent's deadline, her stubborn fears. It felt real, so much more than the mechanical scenes she'd been stuck in. They lingered, the tension almost a tangible thing. He held her gaze like a dare.

"Yes." She said finally, and the release of the word sent a shiver through her. He let it hang there. The power of it. The promise.

"Cassie," Logan broke through, shattering the suspended moment with abrupt clarity, "what's the book about?" She stared, her heart in her throat, stunned that the spell had been so easily dissolved, anxious that it meant this new world they'd created wasn't as solid as it seemed. She'd said yes. She'd let the word fly between them like a promise, and now here he was, casual, unfazed, asking questions like it hadn't been the most intense moment of her life. Asking questions like it hadn't shattered something crucial in her.

"The book." She blinked, suddenly unsure of how to answer, his gaze expectant, amused. The scene had been so real, more real than anything she'd written or lived, and now she wasn't sure where to go from here, what to say, how to move past a line she thought she'd never cross. The uncertainty gnawed at her, but Logan sat with the same infuriating satisfaction, as if all of this was exactly what he'd intended. As if he knew everything she didn't about herself, and had known it all along.

"Yes," he smiled, "your book."

"It's a sequel. Desmond and Charlotte. They—" She trailed off, her words catching in her throat as if the sudden admission was forbidden. But people had loved it, and it's why she was writing a second one.

"It's kind of romantic, but basically porn," the truth, loud and clear, came from her with all the confidence she knew how to muster, "the first one was a hit. My agent says there's been some interest in turning it into a TV show, but only if I can get the sequel right. They want more—"

"Sex." Logan interjected, the glimmer in his eye reading her as if she was an open book.

"Yes," Cassie replied quickly, sinking back into her chair, "the first one was romantic, with a bit of raunchiness to it. It finished with Desmond and Charlotte parting ways. My agent wants more sex, more fire, more—"

"And you need help with that?" Logan mirrored her, leaning back into the chair with a casual ease that left Cassie feeling unsure.

"Cassie," Logan suddenly leaned forward, peering at her with his dark eyes, "I think you need help of a different nature."

"Oh?"

"Stories are easy. Conversation flows naturally. I think you need help with some of the scenes you're afraid to write." He had barely scraped the surface, and yet somehow he was reading into her thoughts as if she had given him the manuscript to her life. Her first book had come so naturally, so at ease based on her experiences. Love, devotion, a whirlwind romance that had swept her off her feet. Late night dates and spontaneous adventures wrapped up in long evenings of sex and pleasure. But it had been mundane. It had been safe. And then it was over, and she knew how to write the heartbreak too.

She had no idea how long they sat, suspended in that strange, wonderful place. All she knew was she didn't want it to end. And then it did, the silence echoing as loudly as the words had. She didn't know whether to thank him or kick him out, but her mind raced with more possibilities than it had in months. Logan stood, that infuriating smile still in place. He was a great muse, that much was certain, but not in the way she had intended. He had inspired her, mildly, yet it was enough for now.

"Shall we do this again?" He asked, halfway to the door. Cassie nodded, her voice barely working.
"I'll let you know." The door closed, and she was left with only the memory of the scene and the rush of inspiration it gave her. She sat at her laptop, unable to type fast enough, unable to remember why she'd been blocked at all. Cassie wasn't used to being this inspired, wasn't used to feeling this alive. And she definitely wasn't used to opening the door for men like Logan. Yet here she was, the keys of her laptop hot beneath her fingertips, words pouring out of her like they'd been waiting, like they'd been denied.

It was exhilarating. It was terrifying. It was nothing short of a revelation. Her agent would think she was possessed, and she was looking forward to the disbelief. To being the woman who shocked everyone, herself most of all. She set a pace that left even her breathless. If the agent thought her steamy manuscript was nowhere near finished, he was right. But the joke was on him now. Their sessions continued, each one more intense than the last. Each one chipping away at her resolve, exposing the parts of her she pretended didn't exist. Logan was due any minute, and she should have known by then what to expect. Should have, but didn't. He rang the bell and she answered with more composure than she felt, her confidence rattling around inside her like a trapped bird.

"Any sex scenes you want to act out today?" He asked, and she loved and hated that he assumed it would happen, that she couldn't bring herself to correct him. He put her at ease, joking around in a way that made her laugh like she hadn't in a long time.

"I was thinking the bookshop meeting," she said as he followed her inside, "Cassie is still reeling from the breakup and she's in a bookstore trying to fill the void with a new novel."

"Cassie?"

"Charlotte," she suddenly corrected herself, feeling a flush of red wash over her cheeks, "Charlotte is the one still reeling from the breakup. I'm Cassie."

"I know," he laughed, setting onto the couch and leaning back into it, "you need to relax, Cassie. You have nothing to be nervous about." She didn't know why, but he seemed to fill the space with the weight of his presence, the lightness of his stride.

"I have plenty to be nervous about." She caught a glimpse of his full lips as he smiled, wondering what they would taste like before shaking the thought from her mind. They got right into it. The air between them electric and uncertain. Cassie knew she was in trouble the moment they began. Logan added new lines, a knowing smile tugging at his lips as he did.

"The first edition of Pride and Prejudice," he said, lifting an imaginary book from an imaginary shelf, "I didn't know anyone read that anymore."

"Some of us are old-fashioned." She replied, sticking to the script, but only barely. The heat rose in her cheeks.

"The best things are." He stepped closer, his voice low. Cassie's pulse quickened, the words a tangible thing, the world a blur. He kept at it, relentless. It was suddenly too warm, too close. Her heart thundered in her ears. She didn't remember writing this intensity. Didn't remember feeling it until now. He was there, so completely there. She wasn't sure where the script ended and she began.

"Can I buy you a coffee?" He asked, the simple line making her skin prickle with its boldness, its potential. She stumbled over the next sentence, getting tangled up in the desire she refused to name. The loft felt too small, too charged. The look he gave her sent a thrill through her. It took everything she had not to call the scene, not to break under the weight of his gaze. It wasn't supposed to feel like this. This intense. This overwhelming. She felt embarrassment and exhilaration all at once. It was hard to know where one ended and the other began. When they finished, she felt like she'd run a marathon, heart pounding, breath unsteady. Her fingers itched to get the words down before they vanished. But Logan was still there, watching, waiting. She couldn't send him off yet. She didn't want to.

"I know our time's up," he said with a casual smile that sent shivers down her spine, "but admittedly I am having fun. It's not often people pay for my time to act out scenes from a book."

"It's not a book yet," she quipped, moving to her laptop and opening the screen, "but I need to get these ideas down before they vanish."

"I'll tell you what," he stood, his voice smooth and confident, each word carefully chosen, "you need to eat, as do I. Why don't I go grab us some dinner while you write, then we can eat and continue with our next session tonight."

"Tonight?" Her surprise was written all over her face, shock and disbelief at the notion that he wanted to stay.

"Any preference?" Logan stood tall and lean, his posture relaxed and confident.

"I'm not picky," she bit her lip, glancing between Logan and her laptop, "are you sure?" His dark hair was tousled yet perfectly styled, and his deep eyes were both intense and playful. He smirked as he left the loft without saying another word, the door clicking shut with a finality to it that made her jump. She didn't have much time, and not wanting to lose her thoughts, she got stuck into her notes, her fingers flying across the keyboard like they were possessed. And before she knew it he was back, knocking at her door with demand.

"That was quick." She breathed, letting him in urgently, the need to continue her story becoming more rampant, more imperative.

"I was gone for two hours," he held up both hands, one carrying a paper bag that wafted the smells of delicious food, the other holding a black duffel bag, "I figured if we're gonna spend the night banging out your book, I might as well grab a few things."

"Cute," she pushed him in and closed the door, "what did you get?"

"The best Chinese in town," he set the bag on the table, "now sit down, finish your notes, and I'll fix you a plate."

She watched him as he slowly made himself at home, kicking off his shoes and going through her kitchen as if he had just moved in. But he had, she thought, he had moved into her life so easily and this night, this one perfect night was going to ensure she met her deadline. They moved on, every minute ramping up the stakes, every second drawing her in deeper. She let herself get swept away by it, helpless and reckless and wanting more. And finally another scene, the one she had been dreading - a stolen kiss at a party. He played his part too well. His eyes locked onto hers, the words an unnecessary formality between them.

"I can't do this." She told him, her voice breaking on the line, a tremor in the facade. He closed the distance, placing a gentle hand on her arm.

"Do what?"

"The kiss," she pursed her lips together, "it's too—"

"Do I need to brush my teeth or something?" His laugh was deep and infectious, making her own nerves melt away.

"No, it's not you," she laughed in return, feeling her walls melting slowly, "I just feel like it's too impersonal."

"Between us?" Logan stepped closer and she imagined his lips tasted like coffee and tobacco, a mix of sweetness and bitterness that was irresistible.

"Here," he said, taking her notes from her hands and throwing them on the couch, "we need an icebreaker."

"We do?" Cassie watched her notes flap and fly in the air, landing on the couch with a decisive thud.

"Is this okay?" His lips barely brushed hers, but the impact left her reeling.

"Yes." She nodded, and leaned into him slightly. If she closed her eyes she could imagine it was Desmond, her beloved character coming to life, or the new love interest she had yet to name. She felt the heat of his body, the softness of his lips. And then she couldn't imagine anything else. Their kiss was everything she had wanted, everything she had been missing. It was real and raw, messy and perfect all at once. She leaned into him, feeling safe for the first time in months. Logan slid his hand into her hair, pulling her closer still, and she melted into him without a second thought.

"Are you okay with that?" He whispered against her lips as they parted. Cassie nodded, unable to speak, unable to find the words for what she felt in that moment. He stepped back and looked at her with a new intensity, his gaze searching every inch of her face before he smiled slowly.

"Good," he nodded towards the laptop on the table beside them, "now let's get back to work." But Cassie called for a break, though it was more like a lifeline. The air felt too thick. Her senses felt too raw.

"Coffee?" He asked, back to the calm, composed Logan who seemed to get a thrill out of rattling her. She nodded, silent, desperate for the respite. The mugs felt good against her hands, something solid to cling to while she wrote down her notes for the kiss, for the feeling that had bore itself into her stomach. Then they talked, stilted at first. The words eventually flowed, mirroring the rest of her life. Her work, her heart, both dangerously open to him.

"So how's it going?" He asked. She knew he meant the writing, but it felt like so much more.

"Amazing," she admitted, hating how she needed this, hating how she loved that she did, "you've been a huge help."

"I hope so," his laugh filled the room, the casual and light tone to it making her feel easier still, "or else I'm out of a job."

"I'm sure you have other job opportunities lined up when we're finished here."

"Not really," he remarked, raising an eyebrow at her, "I was taking a break from all of it when you called." He was so disarming that she forgot to be nervous. Almost forgot to be in control. She reminded herself that this was a job, that he was hired for a role, nothing more.

"So why'd you accept my job proposition?"

"Something in your voice—"

"Desperation?"

"No," he laughed, "something in the way you sounded, like you needed help. Really needed help. I'm hired for sex, Cassie. Appearances on someone's arm and a good time afterward. When we met and you were talking about your book, it was different. Something new. I wanted to be a part of that." His charm was intoxicating, but something else had replaced his usual smug demeanour. She saw a glimmer of vulnerability. Something she hadn't seen yet. And then he stood, breaking the spell.

Back to roleplay, and he was there again, new lines, new energy. He caught her by surprise, leaving her breathless, leaving her wordless.

Cassie fought for control but found herself spiraling further each time. They broke character, often too fast, sometimes too slow. He asked if she was okay, and she told him yes, because more than okay was the truth, and she couldn't admit that. Not yet. Another scene, an argument. They held each other's gaze across the dining table that seemed to disappear. Voices rose and tension built, one line, one look, until she was dizzy. She knew the characters had names, but she forgot them each time he touched her hand.

"I'm gonna take a shower, if that's okay," he stepped closer, and the proximity was as breathtaking as it was terrifying, "are there any shower scenes you need to visualise?" She shook her head, swallowing the lump that had formed in her throat.

"Not that I can think of." She whispered.

"You should write down your notes then," he shrugged, the gesture effortless, a shrug that had its own intentions, "feel free to join me if you change your mind." Cassie wrote furiously, the pages flying out in fits of passion. She couldn't remember being this inspired. She couldn't remember wanting anything so much, and she couldn't remember being so afraid of it.

The props were supposed to help, but Cassie stared at the tangled ties and wondered if anything could keep this contained. One blue, one red, like she was color-coding the absurdity. The half-empty bottle of wine seemed more honest than either of them, more of an admission that this was going to be as reckless as she feared. She sighed, rearranging her courage more than the items. She found herself laughing, though she wasn't sure why, though she wasn't sure if it was because of him or in spite of him. Logan glanced at the ties, and she felt their gaze as if they had eyes. He picked one up, fingering it with a look that made her cheeks heat. She busied herself with the other, tying it around her wrist, around her sensibilities.

"I guess this is the scene you were waiting for." She explained, trying to sound like she was confident, trying to sound like she believed in herself.

"I should be doing that," his grin widened, an open door, an invitation, "but are you sure you want to jump straight into that?"

"What?"

"Bondage?" It was both a statement and an explosion. Logan's eyes were filled with amusement and intrigue.

"What would you suggest?"

"I think we should improvise." His hands grazed her arms, a casual touch that sent a tremor through her, a shiver that echoed. She almost forgot herself. Cassie's heart raced. The loft shrank to nothing. The props vanished, unnecessary, meaningless. Her stomach fluttered. Improvisation meant loss of control. Improvisation meant him.

"Just don't go too off-script." She cautioned, already feeling herself careening away from it.

"No promises." Logan said, his eyes lighting a fire under the words. The loft shrank further, and she felt his eyes on her now, scrutinising her, assessing her worth as a worthy companion in the bedroom.

"I don't know where to start." She admitted, her body hot and her cheeks red.

"Let me," he took a step closer, in nothing but a pair of jocks after his shower, "what do you need help with describing?"

"The feeling." She whispered, the words barely escaping her lips. She was aware of everything, the beat of her heart, the heat on her skin.

"That's specific." He laughed, a gesture that made her more at ease, more ready to fall into the next moment.

"I'm serious," she insisted, but her tone lacked the authority to convince him it was a demand, "I'm not sure how to put it into words."

"Why don't we try something different," his eyes searched her face, finding something there that made him sweep her up again, "something you haven't done before."

"Like what?" She was breathless, a confession that was as embarrassing as it was liberating.

"Whatever you want," Logan encouraged, watching her reaction, "I'm the one hired to help, remember?" She nodded, trying to convince herself that he wasn't the only one in too deep.

"Well," she breathed in deeply, bracing herself for what she was about to say, "I suppose I could play around with—"

"Play around," he cut her off with a grin, "that sounds dirty already."

"Not that," she laughed nervously, "but something to shake things up." He raised an eyebrow, inviting her to continue.

"You know, maybe an unlikely circumstance." She was trying to plan, trying to control the way her heart was pacing.

"You can't hold me accountable for what happens." His words were heavy with anticipation. "Something unexpected."

"Like?" The challenge in his voice was just what she needed to go further, to let herself go.

"Well," she hesitated, but only for a second, "clearly I had the bondage idea laid out but you didn't want to start with that." His eyes widened, and she wondered if he was surprised or amused.

"Here," he whispered, taking the cheap blindfold off the table, clearly unused and purchased for the sake of a prop, "try this." He gently took off her glasses, placing them gingerly on the table, and removed her jumper, letting it fall in a heap on the floor. Slowly, every so slowly, he placed the blindfold over her eyes, letting the elastic hit the back of her head lightly with a snap.

"Ow." She whispered, disoriented in the dark. Cassie raised her hand to touch her hair but he grabbed it, holding it above her head.

"What do you feel?" He whispered gently in her ear. She could almost hear his grin, feel the curve of his mouth in the way he asked her.

"What do you mean?"

"Don't touch your hair, don't ruin the sensation from the elastic with your fingers," Logan pulled her close, his breath warm against her cheek, "describe the snap to me. How it feels, physically, metaphorically. You're a writer, use your words." She was silent, aware of her pulse, of his fingers wrapped around her wrist, of the quiet that enveloped them.

"Uh," she stalled, working through it in her mind, trying to decide how much was fiction, how much was real, "sharp at first. And then like everything else is blurry." He hugged her tighter, the motion nearly lifting her from the ground, nearly making her forget to breathe. Logan's voice was low, a gravelly purr that slithered down her spine like a serpent coiling around its prey.

"I can work with that." He said, his breath hot against her ear as he kept her hand pinned above her head, her wrist trapped in his iron grip. She could feel the heat of his body pressing into her, the hard ridge of his cock already straining against the fabric of his jocks, begging for release. His other hand trailed down her arm, fingertips brushing over her skin like a match striking against flint, leaving sparks in their wake.

"Tell me what you feel." He demanded, his voice a dark command that brooked no argument. His lips grazed the shell of her ear, teeth nipping at the sensitive flesh, and she shivered, her breath hitching in her throat.

"I feel," she whispered, her voice trembling as his fingers dipped lower, skimming the curve of her waist, teasing the hem of her tank top, "I feel your hands." His touch was electric, sending jolts of pleasure through her body, pooling low in her belly.

"And how does that make you feel?" He growled, his lips trailing down her neck, leaving a trail of wet, open-mouthed kisses that made her knees weak. His tongue flicked out, tasting her skin, and she moaned softly, her head falling back to give him better access.

"It feels good." She breathed, her voice barely audible over the sound of her own heartbeat pounding in her ears. His hand slipped under her jumper, his fingers brushing against the soft fabric of her bra, and she gasped, her nipples hardening instantly under his touch.

"Good?" He repeated, his voice dripping with mockery as he circled her, his body moving with the predatory grace of a wolf. He grabbed her wrists, pulling them behind her back with one hand, holding her in place as his other hand slid lower over her stomach, slipping between the waistband of her pants. His fingers teased at the edge of her panties, brushing against the damp fabric, and she whimpered, her hips bucking involuntarily against his hand.

"If you describe the physical touch one more time, I'm going to stop," he warned, his voice a low growl that sent shivers down her spine as his fingers pressed harder against her clit, the pressure just enough to make her ache for more, "do you want me to stop?"

"No," she gasped, her voice desperate as she shook her head, her body trembling with need, "please, don't stop."

"Then tell me how it makes you feel," he demanded, his lips brushing against her ear as he spoke, his breath hot and heavy against her skin, "in your soul, in your stomach, in your pussy." His words were filthy, crude, and they sent a wave of heat crashing through her, making her clench around nothing, her body begging for him to fill her. She laughed nervously, the sound shaky and breathless, and he bit down on her neck, his teeth sinking into her skin just hard enough to make her cry out.

"Tell me," he growled, his voice rough with desire as his fingers slipped under the edge of her panties, brushing against her lips, "how does it make you feel?"

"Alive," she moaned, her voice breaking as his fingers dipped lower, teasing her, "it makes me feel like I'm on fire." Her hips rocked against his hand, desperate for more, and he chuckled darkly, his fingers sliding inside her with a slow, deliberate thrust.

"Good girl," he purred, his lips brushing against her ear as he worked his fingers in and out of her, the wet sound of her arousal filling the air, "now tell me what you want."

"I want you," she gasped, her body trembling as he added a second finger, stretching her, filling her, "I want you inside me."

"Good," he growled, his voice rough with need as he curled his fingers inside her, "now go write."

"What?" Her voice hitched as he let go of her hands, removing the blindfold and setting it on the table.

"Before it leaves your head, write about this," he sat across from her place on the table, staring at the back of her laptop, "show me that you've made notes, and then I'll give you more." She sat quickly, typing furiously as he gazed at her over the top of her screen. She caught a glimpse of him, smelling his fingers as he watched her write.

"Describe that to me." Cassie stared between his face and the screen with the same, infuriating sense of delight. Logan leaned back in his chair, his fingers still glistening with her, the scent of her clinging to his skin like a brand. He brought them to his nose, inhaling deeply, letting her flood his senses. It wasn't just the tang of her arousal, though that was there - sharp and musky, a primal call. No, it was something deeper, something that made his gut tighten and his balls ache. Her pheromones were a drug, and he was already addicted.

"It's earthy, almost sweet," he licked his fingers slowly, deliberately, savoring the taste of her, "but not the kind of sweet you read about in dirty books. It's musky, slightly salty, but mostly just like flesh and sweat." His tongue swirled around the tips of his fingers, lapping up every drop, every trace of her. He could feel her watching him, her breath hitching as she typed, her fingers trembling on the keys. He didn't need to see her face to know she was blushing, her cheeks flushed with a mix of embarrassment and desire.

"Describe it," he said, his voice low and rough, like gravel dragging over silk, "describe it like a writer." Cassie hesitated, her fingers pausing over the keyboard. She glanced up at him, her eyes dark with need, her lips parted.

"The essence," she started, her voice shaky and hesitant, "a mixture of desire, pleasure and sweat, and release. Hot and sticky." Logan smirked, his eyes never leaving hers.

"Go on."

""It's, it's like," she swallowed hard, her throat working as she tried to find the words, "like the first sip of whiskey. It burns, but you can't stop. You want more. You need more."

"And what does it make you feel?" He leaned forward, resting his elbows on the table, his gaze intense. Cassie's breath hitched again, her chest rising and falling rapidly.

"It makes me wet," she admitted, her voice barely above a whisper, "it makes me want you. All of you." Logan's smirk widened, his eyes narrowing in on her.

"Good," he growled, "now keep writing." She nodded, her fingers flying over the keys as she tried to capture the moment, the sensations, the raw need that was coursing through both of them. Logan watched her, his eyes dark with lust, his fingers still tingling with the memory of touching her. He leaned back again, his hand drifting to his jocks. He could feel the heat of her gaze on him, could see the way her body trembled with anticipation. He didn't need to touch her to know she was dripping, her panties soaked through, her pussy clenching around nothing.

"Keep going," he urged, his voice rough with need, "don't stop." Cassie nodded again, her fingers moving faster, the sound of the keys clicking filling the room. Logan's hand moved to his waistband, adjusting it slowly, his eyes never leaving hers. He could feel the tension in the air, the electricity between them crackling like a live wire. He pulled his cock out, stroking himself slowly, his eyes locked on hers.

"Describe this," he said, his voice low and dangerous, "tell me what you see." Cassie's breath hitched, her eyes widening as she took in the sight of him. He was thick and hard, the veins standing out against the flushed skin. precum beaded at the tip, glistening in the dim light.

"It's," she stammered, her voice trembling, "it's big."

"Big?" Logan smirked, placing it back underneath the fabric. He stood, circling her slowly until he stood behind her, leaning down and breathing into her ear.

"What did I tell you about using your words?" His presence was intoxicating, the loft charged with a tension that buzzed against her skin, under it, through it. Cassie's breath caught in her throat, her body trembling with need.

"I—"

"Big isn't good enough." Logan's voice was a low growl, a rumble that vibrated through Cassie's bones like an earthquake. The loft was thick with the scent of him - sweat, musk, and something darker, primal, that made her clench in anticipation.

"Use your words." He demanded, his tone sharp enough to cut glass. His eyes burned into hers, a wildfire that threatened to consume her whole. Cassie's breath hitched, her lips parting as she struggled to form a coherent thought.

"You're going to describe it properly. No shortcuts. No lazy fucking words." He sneered, his voice dripping with disdain, his body towering over her. Before she could protest, he spun her chair around with a rough jerk, the wheels screeching against the floor. Cassie's heart pounded in her chest as she gasped, her pulse racing as he dropped his jocks in one swift motion.

"Logan—"

"Touch it." He commanded, his voice a dark promise. Cassie hesitated for a fraction of a second before reaching out, her fingers trembling as they brushed against him. The heat of him was overwhelming, the skin smooth and hot under her touch. She wrapped her hand around him, her fingers barely able to meet, and gave a tentative stroke. Logan let out a low groan, his hips jerking forward as if he couldn't help himself.

"Describe it," he growled, his voice rough with need, "tell me what it feels like." Cassie swallowed hard, her mouth dry as she tried to find the words.

"It's," she started, her voice barely above a whisper, "thick. Like steel wrapped in velvet."

"Better," Logan's lips curled into a smirk, his eyes dark with satisfaction, "now taste it." Her eyes widened, but she didn't dare disobey. She leaned forward, her tongue darting out to lick a stripe along the underside of his cock. The taste of him exploded on her tongue - salty, musky, and utterly intoxicating. She moaned softly, her lips wrapping around the head as she took him into her mouth.

"Fuck," Logan hissed, his hands tangling in her hair as he guided her movements, "that's it." Cassie pulled back, her lips slick with spit and precum.

"Salty," she breathed, her voice trembling, "slightly bitter. Warm and slippery." Logan chuckled darkly, his fingers tightening in her hair.

"Good," he murmured, "now stroke it. Watch me. Feel me." Her hand moved along it, her fingers sliding over the slick skin as she worked him. She could feel the way his balls tightened with every stroke, the way his cock pulsed in her hand like a heartbeat. Logan's breath came in ragged gasps, his hips thrusting into her grip as he fought to keep control.

"Write it down," he ordered, his voice rough with need, "every fucking detail." Cassie reached for a notepad on the desk, one hand still wrapped around his cock as she fumbled for a pen with the other. Her writing was shaky, but she managed to scribble out the words, her mind racing with the sensations coursing through her body. She could fix the notes later, she didn't have time to refine everything in the moment.

"Thick," she said aloud as she wrote, her hands trembling as she stroked him, "hot, hard. Veins pulsing under my fingers. I can feel every ridge, every curve. His balls are tight, heavy with need, and I can't stop thinking about how he'll feel inside me when he fucks me." Logan let out a low growl, his hips jerking forward as he read over her shoulder.

"Keep going," he urged, his voice thick with desire, "tell me more." Cassie's hand moved faster, her strokes becoming more confident as she continued to write and read aloud.

"The taste of him is addictive," she scrawled, her words barely legible, "salty and bitter, but I can't get enough. I want to swallow him whole, feel him pulsing in my throat as he comes." Logan's breath hitched, his hands gripping the edge of the desk as he fought to keep control.

"Fuck," he muttered, "you're gonna be the death of me." Cassie looked up at him, her eyes dark with desire.

"Then let me finish you." She whispered, her voice trembling with need.

"Not yet." He pulled her to her feet, spinning her around and bending her over the table in one swift motion. His cock pressed against her thighs, the tip teasing her as he leaned down to whisper in her ear.

"You're going to feel every fucking inch of me," he whispered, his voice a dark promise, "and you're going to write about it. But we're not done yet." Cassie moaned softly, her body trembling with anticipation. He knelt before her, his breath hot against her skin as he undid the knot of her sweatpants with a single, practiced tug. The fabric slid down her legs, pooling at her ankles like a discarded second skin, leaving her bare except for the flimsy scrap of lace clinging to her hips. Logan's fingers were like wildfire, slow and deliberate, tracing the curve of her thighs with a hunger that made her breath hitch. The room was thick with the scent of arousal, a heady mix of sweat and something sweet, something primal.

"How do you feel?" He murmured, his voice low and rough. She didn't answer with words, her fingers moving across the notepad in quick, jerky strokes, the pen scratching against the paper like a desperate plea. Logan didn't need to read it to know what she was feeling. He could see it in the way her thighs trembled, in the way her hips twitched, begging for his touch. He started with her calves, his lips brushing against the soft, delicate skin there, leaving a trail of kisses that burned like brands. His hands slid higher, gripping her thighs, spreading them wider as he moved up, inch by torturous inch. His teeth grazed the inside of her thigh, and she gasped, her pen slipping from her fingers as her back arched. He didn't stop. He couldn't. His mouth found the edge of her panties, and he bit down, tugging the lace down with his teeth, exposing her to the cool air of the room.

She was glistening, slick, begging for his attention. Logan groaned, the sound low and guttural, as he pressed his face against her, inhaling her like it was the only thing keeping him alive. His tongue flicked out, tasting her, and she moaned, her hips bucking against his mouth. But she didn't stop writing, even as he buried his hand between her legs, even as his fingers worked her into a frenzy. She reached for the notepad, her hands shaking as she scribbled something illegible. Logan didn't care what it said. He was too busy drowning in her, his fingers sliding inside her with a groan. She was so tight, so wet, and he could feel her clenching around him, desperate for more.

"Fuck," he growled against her thigh, his voice muffled by her flesh, "you're so goddamn wet for me." He added another finger, stretching her, fucking her with his hand as he bit her skin. She was writhing now, her hips grinding against his hand, her moans filling the room. He could feel her getting closer, her body tightening, her breath coming in short, ragged gasps. But he wasn't done with her yet. Not even close. He pulled back, leaving her trembling and desperate, and stood.

"Write." He demanded, his voice rough. She didn't speak, she couldn't, but her eyes said everything. She wanted him. All of him.

Cassie pulled herself into her chair, wheeling closer to the table, clenching her thighs as she scrambled to collect her thoughts. Her fingers flew over the keys as she tried to capture the moment, the sensations, the raw need that was coursing through both of them. Logan watched her, his eyes dark with lust, his cock throbbing in his hand. He could feel the tension in the air, the electricity between them crackling like a live wire. He knew it was only a matter of time before he couldn't take it anymore, before he had to have her. But for now, he would let her write. And when she was done, he would give her more. So much more. She closed her laptop screen with a snap, more aggressively than she meant to.

"Fuck me," she stood, her voice desperate as she sat back on the table, her body on the edge of release, "please, Logan, fuck me." Logan didn't need to be begged again. He grabbed her hips, lifting her off the ground and slamming her against the wood. Her legs wrapped around his waist, and he thrust into her in one brutal stroke, burying himself to the hilt. She cried out, her nails digging into his shoulders as he fucked her hard and fast, his hips slamming into hers with a rhythm that left them both gasping for air.

Her pussy was like a vice, squeezing him so tight he thought he might lose his mind. He could feel her coming undone around him, her body trembling as she clung to him, her moans growing louder with every thrust. He wasn't going to last much longer, the teasing and playing they had done for hours, and she was too perfect, too tight. She wasn't like his usual clients, she had been different, everything had been different, and he had enjoyed it so much the whole experience had been foreplay to him. He wasn't going to stop until she had come undone, until she was screaming his name.

"What do you feel?" He thrust into her, filling her completely. The sensation was overwhelming, the stretch and burn sending shivers down her spine. She reached for the notebook, her hand trembling as she tried to write through the pleasure coursing through her body.

"I can't write." She moaned, her body trembling. He scrambled for her phone, demanding that she unlock it. He opened her voice notes, slamming it onto the table as he pressed record.

"Say it," he leaned into her, his strong arms holding her back, pulling her into him, "scream it."

"He's inside me," she gasped, her words barely audible, "thick and hard, filling me completely. I can feel every inch of him, every pulse of his cock as he fucks me. It's too much, but I don't want it to stop." Logan's hips snapped forward, pushing her further onto the table.

"That's it," he purred, his lips brushing against her neck pushed into her, "tell me how it makes you feel." His voice was rough as he pressed into her, inch by agonizing inch, his breathing becoming rough and staggered.

"It makes me feel warm and numb," she could feel the heat of him, the urgency, the implication, "my hips are sore but I don't want to stop moving." The air was thick, heavy with the scent of sweat and sex, a heady cocktail that made her head spin. She could feel him, every inch of him, pressing into her, filling her up in ways that made her toes curl and her breath hitch. His hands were rough, calloused fingers digging into the soft flesh of her hips, leaving marks that would bruise later, a reminder of this moment, this heat, this need.

"My body, it's on fire," she could feel the slickness between her thighs, the way she clenched around him, greedy for more, always more, "every nerve ending in me is alight with a desperate, aching hunger." His cock was a relentless force, driving into her with a rhythm that was both punishing and perfect. She was close, the tension coiling tight in her belly, a spring wound to the breaking point. Her breath came in short, ragged gasps, her nails raking down his back, leaving angry red trails in their wake. She could feel the sweat dripping down her spine, the way her hair clung to her forehead, damp and messy.

"That's your orgasm," he growled, his voice dark and possessive as he began to move, his hips slamming into hers with a force that made her cry out, "let it happen. Don't control it."

"It's in my toes. My muscles are cramping."

"Let it happen."

"My stomach—"

"Let it happen," he commanded, "come for me."

"Don't stop," she begged, her voice a hoarse whisper, barely audible over the sound of skin slapping against skin, "please, don't stop." He growled in response, a low, guttural sound that sent shivers down her spine. His hands moved to her ass, gripping her tight, lifting her up so he could plunge even deeper, hitting a spot that made her cry out, a sound that was half pleasure, half pain. She could feel it building, that delicious pressure, the kind that made her whole body tremble, her muscles tightening, her pussy clenching around him like a vice. She was on the edge, teetering, the world narrowing down to just this moment, just him, just the way he filled her, the way he made her feel.

And then it hit her, a wave of pleasure so intense it was almost unbearable, crashing over her, pulling her under. She came with a scream, her body convulsing. He followed her over the edge, his own release hot and thick inside her, filling her up in a way that made her shudder with pleasure. They collapsed together, a tangled mess of limbs and sweat on the table, their breathing ragged, their hearts pounding. She could still feel him inside her, his cock slowly softening, but she didn't want to move, didn't want to let go. Not yet. Not ever.

"Fuck," he muttered, his voice rough, his hands still on her hips, holding her close, "talk to me." She smiled, a lazy, satisfied smile, her body still humming with the aftershocks of pleasure.

"The sweat," she murmured, her voice soft, teasing, "I feel you against me but all I can think about is how fucking drenched we are. My heart, I feel it in my head. My legs feel weak and sore, like I've just done a long workout." He laughed, a low, rumbling sound that made her stomach flip.

"Next time," he promised, his lips brushing against her ear, "I'm going to make you scream even louder." She shivered at the promise, already looking forward to it.

Logan pulled out slowly, watching as his cum slid down her legs. She reached for the notepad again, her fingers trembling as she wrote something he couldn't read. He didn't need to. He already knew what it said. He stopped the recording, laughing as he tossed her phone aside and walked steadily to the bathroom, fetching her a towel to clean herself up. Cassie stared at him, incredulous and overwhelmed. She had wanted inspiration, and she got more than that. She got something that felt uncomfortably real, something that left her too stunned to speak. Her nerves did their usual dance, a jittery two-step with her common sense. Her agent would be delighted to know how rattled she was, how alive, how close to the edge.

The loft felt too small, too big, too much of everything she couldn't name. His presence changed the air, the light, the rules. He stood in the kitchen, his half-smile blazing like an admission she hadn't meant to make. She was laughing when slid off the table, laughing and so far away from who she'd been the last few months. Logan watched her with the intensity she tried not to think about. It was more intense than anything she'd written, more intense than anything she thought she could feel. Cassie had never been so inspired. She'd never been so afraid. She knew it was too real. Too much. The intensity with Logan was ruining her objectivity, threatening to ruin the book. The thought terrified her, almost as much as the truth beneath it.

She could almost hear her agent, a spectre of impatience and expectation. Cassie needed distance, perspective, something she couldn't name. She needed to remember why she'd started this. Why she'd brought Logan in to begin with. It wasn't for this, wasn't for a blur of desire and confusion. Her gaze drifted to the window, rain drawing lines like the ones she couldn't. Like the ones she thought would never come. She decided to pull back. Decided she had to. It was the only way to protect her work, her sanity, herself. It was the only way to stop the inevitable. Cassie hadn't known she was capable of this, of the brilliance and terror of it. She hadn't known how much she'd need him to make it happen. He took a few steps toward her, sensing the tension and nerves that had overwhelmed her.

"Time for me to go." Logan held her face between his hands, his touch tender and rough and exactly what she'd needed to bring her back to the moment. Her skin burned where he touched her, where he didn't. She was lost and found all at once.

"I feel like I should credit you when it's published," Cassie looked at Logan, unable to contain her happiness, unable to contain the enormity of what they'd done, "Logan Horne, the man who brought my characters, and my fantasies to life."

"No," Logan's smile softened with each word, "nothing with my full name on anything, please. But I'm sure you'll find some other way to thank me."

"Other than what I owe you." She looked at Logan, the man who made it happen, the man who made her brave enough to try. His eyes met hers, warm and sure and everything she needed to see.

"I almost forgot about that part," Logan laughed with a wonderful mix of awe and pride that she still wasn't used to, that she still wanted more of, "I'll send you the payment request when I get home. Give you a bulk discount."

"Don't you dare," she'd never been so sure of herself, she'd never been so sure of him, "you were worth every cent."

"Call me," he smiled, pulling her into an embrace, the warmth of him a perfect match for the warmth inside her, "if you end up turning it into a trilogy."

Logan kissed her, and Cassie let the rest of the world disappear, let herself disappear into the life she never thought she'd write, let herself find what she'd never thought she'd want. Logan left as Cassie stood in the doorway, watching him disappear around the corner. She heard his light footsteps down the stairs and listened to them fade into nothing. It was electric. It was maddening. It was better than any scene, any draft, any night she'd spent with anyone. Returning to her laptop, she opened her notes. The pages full with new ideas she couldn't wait to write into the world she'd created. She looked at the notepad, scribbles and ideas she needed to refine. Finally, a glance at her phone and she laughed at the thought of listening to what they had recorded. She thought, for a moment, about how Charlotte's new love interest was yet to be named. And she knew the perfect name to give him.

Still to Come

More information can be found at
www.ceshorland.com